KILLERS OF A CERTAIN AGE

KILLERS OF A
CERTAIN AGE

DEANNA RAYBOURN

THORNDIKE PRESS
A part of Gale, a Cengage Company

LIBRARY OF CONGRESS CIP DATA ON FILE.
CATALOGUING IN PUBLICATION FOR THIS BOOK
IS AVAILABLE FROM THE LIBRARY OF CONGRESS.

ISBN-13: 979-8-8857-8500-6 (hardcover alk. paper)

Published in 2023 by arrangement with Berkley, an imprint of Penguin Publishing Group, a division of Penguin Random House LLC.

Printed in Mexico
Print Number: 1   Print Year: 2023

For P. You were right. I could. And I did.

I have wintered into wisdom.

— Beowulf

AUTHOR'S NOTE

Some of the dates are misleading; some of the names are lies. I'm not trying to protect the innocent. I'm trying to protect the guilty. You'll understand soon enough.

CHAPTER ONE
NOVEMBER 1979

"My mother always says it's common as pig tracks to go around with a run in your stocking," Helen says, eyeing Billie's ripped hosiery critically.

Billie rolls her eyes. "Helen, it's murder, not cotillion."

"It's not *murder*," Helen corrects. "It's an assassination, and you can make an effort to look nice. Besides, they're supposed to believe we're stewardesses and no stewardess would be caught dead with torn pantyhose." Helen brandishes a familiar plastic egg. "I brought spares. Please go change while you still have time. I'll start the coffee."

The run is so tiny only Helen would have noticed it. Billie opens her mouth to argue and closes it again when she sees the tightness around Helen's lips. Helen is nervous and that means her eye for detail is hyperfocused, searching out things to worry about. Better for her to fuss about snagged pantyhose than any of the thousand other things that could go wrong on their first mission, Billie decides.

"Mary Alice is on coffee detail. You go check on Nat," Billie says, plucking the egg from Helen's hand. She pops into the lavatory just long enough to strip off her ruined hose and shimmy into a fresh pair, emerging to hear the conversation from the cockpit. Movies again — of course. When Gilchrist and Sweeney aren't debating the odds of getting Goldie Hawn into bed, they are trying to stump each other with film quotes.

" 'A deer has to be taken with one shot. I try to tell people that, but they don't listen.' " The pilot waits while his copilot pauses the preflight check, screwing up his eyes in thought.

"*Monty Python and the Holy Grail*?" he guesses.

The pilot rolls his eyes. "Jesus, Sweeney, no, it's not *Monty Python*. Did that line sound funny to you?"

Sweeney shrugs. "It could be." The copilot jerks his head towards the galley. "Skirt!" he calls.

Billie steps into the doorway of the cockpit.

12

"Yes, Sweeney?" she asks.

He pulls his mouth to the side, doing his best Bogart as he looks her up and down. "She missed being beautiful by just a hair, but the voice more than made up for it. It was low and smoky, the sort of voice that ordered whiskey neat and told the bartender to keep the change."

"I don't remember that in *The Maltese Falcon,*" she says.

His expression is outraged. "It's original! Come on, I make a great Sam Spade."

"Don't quit your day job. What did you ring for?"

Sweeney repeats the quote. "What movie is it from? Vance just threw that one out and acted like I'd punched his grandmother when I didn't know it."

"*The Deer Hunter,*" she tells Sweeney. She points to the pilot. "And his next line will be from *The Godfather.*"

The pilot grins. "How do you know that?"

"Every other one of your quotes is from *The Godfather,*" she says. She pauses and the pilot gives her an assessing look. She is perfectly turned out, from the crisp, un-creased uniform to the smooth, dark blond hair tucked into a neat French pleat. Her hands don't shake and her eyes don't dart around. But she is nervous — or excited.

13

Something is thrumming under her skin, he can almost smell it. And it is his job to settle her down.

"You got this, Billie," he says in a low voice. "You and the others are good or they wouldn't have given you the job."

She smiles. "Thanks, Gilchrist."

He shrugs. "I've given you a lot of shit in training, but the four of you are alright — provided you make it through tonight," he adds with a heartless grin.

"That's comforting," she tells him as Sweeney laughs.

"Just remember the mission and you'll be fine," Gilchrist assures her. "Sweeney and I will be keeping the bird steady, so you girls are on your own back there unless something goes seriously to shit." His expression says it better not, and she promises herself then that she'd sooner open a vein with a paper clip than ask him for help.

"Got it," she tells him. She watches him for a second as his hands move over the switches and levers, working through the preflight check. He is at ease, loose as an athlete who has trained and drilled until there's nothing left but the big game.

Sweeney draws her attention by giving her a nudge. "Tell the brunette I want a drink when this is all over."

14

"You know the rules. No fraternizing," Gilchrist reminds him.

Sweeney makes a noise like a wounded puppy. "Easy for you to say. You've got Anthea." He drags the name out on three syllables. "Ahhhhn-theeee-aaaah," he repeats in a country club drawl.

"You got a steady girl? Good for you," Billie says to the pilot.

He pulls down the visor to show a small snapshot of a girl with a dark flip like Jackie O's, a serious expression in her wide eyes.

"Pretty," Billie says.

"And riiiiiiiich," Sweeney adds in a sulky tone.

"What's your problem, Sweeney?" she asks.

"I'm jealous, of course. He's got a rich, pretty debutante and all I've got is a stiffy for the little brunette with the curly hair out there."

"The little brunette has a name," Billie tells him. "Natalie."

"The future Mrs. Charles McSween," Sweeney says solemnly. "At least for this weekend." He raises a warning hand. "And don't tell me it's forbidden. That just makes it more exciting. It's like they're *daring* me to take her out."

Billie looks from one to the other. "I'm

15

surprised neither of you is chasing Helen," she says. "She's the prettiest of us."

They both shrug. "Pretty, yes," Gilchrist admits. "Beautiful even. But she's what we Canadians call a Winnipeg winter."

"A Winnipeg winter?"

"Great natural beauty but capable of freezing your dick off if you're stupid enough to get naked," Sweeney explains. He surveys Billie with a practiced eye. "Of course, you would just —"

Billie holds up a hand. "Never mind. I don't want to know. Coffee is brewing. I'll have Mary Alice bring you some."

Mary Alice is pouring two fresh cups when Billie enters the galley. The air smells of burnt coffee and Mary Alice gives her an apologetic look. "I spilled some on the burner."

Billie waves a hand. "Who cares?" She reaches for the foil-wrapped package of mixed nuts and sticks it into the warming drawer.

Mary Alice nods towards the cockpit. "How are our fearless leaders?"

"Quoting films and trying to decide which one of us they get to take home for the weekend."

Mary Alice pulls a face. "God, I hate them."

16

Billie lifts an eyebrow. "They're not all bad. Vance Gilchrist just gave me a vote of confidence, a little pep talk for the evening's adventure."

Mary Alice snorts. "Only because he's in charge and if we screw up, it's on his head."

"Probably," Billie agrees. She reaches out and straightens Mary Alice's name tag. It is printed with the name MARGARET ANN. Her own name tag reads BRIDGET.

Always choose an alias with your own initials, their mentor has told them. *At some point, you will be tired or distracted or simply human and you will start to write or say your real name instead of your alias. It is far easier to correct your mistake without arousing suspicions if you have at least begun with the proper letter. Also, it means never having to change your monogram. Remember, ladies, your lives are lies now, but the fewer you tell, the simpler it is to keep them straight.*

Helen appears, poised and unruffled although her eyes are unusually bright. "Showtime," she tells them. "The Bulgarians are here." Natalie joins them as they hurry to the side of the plane, watching through the round windows as the long black bulk of a limousine approaches.

"Oh god," Natalie murmurs. "It's happening. Finally."

17

Helen lays a hand on her wrist. "Breathe, Nat."

Nat pulls in a long breath, flaring her nostrils as she watches the car glide to a halt. The expected quartet of passengers gets out: the principal — a man they refer to only as X — his private secretary, and a pair of bodyguards.

"Oh shit," Mary Alice says suddenly.

Billie leans forward, pressing her nose to the glass. The bodyguards carry nothing, hands free should they need to draw their weapons. They look like bears, heavily bearded and shaggy-haired, unlike the secretary, with his neatly shaven face and slicked-back hair. He has a calfskin case in his hands, slim body hunched over it to shield it from the light greasy rain that has begun to fall. X himself is cradling a small dog in his arms, an apricot poodle with a tuft of hair gathered into a silk bow.

"Nobody said anything about a dog," Helen says faintly.

"I'm not killing a dog." Nat rears back from the window, eyes wide. "I can't do it."

"You won't have to," Billie promises her. The others stare, and she realizes the flaw in the plan. The four of them have their orders and are supposed to be under Gilchrist's command. But he will be secure in

18

the cockpit, locked away from whatever happens in the cabin. And in the cabin, they are going to need leadership. It isn't like their organization to make such a basic mistake, and Billie wonders if it has been done deliberately, a way to test them on their coolness under pressure.

Billie steps up. "The dog is a complication. But it's not a now problem. It's a later problem. The now problem is getting our guests on board and settled. Stations. Let's go."

To her astonishment, the other three obey, hurrying forward to arrange themselves attractively as the principal starts up the staircase of the aircraft. He is the sort of man who should have been flying on a luxury jet, a Beechcraft or a Gulfstream, something with sleek teakwood interiors and the latest gadgets. But his dossier says he is old-school, preferring twin-engine turboprops, the bigger the better. This one has two engines mounted in front of each wing, and they rumble to life as the propellers begin to move.

The quartet of stewardesses smile at X, a dour-looking man in his fifties who snaps his fingers as he stands just inside the open doorway, shaking the rain from his hair. His secretary waits patiently behind him, still shielding the case with his body. One body-guard brings up the rear, standing with bovine stillness on the stairs while the other moves into the cabin. His neck is thick and his gaze is flat and unfriendly as he pokes a head into the cockpit for a quick inspection.

The pilots turn and Gilchrist flashes him a genial grin. "Jesus, you should warn a person." He waits for an answering smile that isn't forthcoming. Then he shrugs and turns back to his preflight check.

"You are not Henderson," the bodyguard says in an accusing tone.

Gilchrist's reply is cheerful. "Nope. Poor bastard got food poisoning. I warned him not to eat the bouillabaisse, but he wanted to go native. Now he's crouched in the bathroom at the Hilton, spewing out of both ends." He finishes with a laugh and looks at Sweeney, who joins in laughing half a beat too late.

"You are not Henderson," the bodyguard repeats.

"Wow, you're quick," Gilchrist says, giving a good impression of a man whose patience is wearing thin.

"We don't take off without Henderson," the bodyguard tells him.

The principal pushes his way forward.

20

"What's the trouble?"

The bodyguard makes a gesture. "This is not Henderson."

Gilchrist rolls his eyes. "Look, can we skip the rerun? No, I'm not Henderson. Henderson is sick and the agency called me. My credentials are right there," he adds, pointing to the laminated ID clipped to his shirt.

"Let me see," the bodyguard says, making a beckoning gesture with his hand.

"Christ," the pilot mutters, handing over his ID. It is a fake, of course, but a good one, and Gilchrist isn't worried. Sweeney continues to work methodically through the check, focusing on his clipboard and his instrument panel while the little drama plays out. The bodyguard scrutinizes the ID.

"Vincent Griffin," he reads slowly.

"Excellent," Vance Gilchrist tells him. "I see someone's gotten the message that Reading Is Fundamental." He gives the bodyguard a thin smile. Usually Gilchrist prefers an easy-going approach, but sometimes playing the jerk gets better results. And it is always more fun.

He puts out his hand for the ID but the bodyguard holds it close.

"What are you going to do, press it in your diary before you ask me to prom?" Gilchrist demands. "That's my ID. If you have a problem, get on the radio. Otherwise, hand it over."

They stare at each other, bristling like dogs. From behind the principal, Billie speaks up.

"Excuse the interruption, Captain, but I need your order and the copilot's," she says, drawing every man's attention.

The principal turns to look and she gives him a cool smile. "Good evening, sir. Can I get you something from the galley before we take off?" She is inches from him and he steps back to take a better look at all five and a half feet of her. The uniform, dark grey and severe, does her the favor of showing off a fair bit of shadowed cleavage and a knee he wants to get to know better.

He returns the smile with his lips but his eyes are cold and small. "Vodka," he tells her. "On the rocks, and no cheap shit. I pay for the good stuff."

"Of course, sir," she says, holding his gaze a moment longer than necessary. "Would you care to take your seat? My colleague is preparing a selection of snacks and dinner will be served within an hour of takeoff."

She holds out her arm, indicating the cabin behind her. The bodyguard makes a noise of protest, but the principal waves him

22

off with a few choice words in Bulgarian. Billie leads the way to the first row of leather armchairs. The secretary has already taken a seat in the second row, wiping at the rain-spotted calfskin case with a towel Helen provides. Natalie is on her tiptoes, struggling to close an overhead locker while the second bodyguard watches with enthusiasm for the way her breasts bounce against her uniform shirt.

He says something in Bulgarian to the secretary, finishing with a rough laugh, but the secretary prims his mouth. Mary Alice is in the galley, pouring drinks and garnishing small bowls of warm nuts with salt to make the men thirsty. She smooths the uniform skirt over her curvaceous hips and carries out the tray, presenting the refreshments with a smile. She makes certain that the bodyguards have a hefty glass of something cold and encourages them to drink up quickly before the plane takes off.

"Something for every taste," the principal says as he takes his seat, but he isn't looking at the nuts. Billie motions towards the seat belt and he waves a dismissive finger.

"I know the drill. Vodka," he reminds her. He settles the dog onto his lap, working his thick fingers into its coat. The backs of his hands are pale and she can see the veins, heavy blue ridges under the skin. She thinks of everything she has read about those hands, the things they have done, things they can never undo.

He glances up to find Billie watching him and he raises a grey brow at her, imperious, silently reminding her that her place is to serve. She smiles and the poodle lifts its head, giving her a superior look before it turns away. Even his dog is an asshole.

Billie gives him a deferential nod. "Of course, sir." She goes into the galley and emerges a moment later with an icy glass and a napkin. She dips her knees, keeping them together as she lowers the glass to his tray. It is a technique the Playboy Bunnies use, graceful and attractive and a bitch on the knees, she thinks as she rises smoothly. "Is there anything else before we take off?"

He says nothing but drops a lazy hand to cup her ass as she turns. For an instant she stops, her eyes wide. Helen gives a short, sharp shake of the head and Billie collects herself, easing out of his grip with a vague smile that promises him a very companionable trip.

The men exchange a few more rough pleasantries in Bulgarian as the attendants buckle themselves into their seats in the rear. Mary Alice sits next to Natalie while

Billie and Helen take seats opposite. Helen touches Billie's hand while she clips herself into the seat.

"Keep it together," she whispers.

Billie nods once, taking in a deep breath. It is all part of the job and she knows it. Nobody has pretended they won't be harassed or groped or propositioned with ugly words and uglier intentions. In fact, they've been assured of it.

"We knew what we were signing up for," she answers shortly. The phone on the bulkhead behind her rings once and she reaches for the receiver.

"Cabin," she answers.

"Buckle up, skirts," Sweeney says cheerfully. "Captain says we're a go."

"Yes, sir," she says, slamming the receiver down a little harder than necessary as the engines begin to scream. They move forward, slowly at first, then gaining speed as Gilchrist opens the throttle, hurtling them down the runway and up into the twilight sky.

When they level out over the Mediterranean Sea, Gilchrist himself phones. Helen gives Billie a narrow look and takes the call. "Yes, Captain?"

"Cruising altitude. It's time," Gilchrist says shortly.

Helen hangs up without a word and nods to the other three. In unison, they rise, smoothing the creases out of their skirts. Mary Alice produces a case and unzips it. Inside are four hypodermic syringes, filled and capped. It was Nat's idea to use the syringes; Mary Alice chose the payload. Sodium thiopental. In proper doses and administered intravenously, it is an anesthetic. Injected directly into the muscle in a massive amount, it will kill within a few minutes, a gentle, painless death that affords at least a little dignity. And it has the advantage of being quick and tidy, unlike other methods they might have used, Billie reflects, remembering Nat's original suggestion of ice picks.

One by one, they pluck their hypodermics from the case. Helen hesitates, her fingers just brushing her syringe. She is the only one who asked in the briefing why it was even necessary to kill them, given what was going to happen afterwards.

Because one must never leave anything to chance, Miss Randolph, their mentor explained. *This is the only job where overkill is a good thing.*

Helen takes her hypodermic from the case and the four exchange one last look. Holding their syringes carefully, they turn to the

front of the plane. Ahead of them, their passengers are nodding quietly, the chloral
hydrate in their drinks taking effect. The
principal stirs as they approach, putting out
a hand to Billie, gripping her wrist. He lifts
his lids halfway, struggling to form words
against the heavy weight of the chloral
mixed with alcohol.

"Why?" he demands thickly.

Billie reaches out with one smooth gesture
and slides the hypodermic into his neck,
pushing down on the plunger. "I think you
know."

He makes to claw at his neck, but the
sodium thiopental is doing its work. His
eyelids drop. She watches him slide into
oblivion, easing his grip on her wrist as he
lets go of life. She glances at the others, who
are watching their targets with the same
detached interest. After a minute, each puts
a fingertip to the neck of her mark.

"Clear," Billie calls.

"Clear," Natalie replies.

"Clear," Helen says at the same time.

"Shit!" Mary Alice rears back, the bodyguard's hand at her throat, squeezing as he
surges forward, the hypodermic dangling
from his neck. He wrenches it out, flinging
it in an arc that lands it at Billie's feet. She
sees at a glance that the syringe is still full.

Mary Alice hasn't depressed the plunger and the needle has broken off.

Mary Alice goes down hard, the bodyguard on top of her, throttling her as her face turns purple. The dog, startled by the commotion, starts to bark, jumping in circles. Helen scoops it up as Nat launches herself at the bodyguard on top of Mary Alice, landing on his back with as much impact as a flea landing on a dog. He raises one hand to bat her away, shoving Nat hard into the tray table and knocking the wind out of her. She whoops a few times, sucking in air as the dog continues to bark hysterically, struggling in Helen's arms. The smooth, carefully plotted mission has turned into a goddamned circus, Billie realizes, and it is up to her to salvage it.

She reaches down, grabbing the slit in her skirt with both hands, yanking hard to tear it up and open to the waist. Strapped to her thigh is a knife, and she pulls it free as she straddles the bodyguard. Thank god his hair needs trimming, she thinks as she wraps it around her hand and pulls sharply. His head snaps back, exposing his neck. One quick thrust and she is in, severing the jugular as neatly as slicing a piece of steak. A twist of the wrist and she has the carotid as well, both vessels spurting blood in a fountain that sprays Mary Alice where she lies, gasping for air as she rolls out from under him.

"Jesus," Helen says. The dog in her arms suddenly goes still and sends up a mournful howl.

"Don't put the dog down," Billie instructs. "It will lick up the blood."

"Oh god," Mary Alice manages. "I'm going to be sick."

"You damned well are not," Billie tells her. "We're not finished here."

Just then Gilchrist emerges from the cockpit. "What the hell was all that noise —"

He stops short at the sight of the fitted grey carpet, dark and sticky with the spreading pool of blood. "Oh, for Christ's sake," he starts.

"We're handling it," Billie tells him shortly.

"See that you do," he orders. He turns to Helen. "Parachutes."

She retrieves two large packs and two smaller ones — main chutes and reserves — from the overhead locker and hands them over. "Here you go."

He passes them up to Sweeney before turning back. "You know what to do next. Finish up and get out of here. We'll follow. And don't forget the case," he adds with a glance at the secretary slumped in his seat,

29

the result of Nat's quietly efficient handiwork. "Or all of this is for nothing."

He returns to the cockpit before he can
see Billie's upraised middle finger.

Mary Alice, pushing herself to her feet,
gives a shaky laugh as she strips off her
blood-soaked uniform. Nat passes her a
sleekly fitted black suit. It is made of a material developed by a military contractor
happy to sell a few thousand yards under
the table. Mary Alice's skin is sticky with
blood but she forces herself into the suit,
strapping a utility belt and parachute neatly
into place. The others do the same, checking their gear as they zip and buckle.

"We have a problem," Nat announces. She
lifts the calfskin case, raising the secretary's
arm with it. "Handcuffs. And no sign of a
key."

"We don't have time for this," Billie mutters. She strides forward with her knife and
does what she has to do. Natalie looks on
with interest, as if taking notes in a biology
lab, and Billie grabs the case, strapping it to
her chest with the severed hand dangling
like an obscene accessory.

Helen tucks the dog into her suit, zipping
it firmly against her body behind the reserve
chute.

"There is no chance that dog survives the

jump," Mary Alice says.

"There is no chance I'm not going to try," Helen replies coolly. Nat shoots her a look of gratitude and they head to the back of the plane, bracing themselves as Vance points the nose of the aircraft down, lowering the altitude by several thousand feet in a dive that almost stalls the engines.

"Show-off," Helen says.

Just then the cabin lights flicker twice. The signal. Mary Alice steps forward and opens the aft door. Vance has flown southwest out of Nice, parallel with the coast, edging slightly inland before banking hard left to aim the aircraft due south. They are past the bulk of the mountains, flying just over the national park of the Plaine des Maures. It is flatter than the craggy uplands to the east, but it is far from level. According to the topographical surveys they received in their briefings, it is rugged, scrubby, and dotted with parasol pines and dangerous outcroppings. Now it unrolls beneath the belly of the plane, a long, unrelieved patch of black. Far to the west, a narrow line of violet marks the death of the day, and the first stars are winking to life just above the horizon.

Natalie snaps her goggles into place, saluting as she drops away into the night.

31

Mary Alice goes next, flinging herself away from the bottom step like a swimmer setting off for the deep end. Helen is graceful, tipping backwards with a final wave at Billie.

Billie stands on the threshold of the plane, taking a slow, deep breath. The air smells of salt from the Gulf of St.-Tropez and the sharp tang of fuel, and she is grinning as she throws herself into the blackness.

She counts as she floats. Thirty seconds until the chute can be deployed, and it is the most peaceful thirty seconds of her life. She is conscious of counting off the numbers, fingers touching the ring on the rip cord, waiting, half wondering if she should just let it go. From that altitude, there wouldn't be much left of her when she hits the ground and she wouldn't feel or see it coming. Nothing but that beautiful, empty blackness beckoning like the end of time.

Thirty. Her fingers pull hard and instantly she is yanked as the chute fills, stalling her free fall. She dangles, legs loose as a marionette's as she drops to the plain. To her left, she can see three tiny lights glimmering as Helen, Mary Alice, and Natalie drift to the ground. She lands harder than expected, the impact forcing the air out of her lungs.

She makes herself go limp, rolling to her

side as she has been trained. She comes to a hard stop against the base of a parasol pine and the impact wakes a bird that shrieks once or twice before leaving with an angry flap of wings. Billie sees the beacons of the others, winking like fireflies in an uneven line across the plain. She lifts her face to watch two more fireflies drift from the dark bulk of the aircraft. It is flying low, silhouetted against the clouds like a set piece as it heads towards the Mediterranean. The fuel has been precisely calculated to run out somewhere between the Balearics and Sardinia in the darkness before midnight, leaving nothing but a few bits of broken fuselage and a slick of chemicals on the surface of the water. Billie remembers reading it is ten thousand feet to the bottom of the sea, where the bones of ships and sailors have lain for thousands of years. A few more won't matter.

Billie feels something brush her leg — a tortoise? A rat? She pushes herself to her feet and scouts the others, their positions indicated by the large safety beacons they have activated. She activates her own, nearly blinded by the brilliant white light. She shields her eyes as she hears the helicopter approach, lowering itself to pluck her from the rocky plain. She is the fourth to get picked up, shivering with the aftereffects of adrenaline. She trips as she clambers aboard, landing flat on her belly and wishing she had made a more elegant entrance when she sees their mentor and the head of Project Sphinx, Constance Halliday — code name Shepherdess — sitting in a jump seat. Halliday is every day of seventy years old and dressed in a flight suit, a white silk scarf wrapped neatly around her throat to guard against a chill. A walking stick is braced against her leg.

Helen is already buckled in, unzipping her suit to check on the dog, who is barking furiously but apparently unharmed by his adventure. Nat fusses over him while Mary Alice sits back, eyes closed as if in prayer. The men will be collected by a second, smaller chopper, and they will all gather for a post-mission debriefing at an undisclosed location outside of Paris. They will have to go over every minute of the mission in painstaking detail, outlining their mistakes and scrutinizing every decision for how to improve. But for now, they are safe. The first mission is finished with no casualties beyond Nat's cracked rib and the blood still caked in Mary Alice's hair.

Without a word, Halliday gestures and Billie unstraps the case, passing it over with the hand still attached, the blood drained away, leaving it pale and limp, like a glove full of vanilla pudding. Halliday ignores the hand. She produces a tool and opens the case, extracting a file. For the next few minutes, she skims the material inside, allowing herself one very small smile as she finishes.

"Good work, Miss Webster," she says in her clipped accent.

Billie gives her a nod and, without warning, rolls over onto all fours to vomit.

It is the greatest day of her life.

So far.

CHAPTER TWO

Trouble has smelled like a lot of things in my life. A job gone wrong. A one-way street I never should have turned down. A man in faded Levi's with a smile that broke my heart half a dozen times and loved it back together again. On the *Amphitrite,* it smelled like gardenias and money. The boat was a beauty, the latest luxury offering from a company that specialized in mini-liners — fifty staterooms including a pair of owners' suites and a crew member for each of us. The brochures described everything as custom-made or handcrafted or artisanal. They had sent each of us a packet half as thick as a vintage phone book, stuffed with glossy photographs and maps and a welcome letter from the captain on embossed letterhead heavier than a wedding invitation. Everything from the menus for the three on-board restaurants ("featuring the freshest locally sourced seafood and organic, sustainably grown fruits") to the excursion brochures ("glide above the reefs in your own mini-submersible") had been chosen to make us feel welcome and pampered. Tucked into the packet was a personalized letter written in turquoise ink, the *i*'s dotted with tiny starfish.

Dear Mary Alice, Helen, Natalie, and Billie,
It is my pleasure to welcome you aboard the *Amphitrite*! We understand this is a special occasion for the four of you. Happy retirement! Forty years at the same job is a tremendous accomplishment, and we are so happy you are celebrating this event with us. As you turn the page to the new chapter of your lives, please let us know if there is anything we can do to enhance your cruising experience!

Cordially,
Heather Fanning
Executive Guest Services Coordinator
#retirement #luxurycruises #amphitrite

I shook my head. Forty years on one of the most elite assassin squads on earth and it finished like this, with a free cruise and a bouncy letter from a girl who signed her letters with hashtags.

If you expect me to tell you the name of

the organization I work for, stop reading right now. It's a secret — so secret, in fact, that those of us who work there never use the official title. We always refer to it as "the Museum" and we use museum nomenclature to make it a little less obvious to anybody listening in that our job is to eliminate people who need killing.

The men and women who established the Museum were an international conglomeration of former SOE and OSS agents, French, Polish, and Dutch Resistance, and a few of the leftover Monuments Men who had secured the art collections of Europe while stormtroopers stomped their way around the continent. Basically, everyone who wanted to go hunting Nazis and didn't have a mandate from their government got together and decided to write their own.

They were the oddballs and eccentrics, the quirky ones who made brilliant leaps in logic and didn't so much go by the book as fling it out the window. They hunted former members of the Third Reich — everyone from Hitler's shoeshine boy to Treblinka guards. Through Brazilian jungles, Buenos Aires whorehouses, and villas outside Pretoria, they rode down every last one they could find. When they'd exhausted their list of Nazis to bring to justice, they had turned to others — dictators, arms dealers, drug smugglers, and sex traffickers.

It was the Wild West with no law but natural justice, and I suppose those were the good old days. Not entirely, of course. The Museum, for all its high-minded principles, has been a little slow on social justice. I've had my ass grabbed more times than I care to count, and there was exactly one Black field agent in the first twelve years I worked for them. But at least when we joined, there was a hum in the air, the electric fizz of anticipation, of knowing you were doing something worthwhile and doing it better than anybody else.

That's how they got me, of course. They found me in college with my jeans embroidered with peace signs and they dangled the bait of changing history. I was recruited in late 1978 along with Mary Alice, Helen, and Natalie as part of Project Sphinx, the first all-female squad. I put down my protest signs and stamped out my burning bra and let them make a killer out of me.

Helen doesn't like that word, but I always ask her, Why bother with anything else? It's simple and true. We kill for a living. A *good* living, in case you're interested, with a solid base salary, bonuses, and benefits — including full dental and a pension. And we kill

39

who we're told and only who we're told. Let's get that clear right up front. We're not sociopaths. We don't murder for fun or for free. We kill to get paid. Now, Mary Alice loves her idealism and still clings to the notion of us murdering people who need killing in order to improve society. That was the official line when we were recruited, and even though times have changed — more computers and pencil pushers doing cost-benefit analyses — that part is not negotiable. We only kill people who are specifically targeted by the Museum for extermination and we don't freelance, *ever*. We don't murder on our days off any more than a thoracic surgeon will cut your rib cage open for kicks. We have standards.

CHAPTER THREE

The packet arrived in the mail in late November 2018, a predictably gloomy time of year. Contract assassination is surprisingly busy during the holidays — targets are as much creatures of habit as the rest of us, and you can often knock them off when they're traveling over the fields and through the woods to grandmother's house — but I had finished my last assignment the week after Halloween, leaving me rattling around my rented town house like Miss Havisham, only with leftover breakfast tacos instead of a wedding cake. There was no more work on the horizon, the Astros had lost to the Red Sox in the playoffs the month before, and to add insult to injury, it had actually snowed in Houston. In short, I was ripe for anything that hinted at adventure, and an all-expenses-paid retirement cruise embarking the day after Christmas was better than nothing.

I flicked through the brochures, noting the deliberate omission of prices.

It was too much. I gave up after reading about the thread count of the sheets ("hand-loomed from cotton grown in the Nile delta") and threw the packet into my tote bag. It was still there a month later, buried under a bottle of sunscreen, a pack of cigarettes, and a bag of licorice whips, when I boarded the boat in San Juan for a late-afternoon departure that felt like a class reunion. Mary Alice and I had met up in the Dallas airport on our way east; Helen joined us in Miami. Leave it to Natalie to dash on at the last possible minute, spilling lipsticks and miniature liquor bottles from her bag as she ran up the gangplank in the harbor in Puerto Rico.

"She's going to break a hip doing that," Mary Alice said mildly. We were standing at the rail next to Helen, watching as Natalie teetered across the deck on wedge espadrilles that were four inches high and tied halfway up her leg with yellow satin ribbons.

"Or by falling off a porter," I said, nodding to where Natalie was furiously batting her lashes at some poor twenty-year-old who didn't know what had hit him.

"Leave her be," Helen said, a little too sharply. I raised a brow at Mary Alice but neither of us replied. Natalie shifted her gear into the porter's waiting arms and waved him away as she launched herself at us. She was the smallest, barely coming up to Helen's shoulder, but somehow she managed to gather us into a group hug.

"It's been so long!" she cried, pulling back to see us better. "Let me look at you! Christ, you're all so old!"

"It's been six months," Mary Alice told her, smoothing out her linen tunic from where Natalie had crushed it in her exuberance.

Natalie flapped a hand. "Bullshit. It's been longer than that."

Helen was calculating. "It was my last birthday. You all came to Washington," she said. She didn't finish the thought. We'd gone to DC armed with dinner reservations and tickets to the *Camelot* revival at the Kennedy Center to get her out of the house.

I gave her a close look. She'd worried me on that trip. Kenneth's death had hit her hard and I wasn't sure she was going to make it. He'd been gone for three months when we showed up. The blinds had been drawn and the house dark, smelling of gin and unwashed sheets and even more of unwashed Helen. We stayed for four days, rousting her out of the house for spa trips

43

and movies and a baseball game. We made her promise to keep her hairdresser's appointments and her volunteer commitments and signed her up for pottery classes and a meal-delivery service. And then we'd gone home and gotten back to our own lives with a sense of having accomplished what we'd set out to do, like Helen was a chore on a to-do list. Check off the box marked CONSOLE WIDOW and move on to the next thing.

Only Helen hadn't moved any further, I suspected. She was perfectly groomed now, her pale grey-blond hair shimmering with platinum streaks that matched the ostrich Birkin bag hanging from the crook of her arm. But she'd lost more weight. One good hug and I could snap her in two, I thought sadly.

Just then, Natalie's young porter appeared with a basket and a pair of tongs. "Chilled towels, ladies? They're scented with lemon verbena?" Everything the kid said ended in a question.

"Thank you, Hector," Natalie said with a broad smile.

One by one he dealt the little towels out like cards. Mary Alice gave her arms a purposeful wipe while Helen patted her cheeks daintily. Natalie stuffed hers in her bra while I draped mine around the back of

44

my neck with a moan of relief.

"Hot flash?" Mary Alice asked with a sympathetic look.

"Only occasionally," I told her.

"I can't believe you're still not finished with that," Natalie said, plucking the towel out of her neckline. "I haven't had a period since 2005."

"Natalie, please," Mary Alice said, darting a look around to see if anyone was paying attention.

Nat shrugged. "Why do I care if anyone hears me? Periods are a perfectly natural phenomenon."

"I know how periods work, Natalie," Mary Alice said, setting her teeth. "I just think maybe some of the other passengers might not want to know about your gynecological endeavors."

When we were younger, Natalie would have met a remark like that with fire, but she merely shrugged and grabbed two frosted glasses of rosé from the tray of a passing waiter. She shoved one at Mary Alice. "Here, Mary Alice. Drink this and I'll see if I can find you a flashlight."

Mary Alice furrowed her brow. "Flashlight?"

"To find the stick up your ass. Let me know if you need a hand getting it out,"

Natalie said sweetly.

I grabbed another two glasses and thrust one at Helen, raising mine quickly. "A toast," I said, narrowing my eyes at Mary Alice and Natalie. "To us. Forty years on, and still kicking."

They joined in, even Helen, although she hardly seemed to have enough energy to clink glasses. By the time we watched the sun sink over the horizon as we put to sea and moved into the dining room for grilled swordfish, we'd had two more rounds. We polished off an obscene amount of coconut tiramisu and were ready to stagger off to bed when Heather Fanning, as toothy and perky as I'd feared, accosted us with a wide smile.

"I hope you had a wonderful arrival dinner!" she enthused. "I have a special treat for you!"

She beckoned us to follow her, and Mary Alice fell into step next to me. "Ten bucks says that child used to twirl a baton."

"Flaming," I agreed.

Heather took us up to the bridge, where she introduced us to the captain, a man who looked enough like Idris Elba that Natalie made a beeline for him as he gave us a tour of the ship. He took us up stairs and down ladders and around decks, pointing out all the luxurious features and safety measures. He was proudest of his engine room, keeping us standing for half an hour while he explained the intricacies of the NGL tanks — natural gas liquids, in case anyone ever asks you. He talked until my calves were cramping and all I wanted to do was curl up behind the nearest engine and take a nap. But we all smiled and thanked him, and when we returned to the lounge area on our deck a bottle of champagne was waiting with his compliments. It had a tag on it — HAPPY RETIREMENT! — and four flutes. We toasted and immediately the mood turned nostalgic.

"I don't even think I'm ready to retire," Nat said mournfully. "I love my job."

"Me too," I said.

"I'm relieved," Mary Alice commented. "It's time to start a new chapter."

"I would have liked to finish the old one," Helen said, knotting her fingers around her flute. "Properly, I mean. If I'd known the job in Qatar was my last, I would have paid more attention."

"I would have paid more attention to all of them," I said. "It's gone so fast."

"I'm going to miss the adrenaline," Nat told us, her expression wistful. "I mean, how else am I going to find anything that makes me feel that *alive*?"

"You could take up recreational drugs," Mary Alice suggested.

Natalie stuck her tongue out, then turned to me. "I know you get it, Billie," she said.

"I do. It's like going from playing high-stakes poker to nickel slots for the rest of your life."

Natalie threw out her hands in a dramatic gesture. "*Thank* you. It's the kick, the constantly measuring yourself against the odds and figuring out how to zig when you expected to zag, balancing on that knife's edge."

I knew exactly what she meant. No matter how well you planned, no matter how extensively you prepared, something always went differently than expected. And every job was a chance to prove Darwin's simple maxim: adapt or die. We adapted; they died.

I turned to Mary Alice. "Are you going to miss it?"

She thought it over for a minute. "Probably not. Akiko and I have a good life, you know? We have our softball league and Akiko will be starting pitcher next year. I'll be able to join an amateur orchestra finally and dust off my viola. We can travel without always wondering if a job is going to come up and derail everything. I'm down to my last few excuses. I think Akiko is afraid I'm having an affair."

Her voice was light, but I realized how hard it must be to keep that kind of secret from your partner. The job could make demands of you when you least expected it, assignments cropping up without warning. When the notice came, you grabbed your go bag and left. Sometimes for a few days; sometimes for months. There was no way to know.

Mary Alice went on. "Either I'm having an affair or I'm a spy, I'm pretty sure that's what she thinks."

Natalie snorted. "Why would she think you're a spy?"

"Because I am shit at thinking up excuses as to where I'm going when I suddenly have to disappear. The last time I told her I had an accounting emergency."

The Museum paid us annually, a retainer so we'd always be available when they needed us. Bonuses came with each job, which meant we weren't hurting for cash, and being gone for a few months at a time made it hard to hold down regular jobs. But it was easy to get bored and we needed cover stories, so most of us freelanced. Mary Alice had a few accounting clients, Natalie made art that occasionally got shown although she was careful to keep a low profile. Helen was happy playing housewife to Kenneth, while I took translation jobs, usually academic books. If you're imagining it's dull work, you're not wrong. But it kept my languages sharp and gave me something to do with my time.

I turned to Mary Alice. "What the hell is an accounting emergency?"

"Believe me, if I could think of a good one, I'd use it. I usually make up some bullshit about client confidentiality and duck out the door. Or I just say that my mother is poorly."

"Doesn't she ever want to go along?" Helen asked.

Mary Alice hesitated slightly. "She knows deep down I'm lying and I think she's afraid to push because of what she might find out. Besides, you know my family. It wasn't hard to get Akiko to believe she wouldn't be welcome."

I shook my head. "So, for the five years you've been married, Akiko has believed your family is too homophobic to welcome your wife into their home? And that you would just go along with this?"

She shrugged. "It's the best way to keep her safe. The less she knows, the less trouble she can get into."

Helen pursed her lips. "But she must think you won't stand up for her, that you are willing to put up with whatever your family chooses to throw at you."

"Oh, they've thrown a lot, including actual dishes. You should have seen the one time I tried to bring Akiko home for Christmas," Mary Alice said with a sigh. "But maybe someday I'll be able to tell her the truth, now that it's finally over."

"I don't understand why you didn't tell her to start with. Kenneth knew what I did," Helen put in.

"Kenneth was CIA. He had his own baggage," Mary Alice said. She flushed. "I should have told her. I know I should. But I never found the right time. I mean, it's not exactly first-date stuff. 'Well, I'm into chamber music and intarsia knitting, and last week I poisoned the head of a multinational crime syndicate' doesn't quite cut it."

"And there was no chance between first date and your wedding day?" I asked mildly.

She nibbled her thumbnail, looking guilty as hell. "I thought she might leave me. I was afraid, okay? I was worried that if I told her the things I've done, she might decide she couldn't live with that. And I couldn't live without her."

"You should have told her," Helen said firmly.

"I never told any of my husbands," Natalie said.

"None of your husbands ever stuck around long enough for you to tell. You change marital partners like the rest of us change underwear," Mary Alice retorted.

Natalie shrugged. She tended to view monogamy as a suggestion rather than an imperative — something she finally realized she ought to share with a prospective husband after divorce number two. By the time she split from the third one, she'd given up entirely on marriage and decided to keep a string of what the kids call fuckbuddies.

Natalie turned to me. "What about you? Will you miss it?"

"I won't miss the workouts," I said honestly. "Keeping myself in shape because my life might depend on it is getting a little old. My knees are tired."

"What will you do with your time?" Helen asked.

I shrugged. "I have no idea. Maybe I'll take up needlepoint or interpretive dance."

Natalie shook her head. "I can't imagine you ever not being exactly what you are. We're all killers, but you're the Killer Queen," she said, lifting her glass in a toast.

The others laughed and I even managed to drink, but Natalie's remark cut a little closer to the bone than I would have liked. Because she said what I'd already started to fear — that without the job, I was nothing.

The others laughed and even managed
to drink, but Natalie's refusal cut a little
closer to the bone than I would have lik...
Because she said what I'd secretly started to
fear — that without the alcohol was nothing.

CHAPTER FOUR
DECEMBER 1978

There are no job fairs for assassins. Recruitment is a delicate business, and Billie Webster has no idea that her number is about to be called. She is sitting in a holding cell in Austin, Texas. She has spent the night propped against the cinder-block wall, listening to the usual sounds of a city jail on a Saturday night. A prostitute has fallen asleep with her head on Billie's shoulder, and even though she smells like body odor and weed, Billie doesn't make her move.

She hasn't made her one phone call because she has just broken up with the second-year law student at UT who usually bails her out and doesn't know who else to call.

So she waits, letting the prostitute snore on her shoulder until the duty officer comes and barks out a name. "Webster!"

Billie gently moves the prostitute aside and stands. The duty officer jerks his head

54

and opens the cell, cuffing her before taking her arm and leading her down a narrow hall. She is still dressed in the denim flares she wore to the protest, but they are stiff with blood and there are red half-moons caked under her nails. The duty officer takes her through a series of doors until they come to one marked PRIVATE. He unlocks the cuffs and opens the door, gesturing for her to enter as he reattaches the cuffs to his belt.

Inside is a scarred table and a pair of chairs. A man is sitting in one, reading a newspaper as he smokes a pipe. He is dressed in civilian clothes but something about his posture says he's spent time in uniform.

The officer jerks his head for Billie to enter. "I will be just outside, sir," he tells the man, but he looks at Billie when he says it and she knows it's a warning.

She enters and the door closes behind her. The man looks up and waves her over with an unexpected smile. When she gets closer, she sees that the newspaper is the funnies section.

The man chuckles a little as he folds the newspaper. "Marmaduke," he says to himself. He watches as she sits, looking her over carefully as she returns the favor. She is dirty, her dark blond hair tangled and in desperate need of a wash. She is wearing a thin sweater and bell-bottomed jeans embroidered with palm trees and rainbows, and there is something oddly touching about the notion of this girl sitting in her dorm room, setting each little stitch. It pleases him to think of her doing something so precise. It means his instincts about this girl are right.

She sees a man on the wrong side of sixty, she guesses, with the wiry muscles of a whippet and tidy, sandy hair mixed with white. His mustache is thin and dapper, and he wears casual clothes — khaki pants and an oxford-cloth shirt — with the air of a suit from Savile Row. Billie has not yet heard of Savile Row. It will be many months later that she learns about custom clothing and realizes that he has been her introduction to proper tailoring.

His features are set in an expression of calm interest and he seems amused by her scrutiny. "Good morning, Miss Webster."

He looks at her swelling, bloody knuckles and doesn't attempt to shake her hand. It is considerate, and she likes him for it.

"What's this all about?" she asks.

He smiles, a patient, good-natured smile. "All in good time, Miss Webster. I hope you are not in too much discomfort from your injuries? That contusion above your lip really ought to be stitched," he says reproachfully. There is a faint British accent to his words, and she likes him for that too.

"I'm fine," she tells him.

"May I offer you refreshment? A pastry or a cup of coffee? The police canteen does not have much variety, I am afraid."

Billie shakes her head and he sits back, apparently satisfied that the obligatory courtesy has been observed.

"Good, good. Introductions, then," he says, rubbing his hands together briskly. "My name is Richard Halliday. Major, Her Majesty's Army. Retired."

"What does that have to do with the Austin PD?"

He ignores the question and moves the newspaper aside. Underneath is a manila folder with her name on it. " 'Webster, Billie.' " He pauses to look at her. "I admit, that surprised me. I rather thought it might be short for something. Wilhelmina, perhaps." She stares at him and he goes on reading snippets of his notes. He plows through her IQ — 142; her school records — spotty with superb standardized test scores blighted by "discipline issues"; and the fact that she has gotten into college on a scholarship and some institutional pity for the fact that she lived in an unlicensed foster home while in high school. She holds up a hand when he starts on her loner tendencies.

"Major, is this for my benefit? Because I actually know all of that."

He closes the file. "I represent an organization," Halliday says slowly. "A clandestine organization, so if you wouldn't mind keeping this meeting to yourself, it would be greatly appreciated." He pauses and raises his sandy brows to give her a chance to nod in agreement. "Very good, thank you. As I was saying, I represent an organization that is in need of talent — specifically young, new talent that can be shaped and molded in accordance with our purposes for a very special endeavor."

"Is it porn? It's porn, isn't it?"

The narrow mouth almost smiles. "It is not pornography, no."

"Then what purposes?" Billie asks. He flinches a little and she realizes that direct questions are not going to be welcome. She would do better to come at him sideways like a crab.

"That will be clear in a moment," he assures her. "I think it best if I explain the general mission of the organization. Have

58

you heard of the OSS? The SOE?"

"Office of Strategic Services and Special Operations Executive," Billie says. He raises one brow and she shrugs. "I read a lot."

"Indeed." The eyebrow settles back into place. "Then you no doubt know the OSS was founded during the Second World War to coordinate espionage efforts across the branches of the American armed forces."

"Spies," she says flatly.

"Spies," he acknowledges. "After the war, the OSS developed into the Central Intelligence Agency. The story of the Special Operations Executive is a bit different. It was formed under the direction of the Minister of Economic Warfare and largely guided by Churchill himself. Many civilians were involved in extremely dangerous resistance and sabotage work all across Europe."

"The Ministry of Ungentlemanly Warfare," she says.

This time he does smile, but it is insubstantial, a ghost smile, flitting over his mouth and then gone again. "One of many nicknames. The Baker Street Irregulars was another. In any event, after the war, the SOE were not transformed into a government agency like the OSS. A few, a very few, agents were transferred into the other intelligence organizations of the British government."

"What happened to the rest?" she asks.

"Disbanded," is the succinct reply. He strikes a match and touches it to the tobacco packed into the pipe. He pulls hard, sending wafts of sweet smoke into the air. It smells like wood and cherries, the sort of smell that should have hung in the air of a private club or a stately home. It smells like money. He goes on. "After the training, the courageous service, the breathtaking acts of sacrifice, the entire organization was sacked. It was a black day," he adds.

"You were one of them," she says. It isn't a question. The tightness around his eyes tells the whole story.

"Just so," he says briskly. "And instead of going home and licking our wounds, a few of us joined together with some of our opposite number from the former OSS."

"English and Americans joining together in a spirit of 'screw you' to their respective governments," she says with a grin.

"In a manner of speaking, although we like to keep a low profile. We operate best in the dark." He draws a breath, pipe smoke spiraling over his head. "The dissolution of the SOE was distressing, but equally objectionable was the number of Nazis who slipped through the cracks after the war,

60

disappearing without a trace into the ether, frequently taking with them the greatest treasures of Western art. They spent the better part of the '30s and '40s looting museums and private collections, and a mere fraction of what they stole has been recovered."

He looks a little wistful, probably thinking of all those Canalettos and Caravaggios lost to history thanks to Göring's sticky fingers, she suspects. He goes on. "We simply could not endure the idea that these monsters would not face justice, that everything they stole would never be recovered. And without the imprimatur of an official government agency, we were free to do something about it." He pauses to take a drag on his pipe, his mouth tightening on the stem. "When our group was first founded late in 1946, we relied entirely upon word of mouth to gather recruits. We brought in former members of the Polish and French Resistance efforts, Italians and Spaniards who had fought against Mussolini and Franco. Our recruits were Dutch, Belgian. We were open to working with anyone who might share our interests."

"No Russians? They were our allies during the war."

His expression is oblique. "At the conclusion of the war, it was made clear that the Russians, while perfectly content to exact justice upon war criminals, were rather less interested in repatriating stolen works of art to their rightful owners."

"You mean they wanted to keep the art they found."

"As it happens, the Soviets have a gift for looting to rival Göring's," he says dryly. "They decided to keep whatever artworks they recovered and call it reparations. So, when we formed our organization, it was clear that we would have to pursue our mission without the cooperation of our former ally."

"Hunting down Nazis."

"Hunting down Nazis. In the past three decades, we have amassed quite a count," he tells her, his smile grim around the stem of the pipe. "But our original group of agents have grown old and tired, some of them have died in the field. We have slowly been recruiting fresh talent to replace them."

"Wait, you're hunting Nazis *still*?" She blinks. "Aren't they all dead yet?"

"Regrettably, no. Some of them are still at large. But our mission has expanded beyond our original goals. The addition of anti-fascists from Spain and Italy has meant broadening our scope of operation. We have neutralized dictators and other such undesirable persons around the world."

He stops to let the last sentence hang in the air along with his pipe smoke. She keeps her face carefully blank. If she objects or looks shocked, what will he do? Dismiss her politely? Have her returned to her cell? Or has he already told her too much to let her go?

She studies him and he returns the look calmly, drawing on his pipe and waiting, his lips quirking up slightly as if he were faintly amused at her scrutiny and content to let her take her time.

" 'Neutralized' is a pretty bland word for killing," she says finally.

He removes the pipe, setting it carefully into an ashtray before leaning forward a little, lacing his fingers together and looking her squarely in the eye. "Tell me, Miss Webster, haven't you ever thought to yourself that some people simply need killing to make the world a better place?"

"God, yes," she breathes.

His smile is unexpectedly charming. She can see him suddenly as he must have been during the war, thirty years old or so, dressed in a dapper suit, maybe even a tuxedo. He would be betting large in a casino, taking a sip of a dry martini, and making plans to slip into a darkened suite that night to strangle a German general or steal a priceless jewel.

"Miss Webster?" he asks gently. "What are you thinking?"

"I'm thinking if you were thirty years younger, I'd be halfway in love with you."

He retrieves his pipe, settling it comfortably between his teeth. "Well, based upon our reports of you, Miss Webster, I might be a bit of an improvement upon your usual choices," he says with a straight face and a glimmer of amusement in his eyes. "Now," he says, rubbing his hands together, "I have been tasked with finding just the right people for an undertaking called Project Sphinx."

"And what is Project Sphinx?"

"Our recruits are grouped into small training classes, the better to assess them and to foster their talents. Project Sphinx is the first class of its kind in the history of our organization. It will comprise only women, Miss Webster. The first all-female squad of assassins. It will be trained by my sister, Constance, the most highly decorated woman in the SOE and a legend. I'm frankly terrified of her. She was the supervisor of an all-female tactical team that parachuted behind German lines in 1945. They were called the Furies."

"They sound sweet."

"They were strafed by German artillery on the way down," he says evenly. "Constance, code-named Shepherdess, was the only survivor."

"Sorry," she mutters.

He looks at the scattering of freckles across her nose and takes pity on her youth. "They ran seventeen successful missions into occupied territory before they were wiped out. Constance has never been inclined to train an all-female team since, but she has decided the time is right."

He sits back with an expectant air. Billie is confused.

"What does all this have to do with me?"

His smile is enigmatic. "Perhaps nothing. Perhaps everything. I have a friend, a contact here, who happened to take note of you when you were brought in last night. She telephoned, and I flew here first thing this morning."

"Flew here? Where were you?"

"Washington. DC."

She stares. "Why would you fly here for me?"

"Because of this," he says, taking a manila envelope from beneath the folder. Inside are her effects, and he takes them out one at a time. "A wallet with a bus pass, a driving license issued by the state of Texas, seven dollars and forty-three cents, a Mexican peso, and a photograph of a pretty teenaged girl with a baby. There is no inscription, but judging from her dress, I would estimate it was taken in 1958?"

"It was 1959, actually," Billie corrects.

He smiles thinly. "Your mother, I presume?"

"My mother."

He continues on, pulling objects from the envelope. "A half-smoked marijuana cigarette, something called a Bonne Bell Lip Smacker —" He pauses to remove the cap and give it an experimental sniff.

"It's a lip balm," she tells him helpfully. "Root beer."

"Ah. Sarsaparilla," he says with a conspiratorial smile. "I used to love the stuff when I was a boy." He goes on. "And this," he adds, plucking a paperback book from the envelope. It is a cheap edition and well-worn, with the spine broken in a dozen places. The text is marked up with green ballpoint, and he turns to a dog-eared page where a few lines of text have been underscored heavily.

"*A Taste for Death.* By Peter O'Donnell. A

Modesty Blaise fan?" he asks mildly.

"She's my favorite character."

"Why?" The question is fast and so is the answer.

"Because she doesn't apologize for anything. She had a rotten start in life, but she's made the best of it. She lives on her own terms. She knows who she is and what she wants, and she does what she is good at. And she has a good time doing it."

"But without a husband," he says, watching her closely. "Without children."

"I don't want those things either," she says, and although it's the first time she's ever said the words aloud, she realizes they have always been true. "I don't want them," she repeats. "I want to work. To make my own life."

"What sort of work?"

"Anything that doesn't require learning shorthand," she retorts, but he is giving her a long, level stare and she tells him the truth. "I don't know. I don't know what I'm good at yet, but I'd like to find out. And I'd like to travel. I really want to see what's out there."

He purses his lips. "You have made several notes in the book, but this one intrigues me the most." He clears his throat and reads with authority. " 'I am interested in justice,

67

not the law. There is an unfortunate difference.' " He looks over the top of the book with bright eyes. "Tell me, Miss Webster, why have you highlighted that particular passage?"

She opens her mouth to say something brash but suddenly can't. So she tells him the truth. "Because I think it's right. Justice and the law aren't the same thing. You tracked down Nazis, right? What they were doing was technically legal. But it wasn't *just.*"

His expression is suddenly cool. "Is that how you justify what you did last night? I understand it was meant to be a peaceful protest, but you attacked a police officer."

"I didn't attack him. He was trying to provoke us, calling us names and taunting us."

He clucks his tongue disapprovingly. "Now, now. Sticks and stones, Miss Webster. Was that really a good reason to assault a police officer?"

"He was an asshole." Billie shrugs. "He deliberately used his position to target people who had a right to be there. He pistol-whipped a girl, and so I —"

"Took his nightstick and clubbed him with it until he was able to subdue you and take you into custody with only minor injuries

68

— an outcome, Miss Webster, that I suspect has more to do with luck than skill," Halliday finishes. But Billie can see the slight twist to his lips and realizes he is smiling.

"You think it's funny," she accuses.

"I think it is familiar," he corrects. "It is precisely the sort of thing my sister would have done in her youth. Justice over the law," he says.

He settles back with an air of expectation. "Now, do you think that you would be interested in taking the next step towards employment with us?"

She is quiet for a long minute.

"Miss Webster?"

"Who pays you? You don't get taxpayer money because you don't work for any government."

"Does it matter?" His voice is pleasant, but there is no mistaking the fact that he is humoring her.

"It matters," she says patiently, "because whoever cuts the checks calls the shots. Who calls your shots?"

"Among the agents who left the SOE when it was disbanded were several with particular aptitude in finance. They took employment in the City."

"The City?" she asked. "Which city?"

"The City is how we refer to the financial

district in London, rather like your Wall Street. In fact, we have some Wall Street fellows as well. They were able, with the help of a few significant donations from sympathetic benefactors, to establish a fund which has grown to impressive proportions."

"Who runs this organization? What do you even call it?"

"I cannot divulge the official name, but amongst ourselves, it is called the Museum. We have field agents and a research department and a Board of Directors to oversee the Museum's activities around the world, dispatching those field agents to safeguard democracy, to thwart absolutism, and to enact justice."

"Whose justice?" she asks.

"The justice demanded by democratic principles agreed upon by the founders of the Museum — the men and women who were among the original SOE and OSS recruits, although, as I have said, their numbers have begun to thin in recent years."

He is silent a long moment, assessing her, weighing something. She wants to break the silence, but she lets the quiet fill the space between them and he eventually nods. He reaches into the briefcase at his elbow and opens a file. It is dark blue with a small logo of falling stars surrounded by a gold motto: Fiat justitia ruat caelum.

Billie has just enough Latin to translate the motto and she smiles to herself. *Let justice be done though the heavens fall.* He extracts a sheet of paper, which he pushes across the table towards her. "If you decide to work with us, the charges pending against you currently will be dropped. Your arrest record will be expunged and your academic records destroyed. Neither the university nor law enforcement will have any proof you attended this college. If you sign this contract promising not to speak of what we have discussed here, it will be taken as a formal submission to be considered for appointment to the Museum as member of our Exhibitions department." He takes out a fountain pen and unscrews the cap, placing it neatly next to the paper.

"Exhibitions? Are you sure it's not porn?"

"Exhibitions is the name for the department that handles fieldwork. All of our operational terms are taken from museum vernacular. It was a deliberate choice to distance ourselves from our militaristic and bureaucratic roots."

Billie studies the form. It looks like standard boilerplate stuff, the sort of thing covered in a Business Admin 101 course,

71

with a modest stipend to be paid while she completes training. This is to be conducted in an unspecified location, and if she proves satisfactory she will be offered formal employment.

"Training to kill people," she says slowly. She sits back, looking at the pale purple type on the page. It has been mimeographed, like worksheets for a second-grade phonics class, and it smells like soup.

"Training to protect the same values for which every Allied soldier in the war gave his life," he says quietly.

"I'm not a soldier," she reminds him.

He taps the book. "Neither is Modesty Blaise. Neither is my sister. And still they fight."

This time Billie is quiet for a long moment, and Halliday is smart enough to stay quiet too. She looks down at her lacerated knuckles. "Can you teach me how to do damage to the other guy without hurting myself?"

"That," he says with a smile, "is our speciality." *Speciality.* When else in her life is she going to meet a man who says "speciality"?

She picks up the pen. "Alright, Major Halliday," she says, sweeping the nib of the fountain pen across the page in a scrawling signature. "Make a killer out of me."

He reaches for the form, smoothing it neatly before retrieving his pen. He screws the cap on slowly and gives her a knowing smile. "My dear Miss Webster, that is rather the point. We don't make killers. We simply find them and point them in the right direction. We know what you are."

CHAPTER FIVE

Mary Alice and I were bunking together while Helen and Natalie shared the cabin next to ours. Both were elaborate balcony staterooms, and our deck ("the elegant Nereid deck, designed for maximum privacy and serenity") had a small pool and bar that serviced just ten cabins. We made a plan to meet there the next morning for breakfast before heading out on our first shore excursion. I hoped exploring St. Kitts would rouse Helen's interest. Mourning a spouse was one thing, but Helen seemed broken, as if her spirit had died right along with Kenneth.

I said as much to Mary Alice when we disembarked the next morning in Basseterre, but she flapped a hand at me as she rubbed sunscreen into her face.

"I'm sure she's fine," she said, leaving a big white stripe down her nose.

I pointed ahead to where Helen was walking with Natalie. "Mary Alice, she is not fine. Even her hair seems sad. How would you feel if it were Akiko?"

"Well, that's not going to be a problem. Akiko and I have a pact. Whichever one goes first is going to haunt the shit out of whoever is left. And remarriage is not an option. I've already told her if she finds a new wife, I'll go full poltergeist."

She handed me the tube of sunscreen. "Here. Your nose is already going pink. And stop worrying about Helen. She'll get there in time."

Mary Alice pushed me down the gangplank and we spent the day shopping and exploring, eating grilled lobsters and sharing war stories late into the night. Helen perked up a little, which might have been the work of her second mai tai. Between the sea air and the white wine, I slept like the dead, waking to the sound of the gentle chime that indicated the announcements were imminent. The captain came on to greet the passengers and give a rundown on the weather and water conditions, complete with longitude and latitude. There was a detailed map in each room, and I could see that we'd sailed from Basseterre, around the bottom of St. Kitts, shooting the gap between that island and Nevis, a body of water called The Narrows. We had passed the swanky new Park Hyatt resort nestled in Christophe Harbour and were heading southeast now for Montserrat, the captain told us, with a leisurely day at sea ahead of us.

I dragged on a new black swimsuit that promised to hold everything in and smooth everything out. I tied a cotton pareo over it and headed to the pool. Mary Alice was already there, staking out an overstuffed lounger sofa. She was knitting something complicated, her expression intent as she counted stitches. The pattern was next to her, anchored by a stack of magazines and a novel whose cover featured two adorable men in Regency clothing making out enthusiastically.

"I didn't know Mr. Darcy was gay," I said, dropping my pareo and bag next to her.

"Anyone can be gay," she advised as she turned a row. "It's called retconning."

I smiled and slipped into the pool. It was heated salt water and felt like heaven as I plowed through it, lazily racking up laps until my fingers pruned and Mary Alice beckoned me out.

"Food's here," she called. She gestured to the low table in front of the sofa spread with baskets of miniature pastries, bowls of

Greek yogurt, tiny pots of honey and jam, and plates of intricately carved fruits. Pitchers of mimosas and Bloody Marys stood at either end and I motioned for her to pour.

Nat and Helen joined us just then and we toasted the morning, helping ourselves to the food. Helen waited to eat, reaching instead for an osteoporosis pill that she choked down with orange juice and a grimace. Nat's favorite porter, Hector, acted as waiter, bringing out heaping plates of poached eggs with a spicy relish on top of corn cakes.

He winked at Nat as he set them down and she peered over her sunglasses, watching his ass as he walked away.

"What do you think my chances are there?" she asked.

"Maybe he has a geriatric kink," I said, shaking out my napkin. "Dab a little Metamucil behind each ear and go get him, cougar."

"No, no," Mary Alice corrected. "She's too old to be a cougar. She's a saber-tooth tiger."

Natalie flipped Mary Alice off while I started on the fruit salad. We worked our way through breakfast at a leisurely pace. I took three bites of the spicy eggs and sat back, cursing.

"Hot flash," I muttered.

"Get back in the water," Mary Alice advised.

"It's heated," I told her, picking up my napkin to fan myself.

"There's a walk-in fridge behind the bar on each deck for drinks and snacks. You should go stand in it. That'll cool you down," Nat suggested.

"I'm sure that would be forty different health code violations," Mary Alice told her as she peered over her half-glasses.

Nat shrugged. "We're in international waters. They might not even have a health code here."

"Everyone has health codes," Mary Alice retorted.

The hot flash had started mild, a warmth that spread like a good hit of whiskey will do. Usually they hit that point and then crested before ebbing out. But this one hung around, building until the blood pounded in my ears and I wanted to peel my own skin off. Sunshine, alcohol, and spicy food were a recipe for misery, and I was just desperate enough to take Nat's advice.

She had a gift for always knowing her way around. Within minutes of walking into a place, she could tell you the nearest exit,

78

where the bathrooms were, and the best spot to find a drink.

Natalie gestured with her mimosa glass. "That way. Straight behind the bar and turn left. First door. Hector won't mind. If anyone else catches you, tell them you got lost. You're old, they'll believe it," she finished with a laugh.

I headed off, passing the bar where Hector stood polishing glasses and staring out to sea. I would have waved, but he didn't even notice me. That's the thing about being a sixty-year-old woman — no one notices you unless you want them to. That fact doesn't do your ego any favors, but in cases like this, it was damned handy.

Just left of the bar was a door marked SERVICE and I pushed it open to find a massive espresso maker and a sandwich press as big as my first car. Past that was a thick zinc door, and I hauled it open. Out gushed air — cold, luscious air — heavy with the metallic tang of refrigerant. I stood inside, pulling the door almost closed behind me. A light had flickered on as soon as I opened the door, and I spent the next few minutes looking around as my hot flash cooled. It was fitted out with shelves stacked carefully with trays of glasses for white wine and smoothies. Catering tubs of cut fruits stood on one set of shelves while another held crates of fresh produce. One shelf held assorted cheeses and the one below it had vast containers of dips — guacamole, hummus, baba ghanoush. I could smell the garlic from the doorway. I stepped further in, lured by the tray of chocolate-dipped fruit. Instead of the usual strawberries, someone had painstakingly stuck raspberries onto tiny crystal skewers like miniature kebabs and then played Jackson Pollock, spattering them with white and dark chocolate.

It was all too fussy for me, and as the hot flash eased, I wanted nothing more than a whole piece of fruit, nothing carved or glacéed or enrobed. I spied a few citrus boxes tucked under the last shelf and I reached down to tug one free. It was heaped with fresh mandarins, each with a tiny stem and leaves attached. I grabbed two and shoved the box back into place.

I had just shut the cooler door when I heard someone coming down the corridor. Shit. The cruise was inclusive. The food had been paid for and we could eat as much as we wanted. I hadn't taken anything that any crew member wouldn't have happily given me, I reasoned. But I didn't particularly want to get caught like a kid with her hand in the cookie jar. I was too old to get

80

lectured by somebody barely old enough to buy liquor.

I stepped behind the espresso machine, peeling open one of the mandarins while I waited. I popped a segment into my mouth and it was like eating sunshine, sharp and juicy and sweeter than a first kiss. The outer door opened and I stooped, peering around the edge of the machine. I caught sight of a young male form dressed in the liner's uniform of white cargo shorts — tighter than you'd expect — and snug white polo, spotless and crisp. He looked tidy, but a little thicker through the shoulders than most of the crew we'd met.

That heavy ass wasn't built from hauling around crates of tangerines, either, I realized. He bulged in places I didn't like. Forty years ago, men in my line of work were meant to blend in, the muscles slim and practical, fit for shimmying into an upstairs window or slipping out of tight spaces. The new recruits were freighted with gym muscles that did nothing but slow them down in a chase. They relied on guns and grenades, preferring to blow things up and make a mess instead of handling their business with a little finesse. I knew exactly what I was looking at, and when he turned and I saw his profile, I had a name to put with the ass.

Brad Fogerty, a junior field operative from the Museum. I opened my mouth to say hey, but before I could ease myself out of my hiding place, I froze. Brad was here undercover, masquerading as a member of the crew. That meant he was working. And if he was working, he knew we were on board — knew it and hadn't made contact. There were a hundred reasons another field agent might not make contact with us and none of them were good.

He passed close by me, close enough that I could read the name tag clipped to his polo. KEVIN C.

I held my breath until he went inside the cooler. I darted out and made my way straight back to the pool. Mary Alice was eating a croissant, large flakes scattered across her shirt like buttery confetti. Helen was nibbling at an English muffin.

Natalie had taken off her shirt and was staring down in dismay at her drooping bikini top. "I'm telling you, my tits are like two scoops of ice cream somebody has left out in the sun, just melted halfway down my chest with the cherries pointing south." She cupped her hand under one, giving it an experimental lift. She dropped her hand

and it fell back into place.

Mary Alice noticed me then and looked up. "Natalie was explaining to us the state of her tits," she said helpfully. "How are yours, dear?"

Natalie snorted. "Either Billie's had a procedure or that swimsuit is doing god's work. They're jacked up to her collarbones just like when she was eighteen."

Helen's grief laid on her like a fog, but she was always intuitive. She spoke up. "Something's wrong. What is it, Billie?"

"We've got trouble."

CHAPTER SIX

One of the skills we learned in training was how to shorthand a situation. I briefed them in a few sentences.

"Brad and I worked together in Nairobi," I finished. "If he's here, dressed as a member of the crew, he's on a job."

Helen nodded. "He moved into munitions after Nairobi. He's done well there. He and I did a job in Bucharest and his work was impressive. He managed to bring down an entire wing of the embassy with minimal collateral damage to the rest of the building."

I wasn't surprised she remembered him. Helen made notes in a Tiffany address book in her meticulous penmanship, tiny entries for every person she'd ever met, written with a Mark Cross pencil engraved with her initials. Pencil because Helen didn't like scratch-outs. She would carefully erase anyone who died or fell out of her orbit. No

84

matter how many times Helen and I scrapped, I always knew she'd never be really done with me unless she erased me from her book.

Mary Alice's reaction was succinct. "Shit."

Natalie reached for her shirt, buttoning it over her bikini top. "It doesn't mean he is here for one of us."

"Jesus, Natalie, you still don't know how to face a fact," I said. She reared back as if I'd slapped her, and I almost apologized. But I don't believe in saying sorry when you're not.

"There are ninety-six other passengers on this boat and as many crew," Natalie replied coldly. "Any one of them could be his mark."

"Natalie is right," Helen put in. "We shouldn't jump to conclusions until we know more."

Mary Alice purled a few times — or whatever it is knitters do. When she reached the end of the row, she stabbed the needles into the ball of yarn and put it aside. "Alright. So we find out more. One of us will have to discreetly make contact and give him an opportunity to explain."

"I'll do it," I said, reaching for my mimosa. "But if one of us is the mark, approaching him openly is as good as inviting him to take

85

a shot. I'll have a look around his cabin and see if I can get a handle on what he's doing. If he shows up, I'll give him a chance to explain."

Mary Alice nodded thoughtfully. "You need backup. Besides, it will look less suspicious if two of us are found wandering around together. I'll go."

I slid my glance over to Helen. "I think I'd rather have Helen, if it's all the same," I said easily.

Helen looked up, startled, then took a gulp of her Bloody Mary.

"Of course." But her knuckles were bone-white on her glass and I wondered if she was really up for it.

"I could come," Natalie offered.

"No," Helen said. "I'll go." She sounded more certain, but I noticed she finished her Bloody Mary with grim determination and poured a second one like it was her job.

But the Bloody Mary seemed to settle her down and for the rest of the day we stayed by the pool, swimming and sunning ourselves. We might have looked like carefree travelers, but we knew there was safety in numbers and without even talking about it we stuck together, even going to the bathroom in pairs. After lunch we went to our cabins to shower and rest. All of the crew were expected to work the dinner shift, so we decided that was the best time to nose around. While collecting a round of drinks, Natalie had managed to extract the location of the crew cabins from Hector, and I made a mental note of it on the map I slipped in my pocket as we headed down to dinner.

We ate our fill of the starter — "delicate avocado foam on a fire-roasted sea scallop" — and Helen and I eased out of the dining room when the main course was passed. We left our bags on our chairs to make it look like we'd just stepped out to use the powder room. I spotted Executive Guest Services Coordinator Heather Fanning table-hopping with a smile fixed to her mouth as she made sure everyone was having a won-derful time on this wonderful ship and was "hashtag blessed." I gave Helen an almost imperceptible nod. Fanning was senior staff and her key card would be a master.

As we passed her, Helen snaked out a slender arm and retrieved Heather's key card from her pocket. I shot Helen a wink. Her hands might shake a little, but she still had the talented fingers that made her the best pickpocket of all of us. She slid the key card into my hand and I palmed it as we headed downstairs.

I'd dressed for ease of movement in a

black jersey jumpsuit and flats. Helen was wearing a linen shift the color of lemon drops and a pashmina a few shades darker. She'd finished the outfit with a twist of rough-cut amber beads at her throat. They rattled slightly in the hushed stillness of the crew's quarters, just loud enough to attract attention we didn't want. I put out my hand and motioned for her to take them off.

She plucked the seams at her hips. "No pockets," she mouthed silently. I pointed to mine and she handed the beads over.

We found the crew cabins quickly. I had planned to break into the housekeeping closet to find the roster listing the cabin assignments, but there was no need. In college, we had papered the doors of our dorm rooms with brown paper grocery bags cut open and laid flat. Those were the days before answering machines, when people left messages on your door in grease pencil or felt-tip pen, and when the door was too full of notes or too many people had drawn dicks, you tore it off and started over. Here the doors were each fitted with tidy little whiteboards, but they served the same purpose. A dry-erase marker was neatly tethered to each one, and at the top, the name of the crew member assigned to the cabin had been printed in turquoise, the *i*'s dotted with starfish — a Heather Fanning signature touch.

We passed down the corridor, scanning the whiteboards until we came to Cabin 24. Kevin C.

I swiped the key card. There was a brief second of nothing and then a green light blinked; the mechanism clicked. I pushed open the door and we slipped inside, pulling the door closed behind us.

Helen's eyes were round with horror. "Cams?" she whispered.

I looked around the cabin, answering her almost as an afterthought. "I didn't see any."

"But they might have them," she persisted.

"Jesus, Helen, calm down. If they do, we'll just say we're elderly kleptomaniacs looking for something to steal. The worst they would do is slap us on the wrist and send us to bed without any dessert."

She wasn't happy about my flippancy, but she didn't fight me. I turned to search the room, wondering if I'd made a mistake in bringing her. She had lifted the key card well enough, but her nerve was fading and the one thing you couldn't afford to lose in our line of work was your composure.

I motioned for her to check the drawers, but I didn't think we'd find anything there. Or underneath the mattress, though I slid my hands down the length of it anyway. The wardrobe was impersonal, hung with spare uniforms and one set of shore clothes.

Helen made her way methodically through the drawers, feeling her way through neat stacks of underwear — tighty-whities, I was sad to note — and T-shirts.

"There's nothing," she said as she shut the drawer with an expression of disapproval. "Maybe we should just give him the benefit of the doubt and wait to see what he has to say for himself."

I ignored her and moved on. In the bottom of the wardrobe, there was a canvas bag with a printed name tag that said KEVIN COCHRAN.

"Sloppy," I said. In the old days, we always chose our own initials for an alias. It made it easier to cover slips of the tongue. Plus, if you had anything monogrammed, you could still wear it on a job. We had been trained with an old-fashioned attention to detail, but times had changed. Now the training was about gunsights and blast radius, and I hated it. I hated it even more for making me feel like a dinosaur in my own job, and I yanked open the bag irritably.

A book fell out, a worn paperback written by a man who was in love with guns and his own penis and probably not in that order.

90

There was nothing else inside, and I realized it was a very big bag — much too big for the few personal items Fogerty had brought on board. I had just put the bag back when Helen called my name softly.

She pointed under the cabinet screwed to the wall. It was a combination entertainment center, desk, and chest of drawers, everything neat and compact. It was pale wood and reached nearly to the floor. Just below it, pushed right out of sight, was a sleek leather attaché case.

"You always did have good eyes," I said as I bent to retrieve it. My back protested a little and I ignored it, stretching further to get my fingers around it. It was heavy, quality stuff. Nothing like the cheap canvas bag his alter ego had carried; this was custom-made by a specialist firm in Sweden to exact specifications. I knew the bag because I'd carried a few myself when the job called for it. The locks, six-digit combinations, were always set to the date assigned to the job.

I flicked the tumblers to tomorrow's date and tried. No luck.

Helen was watching closely. "The day after?"

I tried it, and the following two dates, but the lock stayed tight. A truly shitty possibility occurred to me and I flipped the numbers to that day's date. As soon as I hit the button, the metal tabs flew open.

"Today," I said. I glanced at the digital clock on the bedside shelf. "And today is over with in about six hours."

I looked at Helen and I swear to god something like relief flickered across her face. I would deal with Helen's death wish later, I decided. I lifted the lid on the case. I wasn't surprised to find a load of explosives and a cheerful little digital display showing five hours and thirty-two minutes. "It's on a timer," I told her. "We've got five and a half hours to figure this out."

If Helen had been slightly tempted to let herself get blown up, she knew the rest of us might object. Besides, there were about two hundred innocent people on that boat who'd go with her, and that was never okay. She pulled herself up. "Then we'll just have to throw it overboard," she said, reaching for the case.

I put out a hand to take her wrist. I could feel the bones, slim and brittle.

"We can't. It's a speedball." I pointed to the explosive. I didn't have to say more. Helen knew as well as I did that speedballs were the special brainchild of the Museum's munitions department. The recipe had been created to be as foolproof as possible, including lavish amounts of ammonium nitrate, ensuring the speedballs would explode even underwater. If we flung the case overboard, it would detonate anyway, regardless of the timer. I glanced at the speedball again. That big of a device would shear off the side of the *Amphitrite,* opening up the vessel like the cross-section of a boat in a kids' picture book. And then it would fill with water and sink, way too fast for anyone to muster the lifeboats.

"So, we have to get everyone off," she said.

"Unless you know how to disarm it," I said. We had all had munitions training. Anyone with an aptitude for blowing things up got moved to Temporary Installations, the Museum's idea of wit. The rest of us knew just enough to stay out of the way when they were working. And we knew that each device was set with a timer that had an override code known only to the operator. Any attempt to dismantle or disarm it prematurely would cause it to blow up, a sort of defense mechanism.

"We could just get the override from Fogerty," I suggested.

"And then what?" Helen asked.

I shrugged. "Hell if I know. I'm making this up as I go along, Helen. But at least we know what we're dealing with now. Let's get out of here and tell the others."

I was half turned away from the door or I would have seen him. In the time it took for me to look up, Fogerty was inside and shoving Helen out of the way with a clothesline arm. She flew back, hitting her head on the wall and crumpling to the floor in a slow slide, her legs straight out in front of her like a discarded doll.

The extra second he took to deal with Helen was enough for me to get my hand around the chair. I didn't have time to swing it and get any proper momentum, so I held it in front of me like a lion tamer and the bastard smiled.

"Nice try, Granny," he said, lifting the chair as easily as if it were made of balsa wood.

I kept my hold on the chair and as he raised it over my head, I lifted my legs, driving the heels of both feet into his kneecaps. He grunted and bent forward at the waist, bringing the chair down hard. But I'd seen it coming and flipped over, taking the hit squarely on my back. I let it push me down, onto all fours, diffusing the energy of the blow. He tossed the chair aside and reached down, his face set and purposeful. I grabbed his hand and twisted the thumb back, causing him to open his stance, exposing his

94

groin. I took a breath and donkey kicked, my heel connecting squarely with his balls. I didn't stop. I followed through, pushing as hard as I could until he choked and fell to his knees.

He would have fallen on top of me but I rolled out of the way and rebounded off the bunk to land on his back. I wrapped one leg around his waist and bent the other, driving the knee into his lower spine. I grabbed the beads out of my pocket and whipped them around his neck, taking a wrap around each palm to hold them tight.

And then I pulled. I pulled like I was trying to stop a runaway horse, fists tight against my shoulders while my knee pushed him into a backbend that made his spine crack. His hands scrabbled at his throat, tearing at the necklace.

"Don't you dare break, goddammit," I muttered to the beads. I tightened my hold and pulled up again and his hand came up, slapping blindly. He caught me on the temple, hard enough to blur my vision for a second, but I held on.

After several seconds, he sagged, but I didn't let up. Helen was moving a little, and by the time she opened her eyes properly, it was over. I was still coiled around him, beads biting into my hands as he jerked one last time and then gave way, relaxing into a huddle on the floor.

Helen knew better than to question whether it was necessary. She eased herself up and came to look, pulling back his eyelid. After a second, she nodded. "Clear."

"Good," I said, easing my grip. Deep red marks streaked across my palms and the backs of my hands. "What the hell kind of jewelry is this, Helen?"

She shrugged. "It was made for the Helsinki job and I liked how it looked with this dress, so I kept it." She pushed a bead aside to show me how it was strung. "Piano wire. I used it on the head of the Finnish national bank."

She fastened the necklace around her neck and looked down at the slumped remains of Brad Fogerty.

"Still want to give him the benefit of the doubt?" I asked.

She pursed her lips. "Billie, far be it from me to criticize, but shouldn't we have kept him alive to get the override?"

I looked at the timer, still ticking away relentlessly.

"Shit."

CHAPTER SEVEN

I doubled over, whooping air into my lungs. Helen stood back until I took a full breath and stood up straight, one hand at my lower back.

"Alright?"

I gave her a short nod. "I wasn't expecting that. I should have stretched first." The truth was, it had been some time since I'd wrapped myself like a pretzel around someone I was trying to kill, to say nothing of choking someone out. It's more a matter of leverage than brute strength, but you always feel it in your biceps and traps as soon as you're finished if you've done it right. Too many people think it comes from the forearms, but that's a good way to end up with a bad case of tennis elbow.

Generally, I was good with my age. Turning sixty hadn't sent me into a tailspin or whipped up an existential crisis. Aging in our business was a luxury most never got.

But it straight up pissed me off when I came up against something I couldn't do as easily as I used to. Every day I walked ten miles and did two hours of yoga. I spent twelve hours a week pounding my fists into a heavy bag and lifting weights. I popped supplements like they were Pez, but once in a while some little shit like Brad Fogerty crossed my path and I felt every damned year.

I dropped to my knees on the carpet and put my chest to the floor, stretching my arms out into puppy-dog pose while Helen surveyed the device.

"Billie, again, I don't mean to sound critical," she said patiently, "but is this really the best use of our time?"

"Helen, my lower back has seized like a son of a bitch and I don't know what the rest of this evening's activities are going to require, so how about you hush up and see if you can figure out how to disarm that thing while I persuade my vertebrae to be friends again."

It was a cranky reply, but I was annoyed. Helen had been one of the best — cool, reliable, unflappable. And now she seemed well and truly flapped.

But she'd regained something of her old spirit by the time I'd worked my way through child's pose and a few sets of cat and cow. I pushed myself to my feet.

"Thoughts?"

She shook her head. "You know I've always hated these things." She pulled a face. Bombs were messy; explosives left bits and pieces of people lying around like so much litter after a Mardi Gras parade. Helen liked things tidy. She took great pride in the fact that she'd once drilled a mark in a stiff wind at eight hundred yards, so cleanly that she put the round directly through the socket of his eye, not even skimming the bone. She'd been given a commendation for that one.

I closed the case, snapping the clasps. "Then we have to take it with us."

Just then Fogerty emitted an unpleasant noise accompanied by a smell I knew too well. The human body has over sixty sphincters, and every one of them relaxes in death.

My usual remedy was a Brach's Star Brites mint — easy to carry and not suspicious — but anything peppermint will do. I went into the bathroom and grabbed his toothpaste, dabbing a bit under my nose. I knelt next to him and went through his pockets. He had his crew lanyard stuffed into one but nothing else.

"He must have stashed his ID and money

with his means of escape," I told Helen. "We should get going."

Helen and I exchanged glances, then she heaved a sigh and dragged the cover off his bed, snapping it out as she draped it on the floor. We rolled him into it, then maneuvered him into the wardrobe. When we finished, Helen sprayed lavishly from the bottle of cheap aftershave in his Dopp kit. I surveyed our handiwork. Anyone taking a quick glance would think he had left a bundle of dirty bedclothes stuffed into his wardrobe. It wouldn't stand up to a close inspection, but it might buy us some time.

Helen took the case, tucking it carefully under her arm and draping her pashmina over it while I closed the door behind us. Helen and I made our way up two flights of stairs to our deck, careful to look like we were having a nonchalant chat as we went.

"Ladies!" Heather Fanning found us just as we reached my cabin. "Everything okay? We're missing a swell dinner! There's even a lovely rose petal rice congee for dessert." She pitched her voice high, the way tiresome people do when they're talking to anyone older than they can ever imagine being.

Helen turned to face her. "Thank you, dear. My friend has a touch of seasickness and I thought I'd see her to her cabin. She just needs a little lie-down."

I hunched over, clutching my stomach, and Heather Fanning's face puckered in distaste. "Oh, that is a shame! If you need the doctor, do let us know. In the meantime, we offer a full assortment of ginger-based natural remedies in the wellness shop on the Hygieia deck."

I growled a little in the back of my throat.

"Thank you, dear," Helen told her sweetly. "But I brought some edibles."

She took the key card from my hand and swiped it viciously, shoving me inside the cabin and shutting the door firmly on Heather Fanning's shocked face before I burst out laughing.

"Edibles?"

She went to put the attaché case down on Mary Alice's bed. "I hate people like her. Talking to us like we're toddlers." Her voice rose in perfect mimicry. "You're missing a swell dinner. Rice pudding for dessert!"

"She said it was a very lovely rose petal congee," I reminded her.

"I don't care what she calls it. It's rice pudding, and I am so goddamned tired of being old." She sat heavily on my bed, and I saw the glimmer of tears in her eyes. I went to the bathroom and got a hand towel. The

101

ice bucket had been filled and left with an orchid on the console. I tossed the orchid aside and wrapped a handful of ice in the cloth. I brought it to Helen and laid it gently on the back of her head.

"You took a crack."

She held it in place. "I suppose it's no use complaining about feeling decrepit when there's a bomb ticking down five feet away and I may never get any older," she said reasonably. "It's just that ever since Kenneth died, I've aged twenty years. I can't even touch my toes anymore, let alone do what you just did," she added in an accusing tone.

"Helen, cut yourself some slack. I didn't lose the love of my life. Mourning is a bitch. And it's a process. You're just not finished with it."

"That's the point," she said. "I think I am. At least I want to be. I am so sick and tired of waking up feeling like someone tore off one of my limbs. Every morning, for just a few seconds, I forget. I wake up and it hasn't happened yet. There's nothing but emptiness and calm. And then it comes crashing down and I hate it. I hate it so much."

I sat next to her, shoulder to shoulder. "I'm sorry. I know that doesn't help."

"No, it doesn't," she said. "Not even a little. It feels like a physical weight, something that somebody thrust into my arms and made me carry. I didn't ask for this. I wish I could break pieces of it off and hand them over to other people. Let them have their turn."

"We all have our turn in the end," I said. I put my arm around her, trying not to feel how little flesh was left on her bones. If I blew hard enough, I could send her tumbling away like a dandelion seed. God only knew where she would land.

She took a deep breath. "Well, I suppose if we die tonight, I'm okay with it. I've had a good life, you know. I was married to Kenneth for over thirty years. Eighteen of them were really happy. That's not so bad."

"What happened to the other twelve?"

"Erectile dysfunction and his abortive attempt to breed Weimaraners."

I burst out laughing and for an instant she bristled like she was getting ready to take offense. But then she laughed too.

Just then the door opened and Mary Alice and Nat appeared with our handbags and boxes of leftovers. "What happened to you two?" Mary Alice asked as Natalie held up one of the boxes.

"Some sort of rice pudding shit with rose,

but it's good," she said. She handed out spoons as Mary Alice looked at the case on her bed.

"What's this?" she asked. I told her the code and she opened it. "Well, hell," she said, stepping back.

Nat shoved a spoonful of rice pudding into her mouth before coming close, bending over the explosive like a fond mother with a newborn child.

"Oh, that's good stuff," she said. "So the little prick was getting ready to blow the boat — with us on it."

"We're either the marks or the Museum doesn't care if we were collateral damage," I said.

"That's hurtful," Mary Alice put in. "We've given forty years to those assholes and this is how they repay us. But why? It doesn't make sense."

"That's not a now problem," I said, reverting to training. It was a reminder to focus on the job at hand and set the priorities where they should be. "Right now, we have to figure out how to dismantle this or how to get everyone off this boat before it blows."

"Easy," Nat said, spooning up more of the pudding. "Override code."

Helen cleared her throat. "Billie removed Fogerty from the equation before we could secure it."

"How far removed?" Mary Alice asked.

"Completely," I said.

"Dammit, Billie —" Nat began.

Helen put up her hand. "Billie did what she had to do," she said. For all her prissiness, Helen was loyal as a lapdog. "And it's done now. We checked his cabin and pockets. He must have memorized it like he was supposed to instead of leaving it lying around."

"Just our luck he wasn't a complete slackass," Natalie said. She tapped the spoon against her teeth.

Mary Alice looked around. "We have to get everyone off the boat."

I pushed myself to my feet. "I'll do it. It's my mistake so I'll clean it up."

Mary Alice gave me a level look. "Fire in the engine room?"

I nodded. "I'll make it good and smoky. One of you hit the alarm. That will start evacuation procedures," I said, remembering the lifeboat drill from the previous day.

"But not everyone will go," Mary Alice objected. "The engine room crew will stay and try to put it out."

"Not if the lifeboats are pushed out. Each one has crew assigned to it, and the engine room boys will have to man their lifeboat.

I'll sweep for stragglers," I promised her. "And I'll set multiple fires to ramp up the confusion. We'll get everyone off in time. The captain will send a mayday before he abandons ship. At worst, people will have a few rough hours in the lifeboats on the open sea before help arrives, and the explosion will be chalked up to an engine room malfunction."

"What about us?" Helen asked.

"What *about* us?" Natalie replied.

"Someone from the Museum is trying to kill us. When the lifeboats are recovered, they will log the passengers to make sure no one is missing."

"And?" Nat still wasn't getting it, but the light was dawning for me.

"We won't be dead," I told her. "We'll be listed officially as surviving the explosion."

"And they'll try again," Mary Alice added. "They might have even assigned Fogerty a backup we haven't spotted yet."

We looked at one another. "Shit," Natalie said.

"So, we need to get off the boat before it blows but not with the other passengers," Helen summed up.

"And we have about five minutes to make a plan," Mary Alice added. "We can't take a lifeboat because they're all assigned."

"That's a very 'glass is half-empty' attitude, Mary Alice," Natalie told her.

I held up a hand. "She's right. So that leaves the rubber launch we rode in to Basseterre. It's got a motor but the fuel tank is small. We'll run out before we get halfway to land, but it has sails and charts. Helen, you're the only one of us who knows how to sail. Grab anything you think we'll need. Nat, you sound the alarm and pitch a wall-eyed fit until people start getting into boats. A little bit of old-lady hysteria will get them nervous. Mary Alice, provisions. Water and any food you can find that's packaged. It may be some time until we're picked up or can get to an island. Leave your phones. No credit cards, but bring all your cash. And leave the passports. From the minute we go over the side of this boat, we're operating off-grid."

Nat groaned and Helen looked resigned. Ditching the passports and credit cards would be a pain when we eventually reached land, but anything that could track us was out of the question.

I started to get up, but Mary Alice stopped me. "You realize what this means? We're burning our identities. Our *own* identities."

We looked at each other, our faces grim. Every assignment had brought cover identities, pseudonyms and papers we tossed aside as soon as the job was done. We never traveled or worked under our own names; it was too dangerous. The aliases gave us a buffer, a layer of protection between our civilian lives and the work we did.

And now the work was forcing its way in, unwanted and uninvited.

"We don't have a choice," I said simply.

She nodded. "I know. I just . . . Akiko."

We were silent again. Akiko would get a call, *the* call. Someone from the State Department, probably. Informing her in short, awful phrases that her wife had been lost at sea.

"Not a now problem, Mary Alice," I told her flatly.

I got up and this time she didn't stop me. I grabbed a few bottles from the minibar and put them into the laundry bag from the wardrobe along with the morning's newspaper and a T-shirt.

My identification and other papers I left. If any scraps survived, they would support the fiction that we had died in the explosion. I pocketed my cash — a few hundred American dollars — along with a tin of Altoids. I stripped the thin neoprene case off of my e-reader and put the case into the same pocket, stopping just long enough to grab a couple of large safety pins out of the vanity kit to secure it closed.

Into the other pocket went the Swiss Army knife I'd brought in my checked bag, but I left that pocket open just in case I needed quick access to it. I grabbed my lighter, heavy and silver, stashing it in my pocket with the knife. There wasn't much in my jewelry roll, just a few pairs of hoop earrings and some diamond studs, which I put into my ears. They were a carat each, so clear and flawless they looked like fakes, but they'd be a useful source of cash if we needed to pawn them. Also in the jewelry roll was a narrow belt of gold coins that looked like replicas but were Pahlavis, souvenirs from a job in Iran and the only other thing of value I had brought. I would have clipped it around my waist, but it clattered like hell so I handed it over to Helen for safekeeping. She stuffed it into her Birkin with her address book and her pills.

By the time I finished sorting my things and turned my attention back to the others, they were on their feet. The change in posture had changed the mood. They were focused now, serious and businesslike. We checked our watches — some things we like to do old-school — and looked at each other. We were in a small huddle, standing close enough to one another that I could smell Helen's Shalimar, Natalie's neroli oil, Mary Alice's green tea shampoo. A wave of love for them hit me so hard, it nearly buckled my knees.

"Screw it," I said abruptly. Emotion is a good way to get yourself killed, the Shepherdess had taught us. I hefted the attaché case.

"You're taking it?" Helen asked.

"It's better this way. The lower down it is when it detonates, the greater the chance it will take out the whole boat." I went to the door and took one last look. "See you on the other side."

"The other side," they said. Three old women, nodding their heads like the witches in *Macbeth*. I'd known them for two-thirds of my life, those impossible old bitches. And I would save them or die trying.

110

CHAPTER EIGHT

I made my way belowdecks, stopping a few times to dodge around a corner when a crew member passed. It seemed to take ages to reach the engine room, but my watch said it had been less than ten minutes. I wasn't surprised. Time always seemed elastic on a job. Seconds felt like eternities and whole hours could pass in an instant. Heather Fanning's key card swiped me right where I needed to go, and I slipped into the room, keeping my ears open for the sound of any engineers who might be hanging around. It was after nine and most of them were probably finishing their dinners or hitting the crew bar. A few would be left to supervise that everything was running smoothly, and they could do that by monitoring the computers. There wasn't much call for them to hang out by the NGL tanks, I realized. It seemed as good a place as any to stash the case, so I wedged it between two tanks, counting on the shadows to conceal it from a casual glance.

Then I headed up another deck to the deserted library. Hunkered behind a chair, I took out the T-shirt and used the Swiss Army knife to cut it into pieces. The newspaper I crumpled into loose balls and piled on top of the T-shirt, soaking the whole pile with the alcohol from the minibar. The newspaper would burn fast but the fabric would smoke like hell, hopefully setting off the emergency warnings. I opened the door and took a cautious look outside. Empty. I slipped out and jammed the door closed.

My third stop was my own cabin. I was out of liquor, but I made do with some nail polish remover from Mary Alice's toiletry bag, dousing the sheets and setting them alight. I fired my bed and Mary Alice's, making sure to drop the security bolt as I exited by the terrace doors. I left them open, the sea breeze already whipping the flames up high enough to touch the ceiling. The curtains were drifting dangerously near and it would only be a matter of minutes before they caught.

I stood on the terrace, waiting for Natalie's signal. Suddenly, the alarm sounded, loud as a trumpet of the Second Coming, and I put a hand to the railing, vaulting over it and lowering myself to the deck below. Another suite was just below ours, and I counted on the guests still being out. They'd even been considerate enough to leave the terrace doors open, and I passed through their suite, emerging into the corridor on the other side.

From there I moved out to the deck where pandemonium had erupted. Natalie was shrieking about smelling smoke and a harried pair of stewards were trying to quiet her down while Heather Fanning urged everyone to stay calm. She was still insisting it was just a false alarm when the captain's voice came over the PA issuing the orders to head directly to the lifeboats.

To their credit, the crew did as they'd been trained, organizing the passengers into their lifeboat queues, trying to check everyone off by name. Helen and Mary Alice hit two lines each, giving their own names to one steward, mine and Nat's to another. Both times they were answered with brusque nods and told to stay close in order to be loaded into the next boat. And both times they slipped away into the scrum.

Nat and I headed towards the back of the boat to rendezvous with them. We'd just rounded the corner of the Theia deck when a voice boomed out behind us. "Ladies!

113

Don't be frightened. I've got seats for both of you."

It was Hector, wearing a lurid fluorescent orange life vest and looking determined to play the hero. "Thanks, but we've got assigned seats," I told him. "Go on to your boat and don't worry about us."

"Absolutely not! My ladies should not be left alone to find their way. Come, I will take care of you."

"Jesus Christ," Natalie muttered. "We're running out of time. We have to get rid of him."

"Then maybe you shouldn't have flirted so much with him," I hissed at her. I turned squarely to face him. "Hector, we're not assigned to you. We are fine. Go to your boat," I said again.

He shook his head and put out a hand to grip my arm. "You're just panicking because you're scared," he said in what he probably thought was a soothing tone. "Now, come with me."

"I don't have time for this patriarchal bullshit," I said, whipping out a right cross that caught him on the sweet spot just below his ear. He went down silently, as if every bone had been filleted out of his body, landing in a heap on the deck.

"Wow. He must have a jaw like porcelain,"

114

Nat remarked.

Together, Nat and I hoisted the unconscious Hector. I grabbed his shoulders while she took his ankles, and we swung him over the rail, dropping him into the water with an enormous splash.

I caught the attention of the nearest steward. "Man overboard!" I shouted, gesturing to the sea below where Hector was bobbing peacefully.

The steward swore and ran to alert someone while Nat and I hustled to the stern of the boat to meet up with Mary Alice and Helen. They were standing by the motor launch, the rubber motorized raft designed to ferry passengers from the boat for a hundred yards or so to the waiting docks. It was meant for harbors, not the open sea, but it would have to do. Together we maneuvered it off the fantail, cutting it loose instead of wrestling with the ropes. It started to drift as soon as it hit the water, the current carrying it away from the larger vessel.

We had seconds to jump, a good twenty feet straight down to a target that looked a hell of a lot smaller than I had expected. Nat went first, landing squarely in the middle of the launch and scuttling out of Helen's way as she dropped. Mary Alice didn't even try, preferring to take her chances in the water. She went in a clean six feet from the launch, a few strokes pulling her to the side, where Helen and Nat hauled her in. Behind me, the alarms were shrieking and there was a thunderous boom from somewhere deep inside the boat. The noise caused more mayhem, with people screaming and shoving as the lifeboats were launched.

I took a breath and jumped, aiming as Mary Alice had done for the sea next to the launch. The water closed over me, warm and silky, and so dark it was impossible to tell which way was up. I held my breath, letting it out slowly so I could figure out where to go. A slender line of silver bubbles trailed out of my nose, pointing the way. I followed, breaking the surface to see a constellation shimmering just overhead.

Helen and Mary Alice reached out, hoisting me under the arms until I flopped into the bottom of the boat, coughing up seawater.

Helen looked up into the night sky, assessing the stars to determine our location.

"Got it?" I asked her.

She nodded.

"Good. Aim for Nevis and let's get the

hell out of here."
And that's exactly what we did.

CHAPTER NINE
JANUARY 1979

It is raining when the plane touches down. The quartet of girls who spill out of the plane, yawning widely, might be mistaken for school friends as they collect their bags and lie, smiling, to the official who stamps their passports and asks their purpose in visiting the United Kingdom. A man in a tweed suit with a printed sign is waiting for them and escorts them to an estate wagon, where a hamper of sandwiches is waiting. They eat as he drives them into the country. An hour passes, then another. By the time they arrive, it is getting dark and the girls are cramped and jet-lagged. They stagger out of the car to stand in front of a mansion — or at least it seems like a mansion to them.

The house is a Victorian monstrosity of red brick surrounded by gardens and a big lawn that rolls down to the cliffs. It is scruffy, from the worn brick paths to the streaky windows of the glasshouse attached to one side. The trim could use a lick of paint, and the brass door knocker is black with grime.

But the door opens and none of that matters. *She* is standing in the doorway, looking them over with the air of a general inspecting her troops. Constance Halliday. Code name Shepherdess. They do not know yet the full extent of her legend. They will learn her story in pieces, and what they will hear is as much myth as truth. She wears her thin white hair closely cropped to her scalp and she walks with a stick, not for balance, but for hitting recruits who don't move fast enough.

As a young woman, she studied Classics at Cambridge and would have taken a First if women had been allowed degrees. Her brother, Major Halliday, has told each of the girls about the Furies, Constance's squad of all-female operatives, and how they died — parachuting into Germany as Nazi sharpshooters picked them off in midair. He has told them Constance survived, but he never mentions she was injured in the drop. Upon being captured, she was sent to Ravensbrück, where her broken leg was set badly. She escaped from the camp, walking halfway across Europe on it before it was fully mended, and her limp is a badge of honor to others, but to her it is a reminder of everything she has had taken from her. When Churchill singled her out for honors, she returned her letter of commendation in pieces with a pithy note in blue pencil about his collective failures.

Her time as a founding member of the Board of Directors at the Museum bored her. She put herself back into the field within months, spending three decades training the best assassins in the business — all of them men. It is her idea to freshen up the talent pool by finding a group of young women to train together. A series of small strokes has slowed her, and she realizes properly that she is growing old. For the first time, Constance Halliday takes stock of her life, and it occurs to her that she would like to leave a legacy to her own sex. She misses the Furies, the camaraderie of women at war. It takes three years for her brother to find her exactly the right sort of young women to train, but she believes they will be worth the wait. They will be the last and best thing she ever does — a fitting coda to the Furies. She will make avenging goddesses of them, killing machines who will fulfill a very special destiny.

But she says none of this when she meets

her quartet. She has read their files until the pages are soft and blurred, but this is the first time she has seen them in person. She stares at them through cold blue eyes until finally she gives a single nod and motions for them to follow her inside. The house isn't much warmer than the driveway, but at least it isn't wet. There is a fire burning in the drawing room and she leads them in, making them stand while she circles slowly before coming to stillness in front of the fireplace.

"Welcome to Benscombe Hall. If you are here, it is because we have seen something in you. It is entirely possible that we are wrong," she says, her eyes pitiless. "But we have been doing this a very long time and we might just be right. Project Sphinx is a very special undertaking, the first chance for a squad of female operatives to be trained together under the auspices of our organization. You will not let us down."

It isn't a question, and the temperature in the room seems to drop about twenty degrees while she talks.

"There are those in the Museum who believe a group of women cannot be trained effectively to do our work. I believe that you can. You can, and you will. Women are every bit as capable of killing as men. And you have advantages that men do not. You are all attractive young women, and your appearance means men underestimate you. You will use this to your advantage."

She pauses to eye Mary Alice's impressive decolletage with a raised eyebrow. "Some of your advantages are more apparent than others, but amongst the four of you, there is something to appeal to most tastes. You, for instance," she says, pointing her walking stick at Helen, "you have an icy, Jacqueline Kennedy quality. Very refined. And you," she says, gesturing to Natalie, "are gamine, like Audrey Hepburn." Helen and Nat exchange quick smiles. Constance Halliday moves on to Mary Alice. "I think I need not enumerate your charms, my dear," she says. "That sort of overripe body was very popular in the 1950s and there are still many men who prefer it to —" She motions vaguely to Billie, who stares coolly back. Constance Halliday wraps both hands around the top of her walking stick. The cane is dark, reddish wood, and the silver head is some kind of bird with eyes made of black glass beads.

"No, you do not have the obvious appeal of Miss Tuttle," she says with a nod to Mary Alice. Billie is impressed that their mentor knows their names without asking, but she realizes there must be reports on each of them, files with all sorts of information, and that makes her uncomfortable.

Constance Halliday cocks her head as she studies Billie. "No, a less emphatic sort of attractiveness than Miss Tuttle," she repeats, "but you look like the sort of young woman who enjoys sex. Do you?"

"Yes."

"Good. Men will sniff that out and it will be quite useful. They have a sixth sense for *earthiness*. But mind you don't let it get out of hand," she says severely. "Sex is a weapon, Miss Webster. Do not permit it to be used against you."

She steps back. "Your rooms are upstairs — you will share. Go and put your things away and wash up for dinner. I will see you in the dining room in quarter of an hour."

The foursome retrieve their bags from the front hall and carry them upstairs. Without much discussion, Mary Alice and Billie take one room while Helen and Natalie take the other. The rooms are simple, with twin beds and plain wool coverlets. There isn't much in the way of furniture, and the rooms are clearly meant to share a decrepit old bathroom in the hallway.

Mary Alice kicks off her shoes and flops down on her bed. "I love this place. Helen says it's just like something straight out of *Winnie-the-Pooh* or *The Wind in the Willows.* And Miss Halliday is a pip. I like her."

"Well, she didn't just call you a slut, so I get that."

Mary Alice laughs. "I suppose that's your superpower. Natalie and Helen can be the cool debutantes, playing hard to get, while you and I . . ." She pauses and does a sort of shimmy that would be fairly obscene if she were not wearing a bra.

After they wash, they go downstairs, ready for their first etiquette lessons. Miss Halliday sits them down for a formal dinner at a table heavy with silver and china. Helen looks completely at ease, but Natalie picks up a fingerbowl and pokes at the lemon slice floating on the water.

"What kind of soup is this?" she demands. "It looks like hot water."

"Because it is hot water, Miss Schuyler," Miss Halliday tells her. She sits on the front third of her chair, back straight as a ramrod as she perches like a hawk, looking at them with raptor eyes. "Your assignments will take you into all manner of company around the world, including into the highest diplomatic circles. You will be prepared to conduct yourselves appropriately," she says, daring them to object. "My code name is

124

Shepherdess because my aptitude is in looking after people, assessing their abilities and making certain they are cultivated. It is my task to prepare you, to anticipate dangers and make certain nothing takes you by surprise. My last squad with the SOE were the Furies, characters out of mythology. Do you know who the Furies were?" she demands, looking around the table.

Helen ventures an answer. "In Classical mythology, the Furies were the bringers of vengeance. They tortured people who had not paid for their crimes."

A tiny smile plays about Constance Halliday's mouth. "Homer said they lived in darkness and had no pity. He called them avengers, the daughters of the night. It was righteous anger that sustained them. It was a good name for my girls."

She takes a deep swallow of wine, leaving a tiny purple crescent on either side of her mouth. "But the world has changed. Anger alone is not enough. You must have cunning and mystery as well as savagery. Do you know what sphinxes look like?" she asks the table at large.

Mary Alice speaks up. "Lions with the faces of men."

"That is an Egyptian sphinx," Constance Halliday corrects. "You are named for the

125

Greek sphinx, a creature with the face and breasts of a beautiful woman, and the body of a lioness. She even has wings."

"No shit?" Natalie asks, her eyes large and round.

Constance Halliday ignores her and sits back in her chair, studying the light playing off the wine in her glass. "Scholars do not agree on the etymology of the word 'sphinx,' but I prefer the theory that says it is from the Greek 'sphingo,' meaning 'to squeeze.' Because sphinxes are lionesses and that is how lionesses kill. They asphyxiate their prey, choking the life from them without mercy, not because they are evil or bad but because they are hunters, and that is what hunters do." She pauses, letting her words sink in. "And you will put a shilling in the swear jar, Miss Schuyler," she adds. "You may swear on your own time. But here at Benscombe, your time belongs to me."

CHAPTER TEN

Helen kept the launch pointed east-northeast for the better part of the night, supervising as the rest of us took turns with the tiller. We held the speed low to save fuel, letting the wind carry us along, gigging the engine only to correct the course. Sometime after we set out, a boom shook the world and a pillar of fire reached up into the night sky. A cloud of oily smoke obscured the moon.

"Well, that's that," Helen said with a sigh. She turned her face to the blankness of the western horizon. Everything, sea and sky, was black and vaguely spangled with stars. We settled into the boat, wrapping up against the breeze that had sprung up.

It wasn't a pleasant night, but we had all had worse. By late the next morning, Helen was steering us into a small cove on Nevis. We grabbed our gear, scuppered the launch so it couldn't be traced to the *Amphitrite*, and headed along the paved road at the top of a little rise, skirting the houses and hotels. After half an hour of walking, I led the way down onto the beach.

"Where are we going?" Nat demanded, struggling. My espadrilles were flat, but she was wearing her wedges, hard going in the loose-packed sand.

"There," I said, pointing to a sign which spelled out SUNSHINE in rope lights that were unlit in the daytime. It was a beach bar, one of the most legendary in the Caribbean. "We're going to order lunch and a round of Killer Bees. Anyone asks, we're on vacation and we're staying on St. Kitts," I told them.

Whether it was the promise of roasted fish or the bar's legendary rum punch, they didn't fuss. We ate and drank until our plates were empty and the last drop of rum punch was gone, paying cash with a tip that was generous enough to be appreciated but not so generous as to be memorable. When we finished, the bartender dialed us up a cab, which dropped us at the water taxi landing. It was directly across The Narrows from the bottom end of St. Kitts, where the Park Hyatt lay gleaming under the sun. The landscaping was lush and the whole resort was tucked between the edge of the sea and

128

the hills rising directly behind it.

The water taxi took six minutes to cross The Narrows, carrying vacationers and commuters. The captain chatted with his regulars, and Mary Alice made a point of flipping through a tourist magazine she had grabbed from a rack at Sunshine's. The water taxi dropped us directly at the Hyatt's dock.

I nodded towards a line of sun loungers on the beach, facing Nevis. "Go and sit comfortably for a minute. I'm going to get a room."

"How do you expect to do that without a passport?" Helen demanded.

I reached into my pocket and pulled out the neoprene e-reader case I'd been carrying since I went off the stern of the *Amphitrite*. A quick flick of my knife along the seam, and it was open. Sealed inside was a Canadian passport with my face but a different name.

"I'll be damned," Nat said slowly. "Do you always travel with extra papers?"

"Ever since Argentina," I said with a grimace. The Argentina job was one of the most dangerous I'd ever done, and an extra set of papers would have saved me a rough interrogation and two months' incarceration in a prison camp on the pampas.

"And how is our Canadian friend planning to pay for her room?" Helen asked.

I dipped back into the case to retrieve a Black Amex. "She has a credit card."

Just then a staff member wearing a striped T-shirt and a broad smile came over with tall glasses of iced water decorated with slices of cucumber. She served Nat and Mary Alice while Helen and I made our way up the hill to the main lodge. In other circumstances, I might have been impressed. It was open-air with koi ponds and a spectacular view across The Narrows to Nevis. The atmosphere was serene, and I wanted to relax, but it was too soon.

The front desk was like something out of *Architectural Digest* — a long slab of polished black concrete with rattan barstools and a lofty arrangement of orchids. Only a slim tablet computer indicated any business was done there. The clerk greeted us graciously. I gave her a thin smile in return. It was important to pitch the tone just right, somewhere between irritation and entitlement.

I eyed her name tag. "Sophia, I hope you can help us. We're booked into a luxury villa on the other side of the island, and I'm afraid it will not do," I said, pinching my mouth to suggest something unspeakable.

"Do you have a room available?"

"I'm so sorry to hear that! Let me see what I can do." She tapped rapidly at her tablet. "I do have a lovely beachside double queen, but I'm afraid it's on the far side of the resort, away from the restaurants and pools," she said, gesturing towards the opposite side of the curving bay.

I sighed a little. "I'm sure that's fine," I said in a tone of mild disappointment.

"It's ready right now," she assured me. "And as I said, it's beachside, so it is on the ground floor with direct beach access."

"That will do," Helen put in, her English very faintly accented with something that might have been Dutch or Danish or anywhere in between.

Sophia smiled gratefully at us. "I'm so glad. I will just need a credit card and your passports."

Helen made a pantomime gesture towards her nonexistent wallet, and I placed my card and passport decisively in the little tray on the table. "No, no. I'll handle it."

"Thank you, dear," she murmured.

"My friend has left her wallet back at the villa. We'll stop by later and let you make a copy after we've sent for our bags."

Sophia hesitated for the length of a heartbeat and then smiled. "Of course. If you'll give me just a moment." She disappeared with the credit card and passport into a back office. If anything was going to go wrong, this was the moment. I took deep, calming breaths and repeated the mantra I had adopted while on assignment at an ashram in Kerala. Helen flipped through a coffee table book on the photography of Lorna Simpson.

A few eternal minutes later, Sophia emerged with a basket of chilled towels and bottles of mineral water. She passed them over with our papers and room keys.

"Welcome to the Park Hyatt, ladies. Enjoy your stay."

We refused the resort tour on the grounds that we were meeting friends for lunch. As soon as we left the main lodge, we collected Nat and Mary Alice from the beachside and followed the map to our room.

"Safe for now," Nat murmured. That had been another of the Shepherdess' dicta. Whenever you were safe, even if it was for a short time, it was important to give yourself a chance to exhale, to take nourishment and rest and live to fight again.

I kicked off my espadrilles and stretched onto the bed, lacing my hands behind my head.

"What now?" Mary Alice asked. "We've

gotten this far, but we're still in the Caribbean with one passport and one credit card amongst the four of us. How are we getting home?"

"Not home," Helen reminded her. "We need a safe house. We need to buy ourselves enough time to figure out what the hell is going on."

We were silent a minute, all of us probably thinking the same thing. For all our experience, we were used to the luxury of an entire organization at our disposal, ready to pluck us out of the field if we were in danger, prepared to clean up our messes, remove us from the line of fire. For the first time in forty years, we were on our own.

I sat up slowly. "I have a friend who can help. Someone with no connection to the Museum at all." I eyed the phone. "But we can't take the chance of using the hotel's phone to contact her. It's traceable."

Instead, I dug out the local directory and dialed an electronics shop in Basseterre. I told them what I needed and they promised delivery of a pack of burner phones within the hour. I stayed in the room to wait while Mary Alice sulked on the patio and Helen and Nat paid a visit to the hotel shop, collecting some toiletries and criminally expensive clothes for each of us, which they

133

charged to the room. When the burner phones arrived, I plugged one into the charger and punched in a number from memory. Minka answered on the fourth ring, and I could picture her, Doc Martens propped on the desk while she fired lasers at aliens in a game she'd designed herself.

I skipped the preliminaries and rattled off what we needed — documents, tickets, etc. She knew better than to ask questions.

Minka promised the package would be to me within twenty-four hours and we hung up. When Nat and Helen returned, I explained what I had done. Mary Alice came in from the patio in time to catch the tail end, rubbing her eyes. She looked like she'd been trying — and failing — not to cry.

"Who is Minka?"

"Long story," I said, waving aside her question. "But she's solid. I'd trust her with my life."

"And ours," Helen pointed out coolly.

"If you have another suggestion, knock yourself out," I told her.

She didn't. We ordered room service and ate in exhausted silence. Helen had bought a few books and magazines from the hotel shop and she curled up with the latest from Reese's book club while Nat surfed the Caribbean news channels, settling on a

Venezuelan soap opera featuring a highly rouged woman who screamed her lines.

"I'm going for a walk," I said to nobody in particular.

Mary Alice got up to join me. We left through the sliding doors and past the patio, out onto a grassy area lined by beds planted out with bougainvillea, banana trees, and pawpaws. A little distance away, a few loungers had been drawn up on the edge of the beach.

"Should we risk it?" Mary Alice asked, jerking her chin towards the loungers.

I shrugged. "Everybody else seems to be at dinner." Sounds of silverware and soft music flowed out from the various restaurants dotted around the resort. At our end of the beach it was peaceful and deserted.

We settled ourselves and I lit a cigarette, the little scarlet glow of it winking like a firefly in the gathering darkness.

"Don't tell me those survived a dunking in the ocean," Mary Alice said with a smile at the cigarettes.

I shook my head. "Helen. From the hotel shop along with moisturizer and dental floss."

"Helen hates it when you smoke." Mary Alice and I sat perched on the edge of the loungers, our knees nearly touching as we faced out to sea. The sun had set off to our right, beyond the headland, and the air was purple

"And she got them anyway. That's friendship."

Mary Alice snorted. For a while there was no noise but the rhythm of the waves. Down to our left, a single palm leaned out over the water, as if listening to the secrets the sea had to tell.

I heard a brisk sniff. "I'm fresh out of tissues, Mary Alice. If you need to blow your nose, you'd better use your shirt."

"Screw you, Webster," she said, wiping her eyes on her sleeve. But her tone was better, her back a little stiffer. "I just can't stand this — being away from Akiko and not knowing what she's thinking. How she's doing." I didn't say anything; it was better to let her keep going and get it all out at once. "This is the only secret I've ever kept from her. Well, the only one that matters," she amended. "She also doesn't know how much I spent on recarpeting the hall stairs."

"Wool?" I asked.

"Organic. From New Zealand," she said. "I'll send you the link."

She leaned over and took the cigarette out of my hand, drawing a deep breath and causing the cherry to glow bright red before she handed it back. She held the smoke in her lungs a good long while before blowing it out in an exhalation that went on forever.

"I miss that."

I flicked her a look and she pursed her lips. "Don't give me that look. I know I can't smoke. One more thing breast cancer managed to take away." She gestured loosely towards her chest.

"They look good," I told her. "Nat said she'd love a new pair."

"Nat can kiss my pretty plump butt. They look good but I was sick as a dog for eight months and my nipples are still numb."

"You're here," I reminded her.

"I'm here." She edged nearer, bumping my shoulder with her own. "The question is, for how long?"

I shook my head as I ground out the cigarette on the sole of my espadrille. I tucked the butt into the pack. "I still can't believe that little shit tried to blow us up. I want to know where he got his orders."

"Who says he did?" she said. "He might have gone rogue."

"To take out four retiring agents? Why?"

"We know things."

"We don't know anything that would be a threat to Brad Fogerty, the punkass little dynamite jockey."

"So, Fogerty had no grudge against any of us," she said, working her way through it. Mary Alice's approach to everything was slow and methodical. She was good at detail, even better than Helen, often spotting what the rest of us had missed even if it took her longer to get there. I rushed in, relying more on instinct than anything else, and sometimes just blind damned luck. It's what made us such a good team. I was her hare.

She smiled, the first genuine smile I'd seen from her in twenty-four hours. "I know. I'm tortoising. Bear with me." She went silent for a while and I watched the lacy edge of the waves, ruffles that flounced up onto the sand and drew back again like a flamenco dancer's skirt. A tiny grey crab scuttled over my foot.

I turned to stare at her. The pale oval of her face glowed in the shadows. If I could have seen it better, I knew I'd find a narrow line sketched between her brows. And suddenly I was impatient with it all. "Mary Alice, you can't whitewash this or find a silver lining or look on the goddamned bright side of life. Either we were meant to be blown up by the same people who cut our paychecks for forty years, or they knew it was going to happen to us and did nothing to stop it because they had bigger fish to fry. And it doesn't matter. They won't let us go. We know too much. In the space of a day, we've gone from possibly expendable to a monumental threat."

"How?" she challenged me, squaring for a fight.

"Knock it off, Mary Alice. You're not this stupid. We know where the bodies are buried — literally. This isn't a footnote, it's a goddamned reckoning, and you don't want to acknowledge that because it means you have to figure out what to do about the problem of Akiko."

I heard her exhale through her nose, sharply, like a bull will before it charges. "My wife is not a problem, Billie. But I don't expect you to understand that."

She started to stomp off, a tricky thing in deep sand. "Hey, Mary Alice," I called after her. She turned back and I stuck my middle finger up.

She flipped me off in response as she stalked away. I dug out a fresh cigarette and lit it, blowing a mouthful of smoke out slowly. "That could have gone better," I said to the crab.

CHAPTER ELEVEN

It was three hours wheels up to touchdown in Miami and we took our time disembarking, careful not to draw attention to ourselves by hurrying. We made our way through Customs and Immigration, but Minka's work was good. We cleared the official channels with half an hour to spare before boarding our flight to Atlanta on another airline. When we arrived, Hartsfield was thronged with the after-Christmas crowds, everybody pushing and shoving. So much for peace on earth and goodwill to men. It must have gotten thrown out with the reindeer wrapping paper.

It was eleven P.M. by then, and we caught the last flight to Birmingham, landing after midnight. Natalie was whimpering with fatigue, but I pushed on, followed doggedly by Mary Alice and Helen, who somehow managed to look perkier than the rest of us. I picked up the rental car Minka had reserved for us, and we settled in for the final leg. Natalie dove for the back seat, crashing into sleep as soon as she landed. The rest of us took turns driving, and five hours later I was at the wheel again, crossing the Twin Span Bridge into New Orleans just as the sun came up. I followed I-10 into the city, keeping with the flow of morning rush-hour traffic until we got close to the French Quarter. Mary Alice was dozing in the passenger seat and Helen and Natalie were curled together like puppies on the back seat.

I poked Mary Alice awake. "Better get them up. We're almost here and we're going to have to move fast when I stop."

She roused Helen and Nat and collected the little baggage we had with us. I left the car running on a side street just off of Rampart. Within half an hour it would be in a chop shop, stripped for parts, leaving no trace of how we'd gotten to the city even if anyone managed to track us as far as Birmingham.

"What now?" Mary Alice asked, shouldering her bag.

"We walk," I said, pointing towards the Quarter. If I'd been on my own, I'd have taken a precautionary lap around the block, but Helen was drooping again and Natalie was barely on her feet. Going without good sleep for twenty-four hours is easy when you're twenty; it's a bitch when you're sixty. I felt every minute of that lost night as we trudged down Ursulines. It was as quiet a block as you could find in the French Quarter. No drunks stumbled down the uneven sidewalks; no vomit pooled in the gutter. It was almost serene.

We stopped in front of a nondescript gate fitted with a keypad. The gate was backed with thick, padded black canvas, obscuring any view into the property. I punched in the code and there was a moment of expectant silence. Then a soft buzz, a clang, and the gate swung open. Beyond lay an arched brick tunnel, softly lit by a single gaslight that flickered. Something scuttled around in the shadows on the damp ground.

"What was that?" Natalie asked, peering into the gloom.

"Probably a rat," I told her cheerfully. I slammed the gate closed behind them, making sure it locked. "Welcome to my place."

The tunnel led into a courtyard bordered by four brick buildings, each one more decrepit than the last. The façades, linked by galleries and staircases, leaned against each other for support like elderly women having one last gossip.

The three women stood, turning slowly as they took it in. An overgrown tea olive reared up in the corner between stacks of crumbling bricks. There were more stacks — slates, boards, bags of cement — and pots full of shrubs in various stages of growth. In the center, a fountain missing its jet was full of green water. The surface rippled a little and Natalie jumped.

"What's moving in that water?" Mary Alice demanded.

"Louie the carp. He came with the house."

"Well, I suppose it's nice to have a pet," Helen said politely.

"It looks like it's about to fall down," Nat said, staring up at the flaking black wrought iron holding up the second-floor galleries.

"It might. Watch your step up there," I said.

"It must have been beautiful once," Mary Alice said with a stab at diplomacy. "I'm sure it could be nice again."

"With a little elbow grease and a few sticks of dynamite," Natalie replied.

"You're staying for free," I reminded her.

Mary Alice put on a brave face. "Does the plumbing work?"

"Sometimes," I said. It was clear Mary Alice and Natalie weren't impressed. I turned to Helen.

To my surprise, she smiled. "It's perfect. Thank you for bringing us here, Billie."

Mary Alice had the grace to look a little ashamed, but Natalie merely yawned. Just then a door — wide, with peeling turquoise paint — opened and a tall, skinny girl emerged. Before I could introduce her, she was on me, wrapping me up tightly and lifting me an inch off the ground. She smelled like maple syrup and burnt toast.

"You scared me. Don't do that," she said firmly as she put me down.

"We're alright," I told her. "You did great."

She kept one hand on my shoulder and turned to look at the others, her head cocked like a squirrel's. "These are friends?"

"Mary Alice, Helen, Natalie," I told her. "This is Minka."

They made polite noises and she nodded back before turning to me. "I made breakfast."

"You can't cook," I reminded her.

She shrugged. "It is not good. But you should eat."

She led the way through the turquoise door into a shell of a house. The brick walls that held it up had been left standing but the interior partition walls had been punched out and the upper floor removed entirely so the ceiling was two stories above our heads. An old door laid onto stacks of bricks made a makeshift kitchen counter to hold the essentials — coffeemaker, hot plate, and toaster oven. There was an expensive electric kettle for tea, but that was my only concession to luxury.

A table that could have seated forty for dinner stood in the center of the room with a small scattering of chairs that didn't match. The windows were stained-glass Bible stories with clear glass in a few places where the original panes had shattered and been replaced cheaply. The rest were mostly cracked, with a long, jagged line marking the upturned face of Mary Magdalene as she knelt before a risen Jesus.

"What is this place?" Mary Alice asked.

"Former convent," I told her as I pointed them to places around the table. A platter was stacked high with cold, burned pieces of toast, and the butter was upholstered with a layer of crumbs. But the coffee and tea were hot.

We sagged into chairs, each of us taking a mug and ignoring the ruined bread. "The sisters belonged to an order associated with Mary Magdalene," I went on. "Down the street is a convent that used to belong to the Ursulines. The nuns who built this house came a few decades after. They were a nursing order and they were wiped out by a yellow fever epidemic."

"It is haunted," Minka put in cheerfully, coming to sit with a cup of coffee.

Mary Alice turned to her. "Haunted?"

"With ghosts," Minka added.

"Nun ghosts," I clarified. "They've driven a few owners away, but they've never bothered me and they don't seem to trouble Minka."

She shrugged. "It is nice to have company when you live alone."

"You live here, Minka?" Helen asked politely.

Minka nodded. "Yes, I am a proper American now," she said. Her features were pure Slav: wide, flat cheekbones and deep-set eyes. Her style changed from week to week, but today she was dressed like an extra from a French film with a striped boatneck tee and a little scarf scattered with polka dots. She'd cut her hair again, cropped short, and dyed jet black with cherry highlights. She was wearing a tiny pair of reading glasses with round frames. All she was missing was the bicycle basket with the baguette sticking out of it.

Helen gave me an appraising look. "Is the house in your name?"

"Nope. A holding company from the

146

Caymans. There's no way to trace it to me."

"I'll be damned," Mary Alice said. "You have your own safe house."

I shrugged. "A reasonable precaution, in our line of work."

"I don't have a safe house." Natalie was sulking, but Helen still looked thoughtful. She didn't say anything else and Natalie turned to Minka. "I hope Billie has at least provided you with an indoor bathroom. It's a bit rustic."

Minka's eyes narrowed like a cat's. "Billie has provided me with everything." She stuck around for a few more minutes, but the atmosphere was distinctly chilly, and when she excused herself, Natalie turned to me.

"What did I say?" Nat demanded.

"It wasn't what you said," Helen told her. "I think it was the suggested criticism of Billie she resented."

Before Natalie could roll her eyes, Helen stood up. "I am about dead on my feet."

I pushed myself up from my chair. "I'll show you where you can sleep."

Mary Alice stayed put. "We need to figure this out. We need a plan."

Helen turned as if to sit down again, but she swayed a little and I put a hand to her shoulder, holding her in place. "Yes, Mary Alice. We do. But we're exhausted and in no fit state to think straight. We sleep, then we eat, then we plan. Halliday rules."

I could tell Mary Alice didn't like it, but she got up and followed as I showed them to the building across the courtyard, the one with the brick tunnel running through the ground floor. On either side of the tunnel were two large rooms, one packed so full of junk, it was impossible to get inside. The other was empty except for a small spiral staircase. Upstairs was a long hallway with a dozen doors opening off of it.

"Nuns' dormitory," I told them. "The rooms are small but at least they're private."

I opened the first door. Inside, the floorboards were wide and scrubbed clean. A twin-sized mattress, still in the plastic, was shoved against one wall, leaving just enough room to walk past. A niche in the wall held a plaster statue of a saint without a head.

Natalie opened her mouth, but Helen gave her a warning look.

"It's very nice," Natalie said faintly. She headed straight for the bed and collapsed down onto it, pulling her sweater over her head.

"Nat, dear," Helen called. "Don't you want to at least put sheets on your mattress?"

"Nope." The word was muffled but the

flap of the hand was clear enough.

We closed the door on her and Mary Alice and Helen took the next two rooms in line without a word. I went to mine and dropped to the bed, falling straight into sleep, the heavy kind of sleep that leaves you feeling gritty all over and worse than if you hadn't tried at all. I woke up at sundown with the sheets twisted around my legs, sweating off a hot flash. I rolled out of bed and had a quick wash, then reached for the small stack of clothes I left in the house. Bootcut jeans and a ratty Janis Joplin T-shirt would do just fine for what I had in mind. I threw on my favorite cowboy boots, a bomber jacket older than Minka, and my sunglasses. I snagged a baseball cap on my way out the door. I hadn't seen any signs we'd been followed, but I wasn't taking chances.

I eased out of the gate and headed down Ursulines towards Decatur. My stomach growled as I passed Central Grocery, calling out for a muffaletta, but the CLOSED sign was out and I kept on walking. I made a circuit of the quarter, zigging and zagging a bit, poking into a few alleys, but nothing triggered my Spidey sense. I stopped by Café du Monde for five orders of beignets and got back to the house with my arms

149

full of paper sacks wilting from steam and grease and smelling like heaven.

Helen must have showered. Her hair was damp and combed neatly into its platinum bob. She was paging slowly through an issue of *Vanity Fair* from 2009 while Nat, wrapped in my favorite kimono, was drumming her fingers on the table. Mary Alice liberated the bags of beignets, passing them out with paper towels and the cups of chicory.

I looked around the room. "Where's Minka?"

"Out," Mary Alice said shortly.

"I think I just ovulated," Natalie said as she lifted the first beignet. She bit into the warm dough with a low moan, puffing powdered sugar into the air. "Heaven."

I shrugged out of my jacket and tossed my cap onto the table. "Beignets in New Orleans is a cliché but it's a good one." They were quiet, eating with studied enthusiasm, and I looked around, sizing them up. They were a little the worse for wear, but hanging in there. Just then Minka returned with bags from the carryout kitchen around the block — gumbo and potato salad, with bottles of red wine from the corner grocery. There was bread and a king cake that was so early for the season, it could have only come from one of the tourist traps on Bourbon Street.

"Bless you, child," I said as Minka unpacked the bags. She turned to get bowls and spoons as I opened the first container. "We can talk while we eat."

Helen took one of the bottles and a corkscrew, giving a narrow look at Minka's back.

"Pas devant la petite fille," she warned me.

Minka didn't turn. "La petite fille parle français, madame," she replied.

"Merde," Helen said.

Minka faced us. "If you don't want to talk with me, I will go to my room."

"Of course not," Mary Alice said, smoothing things over. "We all know what we owe you, Minka."

She shot Helen a warning look and Helen handed over a glass of wine with a thin smile. "Certainly. I just didn't know how much of the specifics of the next steps we wanted to bore Minka with."

It was a bullshit piece of politeness, but I was too tired to call her on it.

Minka shrugged and ladled her gumbo over a scoop of potato salad, digging in her spoon while Nat watched in fascination. "Is that good?"

"Try," Minka ordered.

Natalie did as she was told and took a spoonful, her eyes rolling back. "Holy shit.

151

That's amazing."

Minka grinned and they applied themselves to their food with the enthusiasm of teenagers.

"You're going to need an antacid later," Mary Alice told Natalie when she reached for a bottle of hot sauce.

"I'll sleep sitting up," Natalie said. "It's worth it." She turned to me. "So, what now?"

"Time to take stock," Helen said briskly. She ate a beignet with small, dainty bites, then pushed her sack aside. Not even a speck of sugar on her hands. Her bowl of gumbo was untouched but her wineglass was half-empty.

"Fine," I said. "Let's take stock. We have obviously been targeted by the Museum for termination, but we still don't know why."

"I keep thinking it must be a misunderstanding," Helen offered. "I mean, we've all been competent and occasionally exceptional at our jobs. And we're finished. Why take us out now?"

"That's the $64,000 question, isn't it?" I said. "If we know why, everything else will make sense, because right now, nothing does."

"What is this Museum?" Minka asked through a mouthful of gumbo.

Natalie looked at her curiously. "You know what Billie does for a living?"

"Yes," Minka said. "You are friends from work? You kill people too?"

"They do," I confirmed. "The Museum is the organization that we work for. And it seems the Board of Directors has decided to terminate our existence."

Minka tipped her head. "Explain."

The table was covered with oilcloth that had seen better days. The previous owners had left it behind, probably after taking one look at the dark, unappetizing stains and cigarette burns. I motioned for Minka to bring me something to write with. She found a marker, bright blue and smelling like fruit, the sort of thing My Little Pony would use to sign a slam book. I sketched out three boxes at one end of the cloth and jotted a name in each one.

" 'Thierry Carapaz, Provenance. Günther Paar, Acquisitions. Vance Gilchrist, Exhibitions,' " she read aloud.

"Correct," I told her. I drew a bracket to collect the three together and labeled it *Board of Directors.* Above that I wrote, *Museum.*

"The Museum has a board of three directors, each overseeing their own department." I touched a finger to the first. "Cara-

153

paz is in charge of Provenance. Those are the computer geeks. They do research, deep dives into government databases. They also do digital surveillance. Their only job is intelligence gathering."

"For what purpose?" Minka asked.

"To identify two types of people who are of interest to the Museum," Helen told her. "Potential targets and potential recruits."

Minka nodded and I moved on, tracing a line from Provenance to the board. "Provenance briefs the board at quarterly meetings, introducing dossiers on people they think need to be killed or to be trained to become field agents. The board debates and discusses in closed-door sessions and then they vote. It takes all three agreeing, a unanimous vote, in order for either a kill order or an offer of employment to be issued."

I pointed to the next box. "Once the kill order has been issued, Acquisitions — under the direction of Paar — is responsible for supply and logistics. They can do everything from creating fake social media profiles to building bombs. They provide weapons, wardrobe, travel arrangements. Whatever we need in order to make the mission successful. With me so far?"

Minka nodded and tapped the last box.

"Exhibitions. These are field agents who kill? This is you?"

"This is me," I told her. "This is all of us. We work under Vance Gilchrist and we are responsible for carrying out the missions."

"You forgot the curators," Helen said, peering at the sketch through her reading glasses.

I squeezed three small boxes underneath the directors. "The directors each have a curator who deals with the day-to-day working of their department." I filled them in. "Naomi Ndiaye works under Thierry Carapaz in Provenance. Martin Fairbrother is Günther Paar's second in Acquisitions."

I hesitated over the empty box under Vance Gilchrist's name.

"Who works there?" Minka asked.

"Nobody now," Natalie told her. "The last one died six months ago and they haven't gotten around to finding a permanent replacement. Vance can be persnickety."

"Only women are ever called persnickety," Mary Alice said. "Men get to be 'detail oriented.'" She pushed her empty bowl away, letting the spoon rattle. "Moving on. We need a plan. And fast."

It wasn't like Mary Alice to be quite so brusque, but I knew she was thinking of Akiko. The sooner we cleared up this mess, the sooner she could find her wife and figure out how to patch things up.

"Agreed," I said. "We've bought ourselves some time but we can't stay here forever. We have to figure out why we've been targeted."

"I can't believe the board would turn on us," Natalie said with real bitterness. "After all we've done."

"Maybe it's *because* of what we've done," Helen said. "Maybe we killed someone we weren't supposed to. Or maybe we saw something we shouldn't have."

"There are a thousand possible reasons for the board to decide we're a problem," I said. "They're the only ones who can issue a termination order and they would have done it unanimously. We have to find out exactly why they sent this one."

"Too bad we can't ask," Natalie said.

Mary Alice spoke up for the first time. "Why can't we?"

It was an audacious idea, and I was glad Mary Alice was the one to suggest it. She hadn't completely lost her nerve if she was thinking so far out of the box.

"But ask who?" Helen ventured. "We can't very well go straight to the board. They're the ones who ordered the hit."

Minka picked up the blue marker and

drew a thin line over the names of Gilchrist, Paar, and Carapaz.

"The curators?" Mary Alice suggested.

"No way," Natalie said flatly. "I don't trust Naomi as far as I can throw her," she added, poking at her name. "She's in charge of Provenance, which means she was responsible for briefing the board. Whatever she told them is why they're after us."

"We don't know that," Mary Alice began, but Natalie cut her off.

"When have you ever known the board to do anything that wasn't suggested by Provenance? It's literally their job to propose targets," Natalie argued. "Besides, I try to stay away from Provenance as much as possible. They give me the creeps, spying on people through their keyboards like that. It's weird."

I had met Naomi a handful of times and even liked her a little. She was thirty-something with a couple of kids and a foot firmly on the next rung of the career ladder. Every board member mentored the curator under them, which meant she was in line for Carapaz's job when he retired, and she made no bones about wanting it. She didn't make bullshit conversation just to hear herself talk, and I could see how that would make Natalie uncomfortable.

157

I crossed her off the list. "Martin?" I asked.

"Do we really want to do that to him?" Helen put in. "I feel sorry for the boy." Martin Fairbrother wasn't a boy. Like Naomi, he was mid-thirties, but that was about all they had in common. Where she was confident and took no bullshit, Martin was diffident and preferred his gadgets to conversation. We'd once sat next to each other at a daylong conference on hydro-explosives and he had said exactly one word to me. *Pen?* His had exploded, leaking ink all over his cuff. I'd given him my ballpoint and gone back to sleep. But he was very good at his job, ensuring we had everything we needed for each mission, no matter how small. If Mary Alice wanted peppermint Lärabars or Helen requested hollow-point ammunition with Chinese manufacturing stamps, Martin was the guy.

"He put some calcium chews in my work bag because he heard me complain about my last bone-density scan," Helen added with a smile. "Chocolate macadamia."

"And he got me the sweetest little yawara the last time he was in Nagasaki," Natalie put in.

They looked at me and I shrugged. "He got me a slapjack from a leathermaker in

158

Texas." It was a nice little weapon. It looked like a Bible bookmark but it had enough lead in either end to crush a man's temple. "He's good at details and he's thoughtful."

"See? A nice kid," Helen said. "Look, the board obviously believes we did something wrong, wrong enough to kill over. And by now they know the first attempt to take us out didn't work. They'll realize the natural thing for us to do is ask questions, and whoever we ask is at risk."

"And Martin is the first person we'd ask since Vance's curator is dead," I finished. I rubbed a hand over my face. "Helen's right. Contacting Martin could put him in danger."

"We don't know that," Mary Alice argued.

I held up a hand. "Let's call Martin Plan B. There has to be someone else who might have a line on what's going on. Someone less vulnerable than Martin but with an ear for gossip."

We were silent a moment, thinking. I tipped back in my chair, balancing on two legs as I considered. Natalie picked up the marker and started to doodle on a corner of the tablecloth while Mary Alice plucked at her paper napkin, tearing little pieces off and putting them into a pile. Helen simply sat, staring into the middle distance, and

Minka finished off the last of the beignets.

Suddenly, I set the legs of my chair down with a thump. "Sweeney would talk."

"I haven't seen Sweeney in twenty years," Mary Alice said.

Helen sat forward. "It might be worth asking. He's always been very fond of us."

"He retired last year," I said thoughtfully. "He might not be as inclined to keep Museum secrets now that he has his pension."

"Provided he knows any secrets," Mary Alice pointed out. "If he's not active, he might not be up on the latest gossip."

"Targeting four active operatives is not exactly a story they're going to be able to keep a lid on," I said. "Trust me, people are talking."

Nat looked up from her sketch — a male nude that was in danger of crossing over from tasteful to mildly pornographic. "Sweeney will help."

I flicked her a look. "You sound pretty sure of yourself."

Her expression was smug. "I ought to be. I slept with him last year."

Anybody listening to what came next would have mistaken us for the world's oldest slumber party.

"Euw, Nat, *Sweeney* —"

160

"You don't like redheads."

"Was he any good?"

The last was from me. Natalie grinned. "Better than you'd think."

"But *how*?" Helen asked plaintively.

Natalie gave a satisfied little stretch, remembering. "It was in Osaka. We'd been assigned two members of the same crime family. Somebody in Provenance screwed up and didn't realize they were related because the surnames were different. Otherwise we could have coordinated the job. As it was, when we crossed paths in the Ritz, we almost blew our covers. We had to compare notes, so he came to my room. One thing led to another." She shrugged.

"So, you can get in touch with him?" I asked.

She shook her head. "We had a quickie before the job and then a nice encore after. He was out of my room by dawn. He had an early flight out."

Helen gave a sudden exclamation and dove into her bag. "I've got it," she said, waving her address book. She flipped through the pages. "McSween, Charles. Kansas City."

She jotted down the number and offered it to Natalie. Nat stared at it like she'd offered her a spoonful of roadkill on a cracker.

"I am *not* calling him."

"But why?" Mary Alice asked. "You're the last one who had any contact with him." If she hadn't been so preoccupied with Akiko, she might have snickered at the word "contact." God knows I wanted to. But she was annoyed, speeding up the on-ramp to seriously pissed.

I grabbed the piece of paper from Helen. "I'll do it. Talking to an ex can be awkward."

"You would know," Mary Alice shot back. I didn't flip her off that time, but I made a note to start a mental tally. I headed out, stopping by the drugstore for a fresh burner I bought with cash. I threaded my way through the narrow streets, cutting over to Jackson Square. It was getting dark now, the fortune-tellers and jugglers all packed up for the day, leaving the shadows for the vagrants. I passed a few benches where people had bedded down for the night, although it wouldn't last. The NOLA police station was two blocks away and the cops would be along soon to encourage them on their way. They'd shuffle along to the darker side streets, bunking in doorways with elaborate arrangements of cardboard and moldy sleeping bags to keep out the chill.

One of the benches was empty, and I sat facing the river. I took a deep breath before keying in the number Helen had scribbled onto a piece of paper. I waited — three rings, then four. I was just about to give up when Sweeney answered, sounding a little sleepy. I could hear the annoying squeaks of a televised basketball game in the background. He must have dozed off watching, and I glanced up at the clock face on the front of the cathedral. Ten to seven.

I told him who it was and waited for the inevitable.

"Billie? Hey, it's been a while — *hey,*" he said, drawing out the syllable in a long breath. "You're supposed to be dead."

"Just call me Lazarus," I said.

"What the hell? I mean, what the actual hell?" His voice rose and the volume of the basketball game suddenly fell. He must have muted it as he waited for me to answer.

"It's complicated. I can't explain now, but I think we should meet."

"Meet," he repeated. He was playing for time, and I pressed him a little.

"Sweeney, I wouldn't ask if it wasn't important."

"If you're alive, what about the others? Are they alive too? What about Nat?" God, it was like seventh grade all over again. Next he'd be asking me to leave a note in her locker after gym class. *DO U LIKE ME, CIRCLE Y OR N.*

"Not on the phone," I told him. "I can meet you tomorrow in New Orleans."

"Tomorrow? Not a chance," he said flatly. "It's New Year's Eve."

"Shit," I said. I'd lost track of the time. "Wednesday, then. The second."

"Gimme a minute. I need something to write with. Where the hell are my glasses?" he mumbled.

"On your head," I told him.

"Hey, how did you know? Can you see me?"

"Sweeney, I'm not in Kansas City, peering in your windows. I guessed."

"I gotta say, I'm a little disappointed," he replied. He was quiet a minute and I heard him tapping away on a keyboard.

"Okay, I found a flight first thing Wednesday morning. I'll arrive about three. Where do you want to meet?"

"Jackson Square, four o'clock."

"How will I find you?"

"I don't know yet, but don't worry. I'll find you. If anything comes up or you're delayed, then meet me at the Sazerac Bar at the Roosevelt Hotel at nine PM. If you can't make that, leave a message with the bartender. Got it?"

"Why can't I just call you back?"

"Because I'm throwing this phone away as soon as I hang up."

"Shit, you are in trouble, aren't you?"

"I think so."

He sighed. "I'll be there."

"Safe travels."

I pressed the little red phone icon before he could answer. I powered off the phone as I walked towards the Cabildo, the museum tucked just to the west of the cathedral. A small street with nice wide gutters ran beside it. I didn't even have to break stride as I let the phone slip out of my grasp and into the storm drain.

I cut through the little alley between the Cabildo and the cathedral. Here and there, doorways sat in pools of light with long shadows stretching in between. Most were occupied with vagrants stretched out on their beds of flattened cardboard, but in the last doorway, a clown sat on the steps, holding up a piece of broken mirror as he applied his greasepaint. I pulled out a five-dollar bill and dropped it into his tip bucket as I passed. There was nothing else in the bucket except for a few dimes. Hard week to be a clown, I guessed. I started to walk away, but he called me back.

"Hey, lady." The clown held something

out. It was a laminated prayer card, the kind you buy in church gift stores. This one was worn and soft with age. The picture was of a man in a red robe carrying a toddler across a river, both of them wearing sunny halos.

"St. Christopher," he said. But I already knew that. The image matched the small medal I wore on a thin chain around my neck.

"Thanks," I said, pocketing the card.

"Happy fucking New Year," said the clown.

"You too."

I tightened my scarf as the wind rose, and I headed for home.

CHAPTER TWELVE
JANUARY 1979

The swear jar on Constance Halliday's desk is kept full by Natalie and Billie. Helen is too ladylike to let the profanity fly, and Mary Alice uses bad words like someone speaking a foreign language.

Under Miss Halliday's tutelage, the four learn how to eat fish with two forks and sip from a soupspoon without making a noise. She teaches them how to exit a car without showing their underwear, to waltz like Viennese debutantes, and to hot-wire an automobile in under twenty seconds. They build bombs, decipher codes, learn how to shake a tail and how to kill. They master suffocation and stabbing, the intricacies of poison and garrote. Constance Halliday does not like military-grade weapons, finding them unsubtle and flashy, but she ensures the foursome are thoroughly grounded in firearms although she makes no secret of her preference for bare hands and improvised

167

weapons. Ballpoint pens, jump ropes, sewing needles — they learn lethal uses for all of them.

And each develops her specialty. Natalie loves anything that makes a noise, bombs and grenades and the biggest guns she can get her tiny hands around. Mary Alice discovers an affinity for poisons, slipping harmless substances into the food Miss Halliday serves in order to practice her sleight of hand. Her spare time is spent mixing up enough toxic messes to immobilize an army. Helen, surprisingly, turns out to be a sharpshooter, her eye for detail serving her well as she marks changes in wind and estimated trajectories. She is so skilled, in fact, that Constance allows her to borrow her favorite weapon, a tidy little Colt .38 that has been fitted with a hammer shroud to keep it tucked neatly into a pocket. There are nicks on the handgrip, slash marks that they suspect are kill notches, but no one dares to ask.

But Billie Webster is a struggle for Constance Halliday. She is fair with a grenade and can handle a gun almost as well as Helen, but she doesn't like it. Her attention wanders, and she takes to shooting wide of the targets just to see what else she can hit. When she takes out the eye of Constance

168

Halliday's favorite garden sculpture — an evil-looking iron rabbit — Miss Halliday raps her sharply on the shoulder with her stick.

"My office, Miss Webster. If you please."

Billie mutters under her breath but follows. She has not been in the office since the day of their arrival and she soon realizes this is not a social visit. Miss Halliday doesn't invite her to sit down, so Billie keeps to her feet, gaze fixed on the painting behind Constance's desk — a nymph of some sort with stars in her hands and a regretful expression.

Miss Halliday doesn't say anything for a long minute. She sits instead, tapping a letter opener on the desk and teaching Billie the power of silence.

Finally, Constance Halliday throws the letter opener on her desk. "Miss Webster," she says with a sigh, "I begin to despair. You are not a bad recruit —"

"Thank you."

She carries on as if Billie hasn't spoken. "But you are very rapidly becoming a superfluous one. You shoot well, but not as well as Miss Randolph. You are good with languages, but not as fluent as Miss Tuttle. You are heedless of your personal safety to a degree that one might be tempted to call courageous, but you are not quite as indomitable as Miss Schuyler. In short, Miss Webster, I fail to see the point of you."

She pauses, but there is nothing Billie can possibly say to that. Constance judges the pause perfectly, then continues on, her tone pleasant. It is the casual, matter-of-fact delivery that hurts more than the words.

"We do have a placement with a perfectly good secretarial college in London. We could send you there. I daresay you might be able to pick up shorthand or typewriting without too much trouble. They could find you a nice office job after you earn your certificate. Perhaps you'd like bookkeeping? That can be rather fulfilling, I'm told."

Only the tiniest gleam in Constance Halliday's eye tells Billie she is doing this on purpose, pushing her for a reaction. She doesn't know what Constance is trying to kindle — anger? Denial? But she is determined not to give it to her.

Billie waits her out in silence and Constance finally gives in, smiling thinly. "It must be difficult for you. I understand."

"Understand what?"

Constance has gotten her to talk, but she doesn't gloat. She merely carries on in the same bland tone, tapping a file on her desk. "You've never had to work for it, have you?

170

Never been tested, not really."

Billie thinks about her childhood and tamps down the rising anger. "I don't know what your little folder says, but I'm not like the rest of them, okay? I didn't get the picket fence and the golden retriever."

Constance shrugs. "I am not speaking of the trappings of a happy childhood, Miss Webster. I mean what happens inside — your intellect and what you've done with it. Or rather, what you *haven't* done with it. Your records show exceptional intelligence and mediocre results. It's a comfortable place, mediocrity. Never pushing oneself to the limit to see what you can take. Never staring down your fears, never reaching into yourself to find that last bit of courage. You don't even know what it is that you are made of — and what's more, you seem distinctly uninterested in finding out. You do just enough to get by, and frankly, I would rather have a dozen recruits with less potential and more heart, Miss Webster. I fear my brother has made a mistake."

She continues to smile but this time there is pity in it.

"Bullshit!" The word erupts from Billie before she can stop it.

Constance gives a slow nod. "I appear to have struck a nerve there." She pushes herself to her feet and gestures for Billie to come around the desk. She turns the girl by the shoulders and points to the painting with her stick. "I know you have not had the benefit of a Classical education, Miss Webster. Do you know who that is?"

Billie shrugs.

"Astraea. Have you ever heard the name?"

Billie looks at the slender figure in her gauzy white gown. She is drifting just above a landscape, her toes brushing the grass as she rises into the air. One hand is stretched out towards a group of weeping shepherds, offering them a gesture of farewell, while the other holds a pair of measuring scales to her chest. "I don't think so. It sounds Greek."

"Very good. Astraea was a goddess, the daughter of Dusk and Dawn, gifted by the gods with the tools of justice. She was the last immortal to live amongst mankind. But in the end, she despaired of our wickedness and she left, fleeing to the stars with her scales. She sits among the stars today as the constellation Virgo, the scales of Libra next to her. She waits, they say, for the day she will return."

Billie looks closer at the goddess, at the expression of resigned sadness on her face as she regards the humans who are clearly pleading with her to stay.

Constance Halliday goes on. "All the great English poets wrote of her, Shakespeare, Milton, Browning. Historians compared Elizabeth I to her, and Catherine the Great. And Aphra Behn, Charles II's playwright spy, used 'Astraea' as her code name in honor of her. She has always been there, in the shadows."

Constance Halliday gestures again, pointing to the goddess's feet. A narrow line of silver lies in the grass, almost obscured by the greenery, but just visible. Forgotten but not gone.

"Look closely. Astraea took her scales with her, but she left her sword behind — the sword that was given by the gods to administer justice. The question is, Miss Webster, will you pick it up?"

She doesn't expect an answer. Instead she dismisses Billie and the girl goes to her room, where she stretches out on her bed, smoking contraband cigarettes and thinking until the sun sets and the room falls into shadow.

The next day, Billie tries. She oils her gun and rubs it down just as she has been taught. She loads it and lines up her sights, firing seven times. Six go wide. She knows Constance Halliday is standing behind her, but she does not turn to look. She tries again and it is a little better but not much. Her face is hot and she feels tears sitting behind her eyes. If she gives in, it would be an ugly cry, snotty and heaving. So she chokes down the disappointment that Constance Halliday is right. She is undisciplined and haphazard. And these qualities will get someone killed in the field.

To her surprise, Constance Halliday pokes her gently with her stick. "Everything alright there, Miss Webster?"

She closes her eyes and feels the heft of the gun in her hand. The weight of her embarrassment is heavy but she lets it sit on her shoulders, feeling the downward push of it. And then she has it. She opens her eyes and runs a finger down the side of the gleaming barrel. "I don't like relying on something that can get taken away from me," she tells her mentor.

Constance Halliday gives her a long, assessing look, then nods. "Well, your hands can't be taken, can they?"

Billie waits to be thrown out of the program, shipped off to London with a steno pad and a pencil skirt. Instead, the next day she walks out to the training ground to find a man standing next to Constance Halliday. He is muscular and ugly as sin, wearing

174

sweatpants and an expression like he has a better place to be and is doing her a favor.

Constance Halliday smiles thinly. "You may call him Mad Dog. And you will do what he tells you."

Whatever he is missing out on to be there, he makes Billie pay for it because it turns out that Constance has brought him in just for her. While the other three work at perfecting their respective skills, he teaches Billie everything she doesn't know about hand-to-hand combat. He throws her down a hundred times that first day, landing her squarely on her back and knocking the air out of her lungs every time.

After she is dismissed for the day, she realizes her legs will not support her and she crawls up the stairs on her hands and knees. The bedrooms are freezing, so the four girls have taken to meeting in the big linen cupboard where the pipes keep the temperature warm enough for the boxes of baby chicks Constance Halliday has ordered. It is a tight fit, but the girls spend their evenings in this tiny room with its warm air that smells of chicken shit and lavender. Billie is too sore to lift her arms, so Mary Alice feeds her while Nat fiddles with a set of lockpicks and a basket of locks and Helen cleans the soil out from under her fingernails. Everyone has chores at Benscombe, and Helen's is weeding the kitchen garden between weapons drills. She is also a traveling drugstore and manages to get Billie some prescription painkillers while Nat filches half a bottle of wine from the pantry.

By the next day, the bruises have blossomed and Billie's body is black and blue from neck to ankles, but she hauls herself out of bed and goes back for more. And this time Mad Dog only throws her fifty times.

Four weeks later, on a wet, miserable morning in the garden, Billie catches him below his center of gravity, levering him onto his stomach as she follows him down onto the soggy grass, landing hard on the small of his back with her knee and driving the air out of his lungs. He pops his head up, a reflex to draw in a breath, and when he does, Billie wraps her elbow around his throat. It would have been easy to jerk the head back towards her body, but she pulls him slowly, careful not to loosen her grip. His legs flail behind her, but this accomplishes nothing except to tire him out. He gets his knees under his body and pushes up, trying to throw her off, but she hangs on, jamming her knee into his kidneys. His face changes colors, pretty ones — pink, red, then purple. His nostrils flare white and he keeps opening and closing his mouth, searching for a breath that isn't there.

He finally sags into surrender, tapping the ground as he collapses. Billie holds on a second longer just because she can, and then rolls off of him. He whoops air into his lungs, gasping and shaking. Billie stands astride him, feet planted wide apart, blood humming in her ears. Her hands are curled into fists and she is ready for him to go again. She *wants* him to get up and try again. But he lies there, beaten.

Billie looks up to see Constance Halliday watching them, a smile on her face, and she realizes she is smiling too.

"Finally, Miss Webster," she says softly. "You understand. It isn't your anger that will make you good at this job. It is your joy."

The fighting that Mad Dog teaches Billie is not sporting or fair. It is down and dirty street brawling. He teaches her to go for the balls and the eyes, to drive the heel of her hand into an opponent's nose until the cartilage crunches crisply, like celery. He teaches her how to ram the resulting mess into the brain to finish the job. He shows her on a chicken how to snap a neck with a quick and decisive twist and how to choke someone out using her thighs or the crook of her elbow.

When the training is finished, he has a pronounced limp and an ear that will never be the same, but Constance Halliday is satisfied. Her little flock of Sphinxes has come along nicely, far from what they were when her brother discovered them. Helen Randolph had been an easy choice. Her father had been a founding member of the OSS, and her grandfather a diplomat with a flair for secret negotiations. Clandestine service is in her blood.

Natalie Schuyler is also a legacy. Her grandmother is a child when her family is driven out of the Russian Empire in a storm of bullets and bombs. They settle in Holland, adopt a new name, and attempt to put the past behind them, but Natalie's grandmother never forgets the sounds of war. When it comes again to Europe, she sends her infant son to America with her parents and stays behind, offering her services to the Dutch Resistance. The elderly Schuylers make inquiries for years afterwards, but no one ever tells them what became of her, and it is too heartbreaking to guess. But Major Richard Halliday knows. And the day he shows Natalie the file on her grandmother, she suddenly understands the impulse towards chaos which beats in her blood.

Mary Alice Tuttle is a more straightforward case. She is the youngest of three children, the bonus daughter after her parents have had one of each. She tears through childhood in a whirl of starched petticoats and blond curls as an afterthought, always knowing that her family was complete before she arrived. Until her brother goes to Vietnam and never comes back. His best friend is carried home in a coffin and Mary Alice's sister, his fiancée, faints when she sees it. Her parents are broken, her sister destroyed, and it seems very simple to Mary Alice. Wars are fought by young men who don't get to choose and that is wrong. Anything that can be done to stop the carnage is justifiable. She burns her acceptance letter to Juilliard and enrolls at Berkeley instead. She publishes an opinion piece in the student newspaper that is so inflammatory, a state representative calls for her to be arrested as a traitor. But it is this opinion piece which brings her to the attention of a Museum recruiter.

Like Mary Alice, Billie is recruited because of her idealism, her willingness to bloody her knuckles for a good fight. She has come the furthest in training, and Constance Halliday is reminded of other young women like her during the war. Her Furies. They were scarcely more than children when they were sent off to fight in a war they didn't start. They were gallant, indomitable. And they died for that gallantry, she thinks bitterly. This way is better. The Sphinxes will use cunning and subterfuge; they will even the odds that have been stacked against them. And they will survive, she promises herself.

It has taken nine months of physical training to bring them into fighting shape. Then secretarial school in London to learn shorthand and typing and the rudiments of air hostessing — posing as secretaries or stewardesses is excellent cover. They have taken courses in cooking and health care should they have to pose as domestic servants or nurses. Driving school has given them the essentials of maintenance and evasive maneuvers. A first-aid intensive has schooled them in how to patch themselves up in the field. Courses in language and culture have refined them — French, Spanish, Arabic, opera, wines. A class in method acting has taught them how to develop cover characters and to cry on cue.

For the final touch, they have all been sent to Paris to be made over. Natalie's curls have been smoothed into place, although she complains that this takes half her personality away. Mary Alice's slightly gapped front teeth are capped to make her smile less memorable. Helen is so beautifully groomed there is not much for the consultants to do except trim her hair and give her a pair of glasses to emphasize her seriousness.

Billie lets them cut off her split ends, but when they consult a plastic surgeon to fix the scar above her lip, she walks out. Helen is disapproving, looking through her clear-lensed glasses with concern.

"We're supposed to get rid of anything that makes us conspicuous," she reminds Billie. "That scar is an identifying feature."

"I like it," Mary Alice puts in loyally.

"It's not a matter of liking it," Helen protests. "It could get Billie remembered and that is dangerous."

"I'll take my chances," Billie tells her.

The truth is, Billie is scared. She has let enough of herself slip away already. Elocution lessons have rubbed the edges off her Texas drawl; the reading lists have improved her vocabulary. The art and history they have absorbed have broadened her world to a vastness she has never before imagined. She is not entirely certain who she is anymore. But if she puts a fingertip to the little ridge that sits just above her lip, she can remember herself.

Two weeks later, they are on a plane for Nice.

CHAPTER THIRTEEN

The morning after I called Sweeney, we slept in. We still had rest to catch up on and a rendezvous to plan, but we also had the luxury of a few days to prepare. During breakfast, Mary Alice made a heroic effort to behave normally, wrestling with the hot plate to fix everybody's eggs the way they wanted. Afterwards, I did yoga, stretching out my sore knees and screaming a little inside when my downward-facing dog came out more like a junkyard mutt. I felt about a hundred years old and looked it too, I decided as I inspected my face after my shower. I slapped on some rosehip oil and hoped for the best. I was halfway into a pair of cashmere joggers when I changed my mind and reached for my jeans instead. The joggers were featherlight and warm as toast, but the jeans made me feel like I hadn't quite given up yet. I was crossing the courtyard when I heard a rattle at the gate, like someone was trying the latch. The odds that anybody from the Museum had found us were long, but I wasn't taking chances. I picked up a piece of rebar from the pile of construction material in the courtyard and hefted it. As a weapon it would do in a pinch.

I crept to the gate, balancing my weight on the balls of my feet. I held the rebar in one fist, the grip just firm enough to keep it steady. Most people grasp a weapon until their knuckles turn white, but that just tires out your hand. Like playing piano or giving a good hand job, it's all in the wrist.

I peered through a gap in the privacy screen and almost dropped the rebar.

"I'll be damned," I said, flinging open the gate.

Akiko was standing on the other side, clutching a pet carrier that rattled and thrashed. She shoved it into my hands as she hurtled past me. I grabbed her bag off the sidewalk and took a quick look either direction down the empty street before slamming the gate closed again.

I shouldered the bag and followed her into the courtyard. Mary Alice came flying out of the house, arms wide, and they held on to each other, gulping down silent sobs while the rest of us watched.

They kissed and hugged again and finally broke apart as the carrying case in my arms shook hard enough to rattle the Richter scale. "What the hell is in here, a poltergeist?" I asked Akiko.

She wiped her wet cheeks. "That's Kevin. He doesn't like to travel."

I bent to look through the mesh screen on the front of the case and something inside hissed what sounded like a satanic incantation.

"You brought the cat?" Mary Alice asked, smiling from ear to ear.

"Of course I brought the cat," Akiko said, smoothing her hair. "He's family."

She greeted the rest of us then, and we went into the house. "Am I supposed to let this thing out?" I asked.

Akiko waved a hand. "Just open the front. He'll come out when he's ready."

I put the case on the floor and stepped out of the way while I flicked the front open with one finger. Whatever was inside stayed there, and I turned my attention to Akiko and Mary Alice, who were sitting at the table, hand in hand. Helen and Natalie grabbed chairs and looked expectantly at me while I looked expectantly at Mary Alice.

"You want to explain?" I suggested.

185

Mary Alice might have played it for embarrassment or defiance. She split the difference, lifting her chin but blushing heavily as she talked. "I called her. When you were picking up the rental car at the Birmingham airport. Don't look at me like that — I borrowed a cell phone from a very nice woman who was waiting at baggage claim."

"They could have tapped your home phone," I reminded her.

Mary Alice turned on me. "Don't you dare give me shit about this, Billie. I took all the necessary precautions and I gave her precise instructions on how to make sure she was clean of a tail."

"Yeah," Akiko said happily. "I'm a natural at this spy shit."

"Spy?" I asked politely. I gave Mary Alice a meaningful look.

She turned forty shades of puce and looked at her wife. "I think I have some explaining to do."

"Is this where you tell me you're not a spy?" Akiko asked, still smiling.

"I'm not," Mary Alice said.

Akiko laughed. "That's just what a spy would say."

"We're not spies," I said flatly. "None of us."

For the first time her smile faltered. She

turned back to Mary Alice. "Then what are you?"

"Assassins," Natalie blurted out.

Akiko made a sound that started out as a laugh but got stuck halfway out and ended up a sort of gargle. "Are you shitting me?"

"No, dear," Helen said. "We are most definitely not shitting you."

It might have been Helen's genteel voice forming the profanity that convinced Akiko. She squeezed Mary Alice's hand. "Babe?"

"It's true. We're assassins. We were recruited in 1979. We work for a small international organization that is extra-governmental."

"What does that mean?"

"It means our organization is outside of government," Mary Alice began.

"I know what the word 'extra-governmental' means — don't you dare patronize me," Akiko said, dropping her hand. "I'm asking, what does it *mean*? Who do you kill?"

"Arms dealers, sex traffickers, the occasional dictator, cult leaders, corrupt judges. Basically not very nice people," Mary Alice replied.

"The organization started out killing Nazis, if that helps," Helen offered.

"But it's been a while since we've found

one," Natalie added. "So, it's mostly the folks Mary Alice just listed. Plus drug traffickers. And pirates — we've gotten really into pirates lately."

"But you *kill* them?" Akiko's voice rose as she stood. "Excuse me if I need a minute to process this." She closed the cat carrier and hefted it onto her hip. "Where's my room?"

"I'll show you," Helen said quickly. She led Akiko away to the sound of shrieks from the cat carrier.

"Well, that went better than I expected," Mary Alice said finally.

"Did it?" I asked.

"Oh yeah. If she were really mad, she'd have taken the cat and checked into the Marriott."

CHAPTER FOURTEEN

The day of the meet-up with Sweeney, I was up before dawn, but Mary Alice beat me to it. She was in the kitchen, frying up apple-stuffed French toast on the hot plate to go with the bacon she'd cooked in the microwave. She looked luminous, like the blood was humming just under her skin, and I knew what had her lit up inside — anticipation. Whichever way the meeting with Sweeney went, we were one step closer to being finished with this and getting back to our lives.

At least, that's what I suspected she was thinking. Nobody was talking much at that point. Akiko — still giving Mary Alice the silent treatment — went to a secret vampire speakeasy on Bourbon Street with Minka while the rest of us were busy preparing for the meeting. Mary Alice fixed plates for Helen and Natalie and the four of us went over the plan again until it was time to dress. It was early — hours before we expected Sweeney — but the point was to be in place, making ourselves part of the atmosphere of Jackson Square.

We slipped out separately to take our positions. Helen had made reservations at Muriel's, the restaurant that sat diagonally off the north corner of the square, insisting upon a balcony table in a prime location. She'd gone in person to secure the booking, slipping a fifty to the hostess with a sob story about it being her first wedding anniversary after her husband's death. It was bullshit, of course, but it was good bullshit, just authentic enough for Helen to manage a few watery gulps as she told the story. The hostess promised to seat her there for a late lunch, which Helen intended to spin out with several slow courses and an off-the-menu soufflé for dessert.

From her perch at the small round table, she'd have a perfect view of the entire paved stretch in front of the cathedral. I'd provided her with a pistol, checking the sights myself. I hoped she wouldn't need it, especially at that range, but there was no way to disguise a rifle. At the far end of the paved area, Mary Alice settled herself against the iron railing separating the green space of the square from the more commercial area. She had found a secondhand cello in a junk shop and had restrung and polished and tuned it until it sounded halfway decent. She'd have preferred a viola, but they were thin on the ground. She set an upturned silk top hat at her feet, displaying the shredded scarlet silk lining and dropping in a few coins to give passersby a hint.

On the same trip to the junk store, Natalie had scored several crappy canvases of depressing landscapes and even more depressing portraits. Nat had popped them out of the frames, overpainting a series of rough pictures that suggested New Orleans scenes without really committing themselves. They were exactly the sort of thing street artists hung all over the railings in Jackson Square, and Natalie finished off her disguise with a grey bobbed wig and a tie-dyed fanny pack, a hippy granny in touch with her creative side.

For my disguise, I bought a deck of tarot cards from Esoterica and spent two days shuffling to rough them up, then crayoned a posterboard sign with an evil eye to stick onto a card table. A couple of folding chairs and I was in business. I wore leggings and boots under my long, bright cotton peasant skirt — it was chilly with the wind blowing off the river — and a pair of cheap, gaudy

191

earrings. I finished with a heavy application of kohl and a cascading wig of dark red curls tied with a scarf. Between the riot of hair and the eyeliner, I was unrecognizable.

I'd expected the crowds to be thin on a weekday so early in January, but the post-holiday tourists were still partying off their hangovers. I set up shop in front of the Presbytére, the narrow building separated from the cathedral by a tiny passageway called Père Antoine Alley. I could see Helen if I glanced up to my right and Mary Alice if I looked down to my left. Natalie was around the corner, watching pedestrians approaching from the river as she hawked her ugly paintings. We had debated using comms, but in the end decided to keep it simple, working out a series of signals we could each give that would alert the others to danger. Once an hour, just as the cathedral clock struck quarter past, we did a quick visual to check in, but everything was good.

I saw Sweeney before he saw me. Charles Ellison McSween. He looked like an old man, I thought sadly, watching him lope into the square, his shoulders hunched into his jacket against the cold. The river breeze ruffled the hair just below his baseball cap. The red was faded to the color of rust with a layer of frost on it. I let him walk past me before I called out to him, fortune-teller patter. He half turned back and I gestured theatrically to the empty seat across from me.

"Wouldn't you like to know what the cards have to say about you?" I asked as he approached.

He gave me a narrow look. "I'll be damned," he muttered as he took the chair, testing it a little to see if it would take his weight.

"Shut up, I'm communicating with the other side," I said, smiling as I shuffled.

He grinned back. "God, it's good to see you." The smile faded almost as soon as it came. "Billie, what the hell is going on?"

I shuffled the cards slowly. "Don't use my name. And you should have worn a disguise."

He touched the brim of his Yankees cap. "I am in disguise. Everybody knows I'm a Cards fan." He narrowed his gaze at the deck in my hand. "What's this mumbo jumbo all about?"

"This is a traditional Rider-Waite deck, recognizable to fortune-tellers and emo teenage girls the world over." I pulled the top card off the deck and showed it to him. It was the Star, a naked woman bending over a brook with pitchers while stars hung

193

just over her head.

"Ooh, I like her," he said, pulling a stick of chewing gum out of his pocket. "She's hot."

"She represents hope, opportunity. Maybe you'll choose her," I said, shuffling the card back into the deck. "There are seventy-eight cards, divided into major and minor arcana."

"Say what now?" He unwrapped the gum and stuffed it into his mouth.

"Major arcana — they represent big life lessons. Minor arcana are numbers and court cards like queens and kings. Four suits, wands, cups, coins, and pentacles."

"Pentacles? Like Satan stuff?"

"No, not like Satan stuff. That's pentagrams." I spread the cards into a fan. "Pick three using your left hand. Leave them facedown."

"Why three cards?" He chewed as he considered the cards.

"The first is your past, the second represents the present. The third card is what is yet to come."

"And why does it have to be my left hand?" he asked.

"It's the hand of destiny," I said solemnly.

He laughed and tugged three cards free of the fan. I gathered up the rest. The notes of

Mary Alice's cello drifted over the square. She was playing Fleetwood Mac — "Rhiannon" — and Sweeney started tapping a finger in time with it.

I turned over the first card.

"Hey! I thought you said it wasn't Satan stuff," he protested. The card was the Devil, complete with horns and goat legs and a dramatic set of bat wings.

"It doesn't mean what you think," I told him. The Devil was sitting on a high throne, looming over a naked couple who were bound together by chains. I pointed to them. "They represent something that started out as a pleasure for you but became something that chained you up — like an addiction. But it's in the past."

He pointed to the wad of gum in his cheek. "Nicotine gum. I gave up smoking last month. I'm down to two sticks a day."

"Well, there you go," I said. I moved towards the second card. "What have you heard, Sweeney?"

"There were rumors," he said. He shifted in his chair, clearly uncomfortable.

"What kind of rumors?"

"That you were taking contracts on the side." I raised a brow. The cardinal rule of the Museum was that freelancing was strictly forbidden. It's one of the things that

195

separated us from hired guns. We killed to order only, targets that had been scrupulously vetted and chosen because their deaths would benefit humanity as a whole. Murders with a mission statement, we joked. But we were convinced it kept us on the right side of the karmic ledger.

"Moonlighting isn't allowed, and even if it were, that's not me. You know that."

He shrugged and I turned over the second card. In the center was an orange disc marked with symbols. Winged creatures hovered in the corners, and atop the disc sat a sphinx.

"The Wheel of Fortune," I told him.

"I don't see Vanna," he joked. "But it sounds good."

"It means a change in circumstances. Could go either way," I said. "What else did you hear?"

He paused, then started talking, fast — like he wanted to get it out before he changed his mind. "Nothing. Just that the four of you had gone rogue and were killing for profit."

"And you thought it was true?"

He held up both hands like he was trying to ward me off. "I'm just telling you what I heard."

I studied him a moment, making a careful

note of the reddened tips of his ears, the quick slide of his gaze away from mine. "Bullshit. You believed it."

I didn't keep the anger out of my voice; I didn't even try.

I flipped over the last card. It was an image of a man lying on his stomach, his face averted. He was wearing a red cape, and part of it — or a puddle of blood — drifted across the card. Ten swords were stuck into his back.

"What the shit is that?" he demanded.

"Ten of Swords," I told him. "It's as bad as it looks. Betrayal. Backstabbing. Utter ruin."

He pulled off his baseball cap and ran his hands through his thinning hair. "Jesus, Billie. Did you put it there on purpose?"

"Me? The cards don't lie," I said simply.

"Maybe they don't," he said. His voice didn't change; he was a pro. But there was something about the shift in how he held himself, some almost imperceptible difference in his arms. I couldn't see his hands, but I knew. He hadn't come to talk. He'd come to kill.

"So where are the others?" he asked, his tone casual. And then I understood. *Of course.* If the Museum's official line was that we had gone rogue, there would be bonuses for taking us out. And Sweeney wouldn't want to stop at one. Four kills would pay for a lot of baseball tickets and Hungry-Man dinners.

Somehow, above the usual crowd noise, I caught the sound of Mary Alice's cello. The melody had changed and she'd crashed into the opening of "Hazy Shade of Winter." She was playing it sharp and up-tempo — the Bangles, not Simon and Garfunkel. She'd spotted somebody who wasn't supposed to be there. Either Sweeney had brought backup or he had competition. Either way, we weren't safe.

Sweeney didn't seem to know he'd been made. He just kept looking at me with the same wide-open, innocent gaze that helped him clean up at the poker table. I gathered the cards and tapped them twice before putting them in a stack on the left-hand side of the table. That was the signal to Helen to take him out.

I resisted the urge to look up to where Helen would be eyeing Sweeney along the barrel. I only hoped she wouldn't go for a head shot. It would be messy as hell and not exactly subtle. A neck shot would be just as effective and a little more discreet.

But the bullet didn't come and I realized Helen must be having trouble getting the shot off. I had to buy time.

I grabbed Sweeney's left hand in mine and turned it over. "Let me read your palm. Then I'll take you to where the others are. They'll be happy to see you."

He smiled and something behind his eyes eased. He was ready to play along if there was a chance he'd get all four of us. I traced lines, making up bullshit about his life and heart, waiting, waiting for Helen to pull the trigger. By the time I got to the Mount of Venus — which sounds dirty but just means the part below your thumb — I was getting antsy. I flicked a glance up to where Helen sat on the balcony, hands gripping the railing. She wasn't in shooting position; she hadn't even gotten her gun out. She was frozen, a rabbit in the headlights, and I knew then I'd have to take matters into my own hands.

I stopped bullshitting and looked him dead in the eye. "Give it to me straight. There are bounties on us, aren't there? Bonuses for every one of us that get killed."

He shrugged. "I'm sorry about this, Billie. I really am. But yeah."

"How much?"

He told me. I was still holding Sweeney's left hand in mine as I spoke. It kept him from noticing that I was reaching into my skirt pocket with my right. My finger touched the trigger and I squeezed.

CHAPTER FIFTEEN

The thing about gunshots is they don't sound like they do in the movies. It's a pop, like a firecracker, higher-pitched and faster than you'd expect. A few people in the square looked around, curious, but after a long minute when nothing happened, they went back to their Hurricanes and their pralines. The gun was in my hand and I'd fired through the table, taking a blind shot and hoping for the best, but I'd been lucky. The small-caliber bullet had entered the front of his chest and stayed there, leaving a single hole under his collarbone and a spreading patch of wet darkness across his navy jacket.

"Sweeney?" I still clutched his hand, but the pulse was already gone, even before his eyes fluttered closed. He slumped in his chair, looking like he had just dozed off in the middle of having his cards read.

I looked up again at the balcony and

Helen was staring down at us with wide eyes. Suddenly she seemed to pull herself together and stood, throwing money on the table and disappearing inside. Nat would have heard Mary Alice's signal and left her paintings, she and Helen making their way back to the house via the twisting routes we'd mapped out. Mary Alice could continue to play, invisible as street performers are. I lifted my skirt and ran, ducking into Père Antoine Alley. I still didn't know why Mary Alice had signaled, but it was a safe bet she had spotted someone who wasn't supposed to be there — someone who would now be on my tail if they were following Sweeney. I ripped off the skirt and wig, leaving them in a heap next to a woman sleeping in a doorway. I had sunglasses in my pocket and I shoved them on as I walked away from the square.

With Sweeney's corpse cooling behind me, I headed up to Royal Street and hung a left, away from the direction of the house. I expected to make a large square and end up at home, but as I crossed Toulouse I saw him. He was dressed like a tourist, his T-shirt tucked into belted jeans like a sociopath. He was wearing only a thin windbreaker, black and gold with a gaudy Saints fleur-de-lys, but there was a fine mist of perspiration on his face. He had a good head of white-blond hair, the sort that everybody else outgrows after toddlerhood but Norwegians keep all their lives.

He was approaching from my left, and on instinct, I cut down St. Louis to Chartres, walking just briskly enough to make it seem like I had business but not fast enough to make it look like panic. I didn't dare look back. I couldn't hear footsteps behind me, but I knew he would be wearing rubber soles. I turned right on Bienville and crossed over, making my way to the garage entrance of the Hotel Monteleone. I didn't turn in, but there was a large convex mirror hanging just over the driveway. I flicked up a glance as I passed and saw him, forty paces back and taking his time. The little shit was enjoying this, I realized. He didn't know I'd clocked him and he'd apparently decided to give me enough space to play, planning to reel me in when it suited him.

I swung hard left onto Royal and broke into a trot, beating feet towards the end of the block. The street was lined with antiques shops, expensive ones, with crystal chandeliers shimmering in the windows. I dared a glance behind as I turned into the main entrance of the Monteleone and he was only just turning the corner. I saw him give a start of surprise when he realized I wasn't where he expected. It was check-in time and the hotel's entrance was crowded with doormen and drivers, bellhops and guests. I eased around them into the main lobby, turning immediately to the right to take the short flight of carpeted steps into the Carousel Bar. The centerpiece of the place was the giant carousel, revolving slowly as drinkers perched on their barstools. It was early, but the joint was already crowded, and nobody was going to look twice at a woman of a certain age who blended into the crowd. I threaded my way through the bar and out the back exit via the restaurant, ending up at the elevator bank. I punched the "up" button and held my breath.

I stretched my neck a little and risked a look across the restaurant and through the windows. He was there, standing with his back to the hotel and scanning the street both ways. In a minute, he would think to canvass the bar and lobby, but if I could get to the roof first, I had a good chance of shaking him. The doors opened and I stepped in, forcing myself to breathe slowly.

"Oooh, hold the elevator!" called a woman in palomino mink as she teetered towards the elevator. She had a tiny dog nestled in her cleavage and I didn't even bother to pretend to wait. I jammed the "close door" button with my thumb and heard her screech with fury as the doors closed in her face. I held that button and the roof button down and the elevator skipped calls for any other stops. I emerged at the roof level and hit four random floor buttons before jumping out. If anybody was looking at the display panel in the lobby, the numbers for multiple floors would be glowing.

A long wall of glass stretched ahead of me and I glanced outside to the pool deck. On the left side, a bar and dining area were tucked under an overhang. Dead ahead was the pool, surrounded by loungers and large potted shrubs. It was too cold for swimming, but the barman was still there, polishing glasses and listening with a politely vacant smile to some old guy who was obviously droning on. I had reconned the hotel months ago in case of just such a situation, and I knew the door to the pool deck only opened with a key card.

But I also knew how willing people are to do favors for you if they think you belong and *especially* if you're older than they are. A young woman wearing a hotel badge emerged from the spa and I marched up to her with a harried expression.

"Excuse me, dear, I seem to have forgotten my key and my husband is too busy boring the bartender to let me into the pool area," I said, rolling my eyes towards the boor on the barstool.

"Not a problem, ma'am," she said, smiling as she swiped the key card. I thanked her and strolled in as if I belonged there, paying cash for a drink at the bar.

Beyond the last potted shrub at the end of the pool was a small area sheltered from casual view, a handy little nook that was completely invisible from the rest of the pool deck. I took a lounge chair behind a shrub and sipped slowly as the sun sank in a gory blaze while I surveyed the streets below. My pursuer was pacing in a careful square, taking the streets nearest the Monteleone one by one in a grid pattern. A few minutes after I arrived, I heard the wail of sirens and figured they had found Sweeney slumped in his chair in Jackson Square. Once they cleared up the body, they'd review the CCTV camera footage and eventually they'd work out where I had gone.

But there are lots of ways to disappear in a city like New Orleans. After another quarter hour of ear-numbing wind blowing off the river, I heard a second line parade coming down the street. I hurtled down the stairs to the lobby, taking them two at a time and praying my knees would hold up. In the gift shop I found a pair of oversized Mardi Gras sunglasses and a handful of throws, which I layered over a sweatshirt decorated with a sequined crawfish that told everyone to LAISSEZ LES BON TEMPS ROULEZ. I looked like any tacky middle-aged tourist from Omaha loose in the Big Easy.

I slipped out the door of the hotel in time to join the end of the parade. At the front, two grooms wearing Tom Ford tuxedos held hands up high, showing off their shiny new wedding rings. The band played "Breezin' Along with the Breeze" and everyone sang along, waving handkerchiefs and holding up champagne flutes to toast onlookers. A bridesmaid who was three sheets to the wind was drinking directly out of a bottle of Veuve Clicquot and she held it up to me.

"Hey, stranger! You need to party with us!" She handed the bottle over and I took a swig. The champagne was tepid and nearly flat, but I didn't care. I passed it back and raised my voice as we stepped down Royal Street and into the night.

CHAPTER SIXTEEN

I left the parade just behind the cathedral, where a floodlight casts a giant statue of Jesus on the church's back wall. Shadow Jesus had his arms outstretched as if asking for a hug, but I walked on by, taking the long way around until I finally got to the gate on Ursulines, buzzing myself in. The others were in the kitchen, hunkered around the table with cups of coffee so cold they had scummed over on the top.

Minka hurled herself on me, exclaiming in Ukrainian, until Mary Alice pried her off to hug me. Helen took a turn, but Nat was the most practical, shoving a hot cup of tea into my chilled hands. "Drink," she ordered, and I raised a brow.

"What?" she demanded. "I can nurture."

"Yes, you can," I agreed, wrapping my numb fingers around the cup.

"Are we safe here?" Helen asked. She was clasping and unclasping her hands, as if she needed something to hang on to.

"For a little while. I had a tail but I lost him. Nielssen."

Go bags were piled by the door along with the cat carrier. Kevin himself was in Akiko's arms, lapping at her cup of coffee while she stared straight ahead, her expression blank. I looked at Mary Alice and jerked my head towards her wife.

"She okay?"

"I'm processing," Akiko said in a stilted voice. "You just killed someone. They said you killed someone."

"He was going to kill me. Actually, all four of us," I assured her. "I mean, if that helps."

She nodded slowly. "I think it does."

I turned to the others. Natalie gestured towards my sweatshirt and throws.

"I like the new look. Not everybody can pull off Shitty Tourist, but you really make it work."

"Thanks, I'm getting you one tomorrow."

Helen fixed me a plate of food — I didn't even bother to notice what it was. I shoveled it in while Nat kept the tea coming.

As I ate, Mary Alice looked around. "Time for a postmortem?"

"Tacky," Natalie said.

Mary Alice's expression was mystified. "That's what we've always called it."

"A friend is dead," Helen reminded her. "Maybe we should just call it a discussion."

Mary Alice shrugged but didn't argue.

"A friend who was ready to kill me," I corrected. I filled them in on what Sweeney had told me, and their reactions were predictable. Affronted — Helen; outraged — Natalie; and practical — Mary Alice.

The one part I left out was Helen freezing when I'd signaled her to shoot.

Natalie folded her arms over her narrow chest. "Are you sure it was necessary for you to take him out? I mean, it was supposed to be up to Helen to take the shot."

I glanced at Helen but she said nothing. "I made a choice."

Natalie snorted. "Well, it wouldn't be the first time you poached a target."

"No, Natalie, it wouldn't. I have occasionally taken point on a job when it wasn't my responsibility because —" I looked at the naked, broken anguish in Helen's eyes and swerved from what I was going to say. "Because I made a judgment call. He was planning on eliminating all four of us. He only delayed because he was trying to get me to tell him where the rest of you were," I finished.

"You didn't have a choice," Mary Alice said firmly.

"Poor dumbass Sweeney," Natalie murmured.

Helen looked down at the ground and continued to say nothing.

Akiko roused herself when I finished. "Shorthand this for me," she said. "Please. I want to understand."

I wiped my mouth on a napkin and put it aside. "When we realized the organization we work for —"

"The Museum," Akiko put in.

"The Museum." I nodded. "When we realized the organization we work for targeted us for termination, we contacted a former associate of ours to find out why."

"And that was this Sweeney person?" she asked.

"Correct. Our rendezvous with him was supposed to give us information about what was going on. We were careful enough to meet him in a neutral location, but it turns out we shouldn't have trusted him at all. He came to kill us, Akiko."

"So what happens now?" she asked. "They tried to kill you and they failed. I mean, they don't just say, 'Fair enough, our bad,' and let you go home? Right?"

I heard the note of hope in her voice, and so did Mary Alice, who winced a little as she spoke. "We can't go home again."

"Ever," Natalie said.

Akiko turned to her wife. "Are you *shitting* me? Mary Alice."

Mary Alice was rubbing her hands together, the knuckles white and then red. She was one of the most accomplished killers I knew, but sitting next to her wife, she looked small, crushed down by the weight of the secret she had carried and what it was doing to them now.

Akiko persisted. "Mary Alice, *look at me.* What happens now?"

Mary Alice took a deep breath. "We need more information."

"You have information," Akiko countered. "You said they wanted you dead because you broke some code — you were killing people for money instead of on assignment."

"But we weren't," Helen said in a patient tone. "That means they have bad intel on us. Somebody is setting us up."

"So tell them the truth," Akiko shot back. "Tell them. They will listen. They have to listen."

Natalie sat forward, her expression sympathetic. "I know you're having a bit of trouble with this, but they won't listen, actually. It's not really what they do."

Akiko turned on her. "A bit of trouble

212

with this? I'm having a goddamned nervous breakdown. The woman I love most in the world has — after five years of marriage — decided to finally tell me the truth about what she does. That's five years of lies. That's a *shit-ton* of lies."

"I was trying to protect you," Mary Alice said feebly.

"I think," Akiko said in a voice like acid, "that ship has sailed. I am on the run for my life with a cat who hates to travel, and I don't know when I can go home again. So fix this, Mary Alice." She got up, Kevin struggling in her arms, and leaned close to Mary Alice. "I mean it. *Fix this.*"

She left us then and Mary Alice blew out a slow breath.

"She'll come around," I said.

Mary Alice gave me a doubtful look as Helen cleared her throat. "Alright, we need to make a plan."

"Maybe Akiko had a good idea," Helen said. "Maybe we should try to talk to them."

That bought us half an hour of arguing over how exactly we were supposed to approach an organization that was actively trying to kill us. We discussed each board member at length before deciding it was pointless.

"What about the curators, then?" Mary

Alice suggested. "I know we discussed it before, but maybe it's time to circle back to the idea."

"Not Naomi," Natalie said. "If they've got bad intel about us, it must have come through Naomi's research. She does the briefings for the board and she would have been the one to tell them we were on the take."

"Not Naomi," Mary Alice agreed. "But Martin?" She raised her voice hopefully.

"Martin," I agreed. The others nodded along, and Helen produced her address book, where his number was neatly written in pencil. We drew straws to see who would call him and I lost. I ripped open a new burner and punched in his private cell number. I halfway expected it to go to voicemail, but he answered on the second ring, a little caution in his voice.

"Martin," I said. "It's Billie Webster."

There was a sharp intake of breath, almost a gasp but not quite. "Oh my god," he said, "give me a second. I'm in public."

There was a muffled sound as he must have clapped a hand over his phone. Eventually I heard clinking and distant chatter, restaurant noises, and then a shift to honking horns and a faint siren.

"I'm on the street now," he said finally.

"Holy shit, Billie. Are you okay?"

"I've been better," I told him. "I assume you know why I'm calling."

"Yes, and I know better than to ask questions. Just tell me, are the others okay too?"

"Yes."

He breathed a deep sigh into the phone. "Good. Listen, I can't talk long. I don't think they monitor my calls, but if they do —"

"I'm not asking you for anything except a bit of information," I promised him. "A little bird told me the board had intel we were taking jobs on the side. What do you know about that?"

"Nothing," he told me. "The board has been extremely close-lipped. You know how paranoid they are about secrecy. They've locked this down tight."

"Martin," I said, sweetening my tone to something warm and coaxing. "I know how good you are. That board doesn't order so much as a paper clip without you knowing about it. The last thing I want is to get you into trouble," I assured him.

He pulled in a breath. "All I know is there is a dossier that somebody in the Museum compiled on the four of you and submitted directly to the board. It didn't come through the usual channels."

"So it didn't originate from Provenance?"

"If someone in Provenance put it together, it was sent up without going through the regular protocols or I would have known about it."

"And you have no idea where it came from?"

"None," he said grimly. "And believe me, I've dug. Nobody is supposed to be able to do an end run around Naomi or me, but it looks like they did. Billie, I can't tell you anything more —"

He was winding down, so I cut in quickly. "Is there any chance of calling this off?"

"Billie —"

"We're not dirty, Martin. You know that," I said.

"Of course I know it," he said, indignant. "But you know what the board is like. If they rescind an order, it would be admitting they're wrong. And you know how much they hate being wrong. Besides" — his voice dropped and he sounded regretful — "they would want proof that the four of you are clean."

"There's my word," I told him.

"Billie, that's not good enough."

"It would have been forty years ago," I said. He didn't respond to that, but he didn't have to. Times had changed and I could swear on a stack of Bibles but it wouldn't make a difference. "So what now?"

He hesitated. "I shouldn't be telling you this, but they know you're in New Orleans. It will be more than my job if they ever find out I warned you, but they're sending Nielssen. If you can, you have to get out of there."

"Our paths have already crossed," I said. "And Sweeney decided to pay us a visit too. I guess he thought he could collect on that bonus." I didn't mention that we'd called Sweeney ourselves. It wouldn't do much for Martin's confidence at that point.

He drew in a shaky breath. "Shit, shit, shit. And you're sure you're okay?"

"For now."

"And Sweeney and Nielssen?"

"Sweeney is leaking blood into Jackson Square and Nielssen couldn't find his ass with both hands and Google Maps. We're fine."

He laughed, but it was small and forced. "So, I guess Sweeney was your little bird?" He didn't wait for an answer. "That won't be the end of it, you know. They'll keep sending people until someone succeeds. They won't stop, Billie. Not until they eliminate all four of you. You have to know that."

"So it's either us or them is what you're saying."

217

"No," he replied, his voice grave. "I'm saying it's them. I know the Museum isn't what it used to be, but it's still an elite organization. They know what they're doing, Billie. And there are only four of you. Without resources."

"Well, it sounds less than ideal when you put it that way," I said.

He sniffed hard. "Billie —"

"It's okay, kid," I said. "This is where I say it's been nice knowing you and you tell me that you can't risk talking to me again because they'll come after you too." I rattled off a number. "That's an answering service I use for emergencies." Not so much an answering service as Max, a phone sex operator in Scottsdale who was happy to collect a little extra money just for letting me have the occasional use of one of her lines. "If you ever need to get in touch, leave a message at that number. I'll call in once a week, okay?"

I heard a noise like a sigh down the line, and I didn't know if he took the number or not. "Good-bye, Martin. Thanks for everything." Before he could answer, I hung up the burner phone. I told the others what he'd said — and more importantly, what he hadn't.

"So we don't know who put together the

dossier on our 'activities,' " said Natalie, making air quotes with her fingers.

"Nope," I replied. "And we don't know why the board has gone so hard, so fast."

"What do you mean?" Helen had been sitting quietly, hands tucked between her knees, but she stirred to life to ask the question.

"I mean, a kill order is extreme. Why not haul us in to question us? Or send someone else to do it?"

"The Museum is an international organization of assassins," Mary Alice put in dryly. "They're not exactly known for giving people the benefit of the doubt."

"Of course they do," Natalie said. "Nobody is targeted without extensive research from the Provenance team. Months, sometimes years of surveillance and intelligence work go into each hit. But somebody gives them a piece of paper saying, 'Oh, the old bitches aren't playing nice,' and suddenly they put us in the crosshairs? That's insane."

"It does seem a little premature," Helen agreed. "They might have done as Billie suggested and at least asked us."

"Because we'd just roll over and tell them if we were on the take?" Mary Alice was skeptical. She turned to me. "Call Naomi."

"She's Provenance," Natalie protested.

219

"For all we know, she's the source of the dossier."

"Martin doesn't think so," I said, putting out my hand for Helen's address book. I punched in the number and waited.

"Ndiaye." The voice that answered was clipped and none too friendly. I identified myself and waited. A TV was playing in the background and I heard theremin music.

"Is that *Midsomer Murders*?" I asked politely. "Old Barnaby or new?"

"New," she said shortly. "You watch English murder shows?"

"Well, sometimes I need inspiration for work," I said. "I'm pretty pissed they thought of using a wheel of cheese to kill somebody before I did." She didn't laugh, and any thought I had of bonding with her over cozy village homicide fell flat.

"Why are you calling me?"

"Because I need some information and you're the only person I can ask," I said.

"I am not having this conversation," she said. But I could hear the episode still playing in the background. She hadn't hung up yet, which meant she was listening.

"Naomi, I know there's a dossier on us and I have a good idea what it says. I just want to know why the board decided that was worth a kill order instead of bringing us in alive for questioning."

She made me wait a good bit before answering. "I'm on medical leave, you know. I'm not supposed to be getting stressed."

"Well, if the idea of four women being targeted for something they didn't do stresses you out, good news. You can help fix it," I replied. I heard the clinking of a spoon and a bowl. "Are you eating?"

"Pho. It's all this baby wants." The spoon clinked again. "Alright. Pick one."

"Pick one what?"

"One question. You can ask about the dossier, the kill order, who has been sent after you. But only one. That's all I have time for because I'm hanging up in fifteen seconds."

I thought fast. We had a good idea of who had been sent after us — basically anybody who wanted to collect a bonus. What we needed to know was if there was a way to call the order off.

"Ten seconds," she said, her voice muffled — from the noodles probably.

"Is there a way to rescind the order?" I asked.

"Nope." She slurped another spoonful.

"That's it? Just 'nope'? We're under a death sentence?"

"Pretty much." She paused. "Can you go into hiding?"

"For the rest of our lives? No, thanks. I'd rather handle this. Why are they so set on terminating us instead of letting us clear our names?"

She paused. "You know what a gibbet is?"

"I beg your pardon?"

"A gibbet? Kind of like a cage on a pole? The law set them up at crossroads and used them to hang murderers, pirates, sheep thieves. And they left them there, chained up and rotting, for everybody to see while they went about their business. You know why?"

"To discourage other people from committing similar crimes," I finished.

"Exactly."

"So they want to make examples of us?"

"More that they want to make everybody else too afraid to ask questions. They want to be left in peace, and you four are in danger of rocking the boat."

I gripped the phone. "Left in peace to do what?"

"You're well past your fifteen seconds," she said. I didn't answer and she sighed. "I heard a rumor. Someone is on the take, arranging murders for pay. I don't know who. But they're determined to cover it up. If word gets out, the entire organization is in jeopardy."

"Bullshit. We didn't know anything about that before they decided to come for us."

"Billie," she said patiently. "Think."

"The only reason to come for us —" I broke off. "Holy shit. They're going to blame it on us and let whoever is actually responsible walk free."

"Well, it took you a minute, but you got there in the end," she said. "You're expendable to the board. Whoever is arranging the freelance hits isn't, so the board has decided to protect them."

"Why?"

"They could be too highly placed to lose. They could be blackmailing the board. They could have cut the board in on the hits. Those are just the first possibilities that come to mind. I could think of about a dozen more."

"And none of it matters because we're still under a termination order," I finished. "Who is it? Who is arranging the freelance hits?"

"I already told you, I don't know. It could be a member of the board."

"It could be someone from Provenance," I said, my voice heavy with insinuation.

I heard the sound of a spoon dropping into an empty bowl. "You want to accuse me of something, go right ahead. I'm done with this conversation. Your time is up."

I related what she'd told me to the others. Mary Alice sat with her head in her hands while Helen covered her mouth and Natalie swore up a blue streak.

"Those shit-licking *bastards,*" she finished. "What if some of the work *we* did was part of this freelance bullshit? Someone could have been using us to carry out their dirty little side jobs like we were common hit men."

It was all too easy to see how it might have been done — money changing hands, dossiers prepared. The board would be briefed on the prospective targets and the field agent assigned. Once it was passed down to us, we'd have no way of knowing if the job was clean or not. We put our faith in Provenance and the board to identify the appropriate targets. Every piece of information, every decision, every action, was a link in the chain we forged together. Any corruption in that chain was unthinkable.

"Not exactly what we signed up for," Mary Alice said.

"I always told myself we were making the world better, safer," Helen said finally.

"And we did," I told her. I looked around at their devastated faces. "Look, I know it feels like a betrayal —"

"Feels?" Natalie's voice rose.

"It is a betrayal," I corrected. "But whatever we may have done, it was inadvertent. We believed in the organization. We trusted them. If we've made mistakes in who we took out, we can deal with that later. Right now the problem is the board. They've decided to make scapegoats of us to save whoever is behind all of this. The question is, what are we going to do about it?"

We looked at each other, and we knew this decision was going to be bigger than the four of us.

We summoned Akiko and Minka and brought them up to speed. I ate a cinnamon bagel while Natalie pulled hers to pieces, making little bagel pellets with the insides and flicking them around the room.

"Could you not?" Mary Alice asked, shaking one out of her hair and flicking it back.

"I'm just fidgety," Natalie said. "I don't like being on this end of things."

I looked around the table. "We're going to be on this end of things forever unless we take control," I said. "We've never been marks before, but we've also never had to decide on a target before. That's always been decided for us. For better or worse, we've always been the instrument and not the musician. We don't choose the tune.

And you two," I said, eyeing Minka and Akiko, "have no idea what it's like to get your hands dirty."

Minka gave me a cool look. "I maybe know better than you think."

"Maybe you do, but that doesn't change the fact that this is uncharted territory for all of us. We have two choices. One, we can walk away right now. We can get Minka to forge new papers for each of us. This is a big world and with the right documentation, we can disappear. We can start new lives and just let this one go."

"And do what?" Natalie asked. "I'm broke. Thanks to the board, my pension blew up somewhere in the middle of the Caribbean."

"Mine too," said Helen. "After the illness, Kenneth didn't leave much."

Mary Alice and Akiko didn't speak, but the look they exchanged suggested they weren't much better off.

"We could get jobs," I pointed out.

"Doing what?" Natalie demanded. "We've spent forty years assassinating people, Billie. It's all we know how to do, and you can't exactly find clients for that on LinkedIn."

"I think Craigslist would be a better place to find clients," Helen put in.

I held up a hand. "I'm just saying, we can

try to walk away."

"Okay, and what would that be like?" Natalie asked. "We'd spend the rest of our lives looking over our shoulders, wondering if we've been made, if today is finally the day when somebody gets to cash in a nice fat bonus check for bringing back our hides."

"I don't like it any better than you do," I said. "If it were up to me, we'd already be working up a plan to take out the board and end this. But I don't think this is something we should rush into. We can take a day to sleep on it —" I started.

"I'm in," Mary Alice said firmly.

To my surprise, Akiko spoke up. "Me too."

"Really?" Mary Alice asked, sounding hopeful. Akiko didn't return her smile, but it was a start.

"Alright," I said, tallying. "That's Mary Alice and Akiko in." I looked around. Minka nodded and Natalie grinned and sat up straight. "What's the expression the kids use? 'Hells yeah'? Well, hells yeah. I don't know how many years I've got left and I'll be damned if I spend them looking over my shoulder for whichever goon the board decides to send next. Besides, we've got a score to settle."

I looked at Helen. She opened her mouth

227

and closed it again, nodding. She might be less than what she had once been, but she was still worth a hell of a lot.

I closed my eyes and inhaled, holding it for a count of six. I exhaled slowly and opened my eyes. "Then it's unanimous. The Board of Directors is going to die."

CHAPTER SEVENTEEN

When we had finished our discussion, I went to my room to throw a few things in a bag. At some point we were going to have to leave New Orleans and I figured it was easier to pack when I had the chance. I was stuffing clothes into a small duffel when Helen slipped into my room, closing the door behind her.

"That's a criminal way to treat silk," she said, pulling a blouse out of the duffel. She laid it on the bed facedown, smoothing it neatly before making a couple of quick motions with her hands that created a small, tidy parcel.

"It looks like Barbie's Glamour Parachute," I told her.

She tucked it into the duffel. "It should come out fine, but if there are creases, just hang it in the bathroom when you shower. The wrinkles will drop right out."

"Gee, if only that worked for my face," I

said, tossing a pair of jeans into the duffel on top of the blouse. I wadded up a T-shirt until I saw her expression. She put out her hand for the T-shirt and refolded it, smoothing the fabric slowly. "I've been thinking, Billie. About Minka. I don't think she should come."

"You didn't like her on day one and you still haven't warmed up to her," I began.

"It isn't that, Billie. You were right to trust her. She's a remarkable girl. But she *is* a girl."

"She's the same age we were when we signed up for the Museum," I said, snatching back the T-shirt and shoving it into the duffel.

"And my mother was having babies at twenty. What's your point?" she said mildly. "Times change. She should have a chance to see the world. And not the way we did."

I moved to pick up a stack of underwear, but she put out her hand to take mine. "Billie." I stopped moving.

"She's seen more of the world than you can possibly imagine," I said.

"I know. We've had a few interesting chats," she said, her hand still on top of mine. "I know where you found her and how you got her out of Ukraine. You didn't have to do that."

"Yes, I did," I said simply.

Helen smiled. "Contrary to what you think, I like her. Very much. And I don't want to see her end up like us."

"What are you saying, Helen? That we somehow missed out? That we wasted our lives and we're nothing but washed-up cautionary tales?"

"No," she replied. "But aren't there things you wish you'd done differently? Things you wish you'd made time for? People you wish you hadn't let go?"

I snatched my hand out from under hers. "Minka is part of the team and she's coming to England. End of story." I clamped my mouth shut before I said anything I'd regret — probably about her freezing up in Jackson Square and losing her nerve.

I started shoving the rest of my clothes into the duffel, cramming a pair of boots on top of a shirtwaist dress I didn't even remember owning. Helen watched me for a minute, then got up.

"I'll leave you to it, then," she said quietly as she shut the door behind her.

She hadn't said his name, but I knew exactly who she was thinking of, and when I crawled into bed without undressing that night and waited for hours to crash into

231

sleep, it was because I was thinking of him. *Taverner.*

CHAPTER EIGHTEEN

NOVEMBER 1981

Billie has a theory that every life has a soundtrack. Some people are big band people or smooth jazz. Others are pure Baroque opera theatricality. Her soundtrack is not that glamorous. "Delta Dawn" was on the jukebox when her mother left her — age twelve, sitting in a strip mall pizza joint — and never came back.

And "If You Could Read My Mind" is being played by a soft-rock combo in a hotel bar in Chicago when she is passing time, waiting to meet up with her partner for the first job after a debacle in Zanzibar. Vance Gilchrist, her mission leader for the assignment, has been unstinting in his report and she realizes she will be watched to see if she makes a habit of going off piste. This is a chance to redeem herself and she means to make the most of it.

She sits at the bar, nursing a glass of tepid Chablis while the singer invokes ghosts and wishing wells, and feeling faintly sick to her stomach with anticipation as she goes over the coded exchange they are supposed to use to establish contact.

"Is anyone sitting here?"

She glances up and falls — at least that's how it feels. It is a second, maybe two, before she answers. But two seconds is a long time when your life cracks open.

He isn't handsome, not like the polished-up pretty boys Natalie favors. This one needs a second look, but that look is a killer. He has maybe five inches on her, and an easy, loose-limbed way of holding himself that only comes with the bone-deep confidence of knowing there is nothing on earth you're afraid of. He wears a washed-out Henley and faded jeans with a battered leather jacket and a pair of Frye boots that have seen a dozen years of hard wear. A narrow silver bracelet circles one wrist and a knotted cotton braid wraps around the other. He has the sort of light brown hair that goes gold with too much sun, just unruly and wavy enough to bury your fists in when you're kissing hard. His beard and mustache are about two days past needing a trim if you mind about that sort of thing. Billie doesn't.

He has been looking down the bar to

signal the bartender, but he turns to her and gives an almost imperceptible start, a brief widening of deep brown eyes and the slightest parting of the lips.

"Oh." It isn't a whisper; it is an exhalation, a statement. He gives her a long look that seems to say, *It's you. Finally.*

"Yeah," she answers. He turns back to the bartender and lifts his hand as he levers himself onto the stool beside her. A minute later the bartender sets a beer in front of him, the liquid in the bottle fizzing gently. He swings it to his mouth and takes a long swallow, looks hard at her, then takes another.

"I don't think I have it in me to play this cool," he says finally. He takes another deep drink.

"Me either. Or maybe I've just seen too many Streisand movies. I mean, the way she looks at Robert Redford and he looks back . . ." She lets her voice trail off. She isn't wrong about what is happening, and the fact that he feels it too seems like a very small miracle. But she doesn't believe in miracles. She reminds herself they are strangers. Perfect, combustible strangers.

"Shit," he says, putting the beer carefully onto the bar. "As much as I'd like to forget

235

about the job right now, there's no way we can —"

"I know that," she tells him.

"It's my first time leading a mission and there are rules about fraternization," he says more to himself than to her. "I can't screw this up." In spite of the rugged American clothes, there is the slightest lilt of an English accent.

"You won't."

He takes another drink of his beer, pulling down half the bottle while she swallows the lukewarm Chablis. He turns to her. "I already have. We've forgotten the protocol. Do you like baseball?"

She struggles for a minute with the non sequitur, then remembers the code. "Yes, but I'm afraid I'm a Cubs fan. No chance of making the Series this year."

"Not since they traded Burris." He finishes the exchange.

They spend the next few minutes drinking silently. "Christopher Taverner," he says finally. "Kit."

"Billie Webster."

"I know." He lifts one brow and her cheeks go hot. Of course he knows. As leader of the mission, he'd have been given her dossier complete with photos. "They don't do you justice, by the way," he tells her, intuiting her thoughts.

"Well, they didn't get my best side," she says.

He laughs, sharp and sudden, and there is a roughness to the sound that makes her want to drown in it.

"So, what now, English?" she asks.

The brow is back. She will get to know that brow well, always cocked at the same angle as his mouth when he is amused. "English?"

"The accent. I'm very observant."

"I can see that. Well, ordinarily, this conversation would move to a more private place, like my room," he says softly, nodding upwards. "But in the circumstances, I don't think that's a good idea."

"Probably not," she agrees.

He smiles, a crooked, lopsided smile that carries just enough sadness to break what is left of her heart. His gaze drops to her mouth, to the tiny scar just above her lip.

"What happened there?"

"I got in a fight with a raccoon." The smile flickers up, then his eyes grow serious.

"Do I need to kick someone's ass?" He puffs his chest just enough to shift a pendant loose from the neck of his shirt. It is a small medallion of some sort, but she can't make it out. She drags her eyes away from the golden hair on his chest as she answers him. "I already did."

"Good. You can be the muscle in this relationship."

"Relationship?"

"Oh yeah. I figure we'll last a few weeks trying to pretend this isn't happening and then jack it all in to run away together and spend the rest of our lives having lots of sex and babies."

She laughs. "You're ridiculous."

"That's no way to talk to the future father of your children."

"I'm not giving up my job," she says.

"Christ, I hope not. Somebody has to make the money. I'll stay home and do the cooking. I look damned good in an apron."

"I bet you do, English."

They smile like conspirators and finish their drinks.

He takes a deep breath. "That was fun, Webster. But we both know this is as far as it goes. I can't risk it."

She rolls her eyes. "*You* can't risk it? If we broke the rules, which one of us do you think they'd bounce out on her pretty ass? I haven't proven myself yet. I'm expendable and I know it." She pauses. "You've never had this problem on a job before?"

"My last job was with a six-and-a-half-foot-tall Irishman with halitosis and a fondness for milkshakes, which do terrible things to his digestive system."

"He sounds dreamy."

"I'll give you his number when this is finished."

He drops a few bills next to his empty bottle and pushes away from the bar as he tucks his wallet into his hip pocket. "I'll knock when I stick the file under your door. Don't answer it, whatever you do, and destroy the file after you've read it. We'll meet up again tomorrow morning."

He hesitates, then puts out his hand. She takes it and it feels exactly like she knew it would, warm and strong. Lifeline hands, the kind you hold on to when everything else in the world is spinning away. The only surprise is the calluses on the tips of his fingers.

"Garrote wire?" she asks quietly.

"Guitar," he says. "I play a little."

"Of course you do. Now tell me you have a motorcycle so I can eat my heart out completely."

He holds her hand a minute too long, giving her that lopsided grin that makes her heart do calisthenics in her chest. "Tomorrow. Nine AM sharp in the coffee shop across the street. Sleep tight, Webster."

"Good night, English."

He moves behind her, stopping just long enough to bend near, his mouth grazing the curve of her ear. "And I ride a Norton 850 Commando."

She groans aloud as he leaves, laughing the whole way out the door. Bastard.

The following day they carry out the mission, posing as newlyweds in order to get an appointment with a crooked judge and his clerk. They are two hours out of town before the bodies are even discovered, and in another four hours they finally stop and check into separate rooms at a highway motel.

Billie lies awake for a long time, watching the passing lights of cars on the highway and thinking about a strange phenomenon the French call l'appel du vide, the call of the void. It's when you stand up high, staring into an abyss, and have a strong desire to throw yourself into it. It can take other forms. You might be driving and suddenly think about jerking the wheel, sending your car into oncoming traffic. Or you might be out for a hike and fantasize about hurling yourself off a cliff. It is not a suicidal impulse. In fact, it is the opposite. Psychologists say it's actually about how much a person wants to live. They perceive a nearby threat to themselves and they think about that threat because they want so much to survive.

Billie throws back the covers and goes outside before she can change her mind about hurling herself into the abyss. She raises her hand but he opens the door before she can knock. He is shirtless, his jeans slung low on his hips.

"I don't want you here," he says hoarsely.

"Good," she says, pushing him back into the room. "Because I don't want to be here." It is the last thing anybody says for a long time.

She jumps up, wrapping her legs around his waist as his arms come up to catch her. He kicks the door closed and slams her up against it. It is an hour before they make it as far as the bed.

The next morning they go their separate ways. Billie has a plane to catch and Taverner has a man to kill. Before she leaves, he puts his chain around her neck — the St. Christopher medallion, still warm from his skin.

CHAPTER NINETEEN

Making the decision to leave New Orleans was a no-brainer. The Museum knew we were there, and we'd never be able to make a plan and keep ourselves safe if we were always looking over our shoulders. Besides, two of the three board members lived in Europe. We had a pretty good idea of where to find Carapaz and Paar and decided to take them out first. Vance Gilchrist was a little more elusive, but we figured we'd deal with him when the time came. The first order of business was to strike Carapaz and Paar and do it fast, before they realized we were coming for them. That meant getting across the Atlantic and finding a safe house from which to plan and execute three missions. We needed a place that would be out of the way but with decent transport links, big enough for the six of us — and Kevin — and with enough privacy that we could plot a few murders without attracting unwanted attention. None of those things are particularly hard to find on their own, but all together? And with a limited budget? It seemed like a tall order until Helen spoke up.

"We could go to Benscombe," she offered.

"Benscombe?" Akiko asked.

"A country house in the south of England," Mary Alice told her. "It was our training ground. And probably not a great idea since it has a connection with the Museum," she pointed out.

"Kind of a frying pan, fire situation," Natalie agreed.

"But it doesn't have a connection to the Museum, not anymore," Helen said. "The organization never owned it. It was always the property of the Hallidays. When Constance died, it was inherited by a distant cousin who sold it. It changed hands several times."

"Then how are we going to get in?" I asked.

"Well, because I own it," Helen said. We stared at her in amazement as she hurried to explain. "Kenneth and I did a tour of England for our thirtieth wedding anniversary, and I thought it might be fun to show him. So we drove down, and as soon as we got there, I saw the noticeboard. It was for sale. I didn't know it at the time, but Kenneth wrote down the agent's details and made inquiries when we got back to the States. He cashed in his retirement and bought it as a surprise for me. Apparently he got quite a deal because nobody ever cleared it out. I think it's been left as it was when Constance died."

"You think?" I asked.

She shrugged. "I haven't been inside. Things kept coming up and by the time we were ready to go and see about fixing it up, Kenneth got sick and there was no money. But the bottom line is that there is a property in England sitting empty."

"We can't use it if it's in your name," Mary Alice said.

Helen shook her head. "Kenneth bought the property in the name of a holding company for tax purposes. My name isn't anywhere on it, and neither is his. It would take a good deal of research and a great deal of luck for anyone to find us."

I looked around the group. "Then we're off to England. Minka, Akiko needs a passport, and you'd better see about paperwork for Kevin as well. I'll make the flight arrangements. Get your bags together, ladies. Tomorrow is going to be a long day."

As we went our separate ways to pack up,

I noticed Natalie slipping out the front gate, looking furtive. I decided to follow, heading out into the Quarter, walking with a baseball cap pulled low on my head and a scarf wrapped up to my chin. I was moving fast, catching up to Nat just as she crossed the street and disappeared through the entry gate into the Ursulines convent museum. I waited a minute and then followed, paying for my ticket and passing through the line of shrubbery in the courtyard and into the convent itself. It smelled of wood polish with a faint trace of incense. To the right were the tiny rooms that had been turned into a museum and to the left was the passageway leading to the chapel. It was anybody's guess where she'd gone, but I mentally flipped a coin and headed left. Sure enough, she was sitting in the buff and blue chapel with its pretty rococo saints. The incense smell was stronger in here, mingling with the odor of the beeswax votives lit by the faithful. I slid into the pew next to her.

We didn't say anything for a long minute, just stared up at the starry blue ceiling. Next to us was a statue of a woman dressed in white and purple, her dark hair crowned with roses. She carried a skull resting on a book and seemed to be making a beckoning gesture with her hand.

"What are you doing here, Nat?"

"I'm communing with my girl Mary," she said, nodding towards the statue. "Two nice Jewish girls hanging out together. I like her skull."

"Sure. I can see that," I said. "Except that's St. Rosalia of Palermo. Pretty sure she was Catholic."

"Well, shit." Natalie slumped in the pew. "I can't even get that right."

"What's the matter with you?"

She seemed to be having some sort of argument with herself about whether to confide. She decided to trust me, I suppose, because she tucked her hands in between her thighs and took a deep breath. "I wanted to be with my people. Only the nearest synagogue is like an hour walk, so I came here. Catholics understand community, you know? And they get guilt too."

"You're sixty and you're finally feeling guilty over something?" I asked. I was only half joking.

"I'm sixty and I never stopped," she told me. "I'm a woman. Guilt is our birthright. Guilt if we want to be mothers, guilt if we take the Pill instead or choose to abort. Guilt if we stay home with our kids or guilt if we work. Guilt if we sleep with a man, guilt if we say no. Guilt if we're lucky enough to survive for no good reason. I'm so damned sick of it. I've never been so tired of anything in my life. I just . . . I just want to go to sleep forever."

"That won't get you out of the guilt," I said. "I'm pretty sure somewhere in the afterlife, some woman is feeling ashamed of herself because her cloud isn't as silver as the angel next door's."

She almost smiled but didn't quite manage it. "I suppose that's part of the reason I've always hated you. You never seem to struggle with it."

"You've always hated me? This is quite a time to find out, Natalie. We've known each other for four decades. I've literally trusted you with my life."

"And you still can. That's the job. I'd jump in front of a bullet for you and you know it. Besides, only a small part of me hates you. A tiny, tiny part of me."

"What, like a mustard seed of hate?"

"Chia. I have a chia seed of hate. Get with the times," she said, smiling a little.

"You have a chia seed of hate for me. Want to tell me about it?"

She picked at her fingernails. "I always wondered how you managed to just ease through without ever being touched by it all."

"By what?"

"The job. What we do. Who we are. It should leave scars, don't you think? I've got some. Helen does. Mary Alice does. But you don't seem fazed by it."

"Nat, that's some mark of Cain shit and I don't believe in it. What we do for a living doesn't strip us of our souls or make us terrible people. We're exterminators."

"That's really how you see it, isn't it?"

"Yes, it is."

"Do you sleep well at night?"

I thought about that. "Most of the time. Look, if you'd have asked me when I was seven years old and playing with a flea market Barbie knock-off what I wanted to be when I grew up, I'm pretty sure assassin wouldn't have made the top ten list. But it's what I do. And I do it well. And when I'm finished with a job, the world is that much safer," I said, holding up my thumb and forefinger, a quarter of an inch apart. "Maybe at the end of a mission I've stopped a trafficker from getting his hands on some eleven-year-old who will get to sleep in her own bed that night. Maybe I've prevented an arms deal that would have wiped out a settlement of villagers who won't have anything more to worry about than getting their crops in the ground. Or maybe I've broken up a cartel that terrorized people into leaving their homes so they could have free run of the farmland to grow their shitty crops. I think about the people we've saved before I sleep."

She was quiet, looking at her new friend, St. Rosalia, for a while before she turned back to me. "I should have called him. Sweeney, I mean. I should have called him and maybe asked him out for dinner. I should have asked him to stay for breakfast. Hell, I should have at least slept with him again."

"Really? Was he that good?"

She shrugged. "Average-sized dick but he really knew what to do with it. I just feel bad I dodged him. And now I won't have the chance to let him know that he was pretty good."

I leaned back and looked at the ceiling. "You know," I told her, "most of the decorations here are trompe l'oeil. All those moldings and stars aren't wood or plaster. They're just paint. They're not really there, but it looks like they are and that's enough for people."

She turned to me. "Really? Metaphors?"

"It's all I've got."

"Sweeney's dead," she said. "And it was a shitty way to go."

"He made his choice. He chose wrong. Unless you think you'd have done any differently if he'd pointed a gun at you."

She forced herself to take a deep breath and shake off the gloom. "I'd have killed the asshole with my bare hands. You were right to take him."

I cupped my hand over my ear. "Say that again. The part about me being right."

She nudged my shoulder with hers. "Bitch."

"Said with love?"

"Always." She breathed deeply, a slow, tired breath. "I kind of wish we could stay here, you know? Get Minka to make us up some new identities. Maybe get jobs. Turn the page and write some new story. Just walk away from it all."

"Okay, let's call that door number one," I said evenly. "But we've already agreed on door number two. If I remember, you were pretty enthusiastic."

I looked at St. Rosalia's sweet smile and unnaturally long toes. And then I shifted my gaze to the front of the church to the statue of St. Michael. He was a very casual St. Michael, one arm upraised like he was hailing a cab, his hair tousled by an invisible wind. But his spear was thrust right through the heart of the dragon at his feet.

The sculptor had caught it in its death throes, head back, tongue lolling out as it gasped its last breath. It looked pretty cheap; I was pretty sure I could order something better from the Toscano catalog. But that wasn't the point.

"He knew what the job was," I said, pointing to St. Michael. "Get in, kill the bastard. Get out alive."

She nodded. "Door number two." She lifted her pinky and I linked it with mine.

"Door number two."

CHAPTER TWENTY

Dawn was just beginning to break over the quarter when the six of us went our separate ways. We stood around the kitchen table with our packed bags and reviewed the next stage of the plan.

"Alright," I began, "today we're taking the first real step towards making this happen. If anybody wants out, this is the time. After we walk out that door," I said, gesturing vaguely towards the street, "we're all in."

I looked around the table at each of them in turn. Helen's face was cool, remote. Natalie was fairly vibrating with excitement, and Mary Alice's jaw was set. Akiko and Minka each nodded, and even Kevin looked committed — although that may have just been the kitty Valium Akiko had forced down his throat.

I gave Minka a sign. "Since we're travel-ing separately, Minka has gotten everybody phones. They're preloaded with contact info for each of us so we can get in touch."

Mary Alice was the first to power up her phone. She clicked into the contacts list and frowned. "The address book is empty."

"Not there," Minka said, scrolling through the apps until she came to a gaudy pink cartoon kitten wearing a big yellow bow and waving a paw.

Helen peered at the screen. "Is that one of those Japanese lucky cats?"

"A maneki-neko!" Natalie said, pulling up the same icon on her phone. She looked at the caption and did a double take. "You have got to be joking."

Below the waving kitten was the word "Menopaws!" in a font that looked hand-lettered. Natalie touched the cat and it meowed and twitched its ears.

"What in the name of hormonal hell is this?" Mary Alice demanded. She opened the app and scrolled through the features. "Hot flash tracker? Last menstrual period? *Vaginal dryness log?*"

Helen let out a little moan of protest, and Minka reared back as if she'd been slapped. "I worked many hours on this!"

"I can tell," Helen said, making an effort to smile.

"There's a sex chart," Natalie said. She hit the button to open that page and the

253

kitten threw back its head to yowl, sending Kevin diving under the table. Soon everyone's phone was meowing, purring, hissing, and generally making more noise than a herd of howler monkeys.

"It's awful," Helen said, hands clamped over her ears. I picked up her phone and closed the app, cutting the kitten off mid-screech.

"It's perfect," Mary Alice said, demonstrating the direct message feature. "Look here, we can communicate with each other without texting or emailing. Minka has set us each up with a profile and we're connected already."

She flashed her screen where the pink kitten was strolling past a blue postbox, its tail swishing as it pointed to the letters stuffed in the box.

"Oh, that is smart," Natalie said. "Look, I made my kitten striped. It looks like a tiny ocelot now."

"I added personalization feature," Minka said sulkily. "Kittens can be made to look different."

"It's very clever, Minka," Akiko said. She'd made her kitten white and gave it a pair of glasses.

"It's exactly what we needed," Mary Alice said, closing the screen on her calico and its tiny top hat.

"What about you?" Helen asked me as she added a sparkly necklace to her Siamese.

I sighed and hit a button. My kitten turned coal black with green eyes. "There. It's a plain black cat. Now, this is how we will communicate and this is the *only* way we will communicate," I said, giving Akiko and Mary Alice a long look. "If you need to talk, buy a burner and send the number via direct message on the app — and that is strictly for emergencies. Got it?"

Everybody made noises of agreement with varying degrees of enthusiasm.

"How in the hell did you develop something this complicated in two days?" Mary Alice asked.

"Minka is an app developer," I told her. "She's been working this up for months, and I asked her to let us have the prototype with a few tweaks."

"It does work, though?" Helen asked, an anxious line etched between her brows.

"Oh yes," Minka assured her. "But the STD warning is buggy and makes everything crash, so do not open."

"Why a menopause app?" Akiko asked.

"Because security people are men," Minka told her coolly.

"Most often," I agreed. "And most men

are terrified of periods." I couldn't count the number of times we'd stashed weapons in maxipads, douches, or vaginal itch creams. "We're all traveling under false papers, and there is always a chance one of us could get stopped. If that happens, make sure the app is open, preferably to something like your flow rate or how many days it's been since you last menstruated."

"Every day without a period, the kitten gets bigger," Minka added helpfully.

Natalie eyed Minka's clear, unwrinkled skin and pert boobs. "No one is going to believe you need a menopause tracker app."

Minka smiled and opened her phone. "Mine is Period Poodle." An animated French poodle with a tiny beret trotted across the screen. "Bonjour! You are on day 14. Bienvenue to ovulation!"

"Oh my god," Helen said faintly.

"I will put it on the App Store when it is finished," Minka told her. "It will be a very big success. You will see."

We said our good-byes inside the house before slipping out in pairs. We had learned through experience that anything more than two women traveling together attracted attention, and it seemed easier just to split up rather than sort out a group disguise for all six of us. Akiko and Minka left first, taking a cab to the airport with Kevin for their flight to Toronto, changing for London Gatwick, where they would pick up a rental car and follow Helen's directions to Benscombe. Helen and Natalie left next, flying to Newark and on to London Heathrow. Mary Alice and I sat on opposite sides of the departure lounge before catching our flight to Boston en route to London Heathrow. We staggered off the plane at seven in the morning, pretending we were traveling solo until Mary Alice collected the rental car and I met her at the curb. Helen and Nat took a train as far as Basingstoke, where we nipped off the M3 long enough to grab them. We were bleary-eyed from spending the night slumped in coach seats, and the weather was predictably awful for January in England — cold and grey and pissing with rain.

But in spite of our fatigue and the weather, we were almost giddy with excitement. Mary Alice checked her tracker messages and Akiko had confirmed their arrival at Gatwick. She tapped a message back and flipped on the satellite radio, punching buttons until she found a '70s station with ABBA. She banged out the piano part of "Waterloo" on the steering wheel while we sang the chorus at the tops of our voices.

Helen mapped our route although we'd been there before. It had been a lifetime ago, I realized, and much had changed — mostly us. We weren't the same girls who had been driven down this highway in 1979.

There were no motorway services where we were going, but we found places to stop twice to pee and get cups of tea and thick bacon sandwiches slathered with brown sauce. We kept the car pointed southwest, eventually looping around Southampton and changing from the big motorway to smaller highways and finally to country lanes. We were deep into Dorset, following the signs for Swanage and eventually the Purbeck coast. Finally, we turned off near Worth Matravers, a village whose name sounded like the perfect place for Miss Marple to find a murdered vicar.

"Turn here!" Natalie yelled suddenly, and Mary Alice stomped on the brake, yanking the wheel to the left. The gate was open, each side hanging from a tall brick pillar topped with a stone finial. Thick ropes of ivy wove between the bars of the gates, anchoring them in place. One pillar still held a bronze plaque that was discreetly lettered. BENSCOMBE HOUSE. The drive was washed almost clean of gravel, leaving a wide swath of mud and puddles for Mary

Alice to navigate as she edged the car in towards the house.

It was late Victorian, modeled, we had been told, after Thomas Hardy's house of Max Gate. The red brick had been homey and welcoming once. Now it was austere and grim, the roof just a little too peaked, the chimneys just a bit too ominous.

Mary Alice stopped the car in front of the house and we stepped out, making various noises as we stretched out our sore backs and rubbed feeling back into our sleeping legs.

"Don't we need a key?" Mary Alice asked.

Helen stood on the doorstep, looking around helplessly. "I didn't think of that."

I tried not to remember how good Helen used to be at details in the old days. A small matter like how we were getting into the house would never have slipped her mind then. But age and grief are both blunt weapons and they'd worked her over pretty well. I turned to Natalie. "You want to take care of the lock?"

"Sure." She picked up a stone from the driveway and tossed it through a window.

"I meant pick it, but okay," I told her. She grinned as she wrapped her hand in her sleeve and reached through the broken pane, feeling for the lock. She flipped it and slid the window open. "I'll come around and open the door," she told us, disappearing into the shadowy interior.

When she opened the front door, it gave way with a shriek of the hinges that scared the birds out of the overgrown laurel bushes next to the front steps. Helen took a deep breath and followed Natalie inside, but Mary Alice hung back, grabbing my sleeve. She pointed to the dark windows, the trim paint peeling off in long fingers. Through the grimy glass I could just make out the shapes of furniture shrouded under white dust sheets.

"Doesn't it look haunted to you?" she demanded.

I took a deep breath and smelled the odor of damp decay and long neglect from inside the house. And something else, much fainter, but still there — the familiar note of beeswax and lavender.

I shrugged. "Well, if it is, at least we know the ghost."

Chapter Twenty-One

APRIL 1980

It is a sunny morning in Rome, and the apartment in Trastevere has its windows thrown wide open to the spring breeze rolling in from the Tiber. It is chilly in the small kitchen, but the fresh air is necessary and Mary Alice is wearing gloves as she surveys her handiwork.

"What do you think?" she asks Billie.

Billie looks over the pans of fruitcake, careful not to touch them. "I think they look like fruitcake."

Mary Alice has baked them as tiny tea cakes in four small pans and eases the miniature loaves onto a cooling rack. They are dark with molasses and studded with dried cherries and apricots, the tops shingled with thin slices of almond. While Billie watches, Mary Alice opens a sealed bottle of Tennessee whiskey and pours a generous amount into a bowl. There is a small jar of white powder at her elbow, and before she opens it, she fits a respirator over her mouth and nose, motioning for Billie to do the same. The door to the rest of the apartment is closed, and the others know better than to disturb them.

The white powder looks a little like granulated sugar. It has been brought into the country in a flowered jar labeled *Lady Fresh Intimate Powder,* tucked into Billie's toiletry bag. In the airport, she is prepared to flirt with the Customs official who processes her, but he never unzips her suitcase. It has been Constance Halliday's idea that the foursome should travel under the cover of flight attendants, and Billie is wearing the blue Pan Am suit, cut just a little bit too snug. The Customs officer is on the point of asking her for a date during her layover when Günther Paar, dressed in a snappy pilot's uniform, puts a casual arm around her waist. The Customs officer makes a mournful face and waves her through with her poison.

They go directly to their rented apartments, a small studio for Günther and a larger one for the women. For two days they play tourist, trudging dutifully from the Colosseum to the Forum, tossing coins in the Trevi and paying too much for pasta in a rowdy café on the Piazza Navona. They take the kind of photos that casual travelers always take, posing with their hands inside the Bocca della Verità or arranging themselves by height on the flower-decked Spanish Steps. They buy postcards and tea towels stamped with the sights, and they drink cheap red wine from bottles wrapped in straw.

But the third morning, Mary Alice goes into the kitchen to put their plan into motion. She bakes the cakes according to the recipe she has been given, one she has practiced a dozen times in preparation for this moment. The pantry in the apartment has been stocked with everything she needs — even the American ingredients that will make the cakes unique. Through the respirator she can no longer smell them, but the aroma of spice and orange wafts out the window to the city beyond.

Taking the jar from Billie, Mary Alice stirs the powder carefully into the bowl of whiskey. When the granules are fully dissolved, she fills a syringe and injects the cakes with the poison-laced whiskey. It was Mary Alice's idea to use thallium, and she is pleased at how well it disappears into the cakes. It is a heavy metal, odorless and tasteless, but deadly if inhaled or absorbed through the skin.

When she finishes injecting the four cakes, she wraps them carefully in waxed paper and fits them into a cardboard box stamped with the gilded logo of a vaguely Gothic-looking convent. Billie sets a fan to blow any lingering fumes out the kitchen window, and they discard their gloves, wrapping them up with the empty jar, the syringe, the pans, and the respirators. The rest of the whiskey is poured down the sink and the bottle is added to the rest of the trash. It all fits tidily into a single garbage bag and there can be no traces left of American ingredients in this small Roman kitchen.

The cakes neatly packaged, they call for the others. The four are dressed identically in the simple habits of an order of nuns that does not exist. Their dresses are modest and dark grey, covering them from mid-calf to neck, their cuffs and collars white. They have scrubbed their faces of makeup and their hair is hidden under light grey veils. They wear thick dark stockings and sensible shoes. They have stripped off all jewelry except thin wedding rings and wristwatches with expensive mechanisms hidden in cheap Timex cases. They look nothing like the glamorous quartet of stewardesses who arrived three days before, but the change is not as superficial as clothing and makeup.

They have been strictly schooled in how to present themselves as modest young Brides of Christ. They walk slowly, hips held tight, gazes downcast, as they have mastered the custody of the eyes. When Günther arrives, dressed in a black suit with a white dog collar and a modest cross on a chain, they are waiting, prim-mouthed and demure.

"The four of you are scaring the shit out of me," he tells them as they collect the box of cakes and follow him out the door.

He is in high spirits, mostly because he has nothing to do on this mission. He is window dressing, necessary because a group of nuns is unremarkable in Rome, but a group of nuns under the supervision of a priest will be completely invisible. After the success of their French mission, they have been allowed to plan and undertake this job, one requiring a good deal of ingenuity. Every step has been reviewed and approved by the Board of Directors. Their only interference has been the addition of Günther, a minor annoyance to the quartet, who hoped to complete their mission from start to finish without anyone's help. But his smile is infectious, and he spends the short walk to Vatican City telling them about what he plans to do with the considerable bonus he is due to receive when the job is complete.

"I am taking the waters in Courtempierre-les-Bains," he says, sketching a map of Switzerland with his hands as he walks. "I go after the Christmas holidays to give myself a complete detoxification process for the new year. And I go again after every job. I am Swiss-German, so you would think I would go to Bern, but no. I am devoted to Courtempierre-les-Bains. It has the thermal baths where you can soak away your troubles and repair your liver," he tells them, listing the various other treatments he intends to indulge in. "Massage, sauna, therapeutic wraps. These missions are very taxing, and the body must be restored."

He is polite enough and passably good-looking, but he has a mild case of hypochondria, and his favorite topic of conversation is the state of his digestive system.

"What kind of therapies do you enjoy, Günther?" Natalie asks, wide-eyed. "Do tell us more about the enemas."

Helen elbows her hard in the ribs, but with Natalie's encouragement, Günther continues to discuss his bowels until they arrive at the entrance to St. Peter's Square. It is impressive, this open-air drawing room designed by Bernini. The long colonnaded wings sweep out and around, enclosing visitors in a way that should feel welcoming but somehow doesn't. It is too large, too grand, intended to evoke awe. There are metal detectors at the entrance, but the guards hardly pay attention, waving them along. The little group of five moves across the vast expanse of the oval, past the obelisk, towards the wedding cake façade of the basilica.

Inside the shadowy marble embrace of the church, it takes a moment for their eyes to adjust to the dimness. Dust motes swim in the shafts of sunlight spilling through the cupola windows, and a tired cleaner is standing in sock feet atop an altar, listlessly pushing a cloth mop. Beneath the marble top of the altar, a glass coffin holds the body of a pope, the face and hands gleaming green. They pause to watch as the cleaner polishes the glass, removing the fingerprints of the faithful. They move on to take a clockwise tour of the church, observed but not remembered by Vatican police and Swiss Guard. They blend seamlessly with every other group, the schoolchildren, the tourists, the miracle seekers. They are nobody within the Baroque grandeur of the basilica.

When they have completed the tour, it is eleven forty-five AM. Every Tuesday at precisely twelve PM, Bishop Timothy Sullivan of the Boston archdiocese crosses in front of the Tourist Information Office on the west side of St. Peter's Square. The four demure nuns and their priest are clustered in a little knot a short distance away, shielded from the nearest Swiss Guardsman by a rack of postcards featuring a pope smiling in Technicolor and ropes of wooden rosaries for sale.

As the clock strikes the hour, tolling twelve times, the bishop appears, his thinning hair combed over his scalp, his cassock billowing behind him as he lopes. He is tall and slender, a little hunched, and could easily be mistaken for an Ivy League academic if it weren't for his expression. He is wearing a faint smile, his attempt to hide the anger that seethes in him at all times. But the smile never touches his eyes, and he struggles to hide his impatience when Mary Alice calls his name.

"Yes?" he asks briskly. He is teetering on the edge of unfriendliness, but even a nun can be useful sometimes, and as he moves closer, he realizes these nuns are young and remarkably pretty. Something surges in his blood and he sets a smile on his lips. He pauses and waits, his eyebrows raised in gentle inquiry.

"Bishop Sullivan! Oh, Your Excellency, please pardon the interruption. We are from the Order of the Sisters of Peace, our chapterhouse is outside Knoxville, Tennessee. Perhaps you've heard of us?"

He doesn't bother to pretend that he has, but his face relaxes still further at the soft Southern drawl of her vowels. "I'm afraid I haven't," he says kindly.

"We are here on pilgrimage," she tells him. "Our mother superior went to school with your sister," she hurries on. "And she gave us strict instructions we were to find you and give you this gift."

The bishop does not bother to ask which sister. He has six, all of them devout Catholics, scattered from Boston to Denver. Mary Alice extends the box and he takes it, his smile deepening.

"How kind," he says.

"They are fruitcakes, Your Excellency," Natalie puts in eagerly. "We bake them to support the order. And every one is flavored with Tennessee whiskey."

"Fruitcakes?" His expression brightens. "Are they moist? I love a moist fruitcake and that's one thing Italians can't get right."

"I promise you," Mary Alice tells him serenely, "they are as full of flavor and moist as you could hope."

He is almost jovial now, and he looks at Günther over the heads of the little flock of nuns. "Father, how do you come to be traveling with the sisters?"

Günther smiles vaguely. "Mother Superior was concerned about the sisters traveling alone, Your Excellency. They have never been out of the States before, so I volunteered to act as shepherd."

"Good man," the bishop tells him. He glances at the nuns and sees how expectant they are, how bright and young they seem. They are pathetically eager, but he likes how deferential they are. It is a balm to an ego that has been badly bruised in the morning's finance meetings. The habits are an atrocity, plain and heavy, but his eye is practiced and he can tell the one who called his name has a lush figure shrouded underneath. He speaks impulsively.

"Would you care to visit the gardens? I could show you my favorite fountain and you won't have to take one of those boring tours."

The five of them are very still for a moment, and the bishop interprets this as reverence. In fact, they are reluctant because they do not wish to be any longer than necessary in his company. When he dies, questions will be asked. Video cameras will be mined for footage. Witnesses will be interrogated. And they want nothing that will connect them in any way to his death.

"Oh, we couldn't impose!" Helen interjects, looking so awestruck that the bishop cannot be offended.

"But," Billie says tentatively, her voice almost inaudible in its modesty, "Your Excellency, we would so love it if you would taste the cake and tell us what you think. Mother Superior will want to know."

The bishop gives a mocking grin. "Well, if there's one person I am afraid of, it is a mother superior," he says, opening the box. He surveys the contents with obvious pleasure. "These look quite delicious." He takes out one tiny cake and opens the waxed paper, sniffing deeply. "I can smell the cinnamon — and is that clove?"

Mary Alice nods. "It is, Your Excellency. You have quite a good sense of smell."

He preens and takes a large bite of the cake. He chews thoughtfully before taking another, and finishes the cake before speaking. "You can tell your mother superior that this is the best fruitcake I have ever had. Outstanding, Sisters."

They exchange happy glances as he starts on the second. "I know it's greedy to eat them all myself," he says through a mouthful of cake, "but I'll worry about that at confession."

Natalie gives him a shocked expression. "Oh no, Your Excellency! These were baked especially for you. Mother Superior would be very upset if she thought you gave them away."

He finishes the second cake and closes the box. "You can tell your mother superior that there is no chance of that. These are mine and I plan on hiding them from everyone. In fact, I won't have time for lunch today, so I'm very sure they'll be gone before the hour is up."

They exchange happy smiles again and Günther looks around. "Sisters, are you ready to go? I think we've probably taken up enough of His Excellency's time."

"Of course," Mary Alice says, dropping her eyes. They take turns murmuring their thanks to the bishop, who raises his hand in a hasty blessing as they leave.

He opens the box and takes a bite of the third cake. It will be three hours before his stomach starts to cramp unbearably and the vomiting and diarrhea begin. When he is completely dehydrated and his consciousness is failing, he will be admitted to a hospital in Rome under the care of a physician who will never think to test for thallium. If he had, he would have prescribed doses of activated charcoal and Prussian blue to stop the cramping and hair loss. But since he does not, the bishop will grow progressively sicker for three weeks, until his heart gives out and he dies. The press release, phoned in from a source that is not the Vatican, will list the cause of death as pancreatic cancer. The doctor who treats him understands the meaning of the mysterious deposit into his bank account. He simply signs the death certificate and asks no questions. He never corrects the press release, and neither does the Vatican. It will be another two years before the collapse of an Italian bank reveals the extent of the corruption within the finances of the Holy See, and whispers of money laundering will continue for decades to come. But a certain bishop's scheme to sell arms to a brutal Southeast Asian regime under the cover of missionary supplies will end, and an energized rebellion will succeed in establishing a fledgling democracy for the first time.

CHAPTER TWENTY-TWO

It took the better part of the first day to get Benscombe in fit state for habitation. It was grim to see what had become of the place. The gardens were a tangled mess, the house was so damp that wallpaper was falling off in sheets, and the less said about the plumbing the better. We stowed our gear in the house, divvying up the smaller bedrooms upstairs. Nobody even suggested taking Constance Halliday's room. The pill bottles from her last illness were still on the bedside table along with the book she'd been reading when she died — *Angela Carter's Book of Fairy Tales.* We doubled up in the smaller bedrooms, brushing aside the worst of the cobwebs and throwing open the windows to the cold winter air.

After Minka and Akiko arrived, we made a trip into Poole to Marks & Spencer, Boots, and half a dozen other places to get supplies to make the house livable. Food, firewood, wine, office supplies, extra sweaters and socks — we piled the back of the cars as full as we dared. We swept the dead beetles and mummified mice out of the kitchen and mopped the floor until our feet stopped sticking to it. Helen had unearthed a few rolls of clearance holiday wrapping paper in the back of a pound store and we thumbtacked long sheets of it over the crumbling wallpaper, giving us a clean surface to write on. Natalie heated up the chicken and leek pies we'd bought while Mary Alice made a salad, and the six of us ate, more to fuel ourselves than out of any real enjoyment. After Minka headed off to play a video game and Akiko went upstairs with Kevin — still hungover from his travel tranquilizers — Helen opened a set of markers also from the pound store. They were Barbie knock-offs in violent, sparkling rainbow shades. She made neat lists under each of our names detailing what we were responsible for researching or securing, reading aloud as she wrote.

"Akiko and Minka, maintaining home base and comms," she said, ticking off HOME BASE AND COMMS from the list. Nat and Mary Alice scooped ice cream for our dessert.

"Are you writing things down just to

check them off?" I asked.

She shrugged. "We can't leave anything to chance. Besides, it makes me feel productive to cross things off. After Kenneth died, there were days I wrote GET OUT OF BED in my planner just to be able to feel like I'd accomplished something."

She stepped back and we surveyed her work. Mary Alice and Nat left the ice cream and came to join us. The entire plan was there in shimmering hot pink ink.

"It looks like a My Little Pony murder plot," Mary Alice said. "Jesus, is that *glitter*?"

"I like it," Natalie said loyally.

"I find it hard to take us seriously as agents of vengeance when our plan looks like a kindergarten craft project."

Helen capped the marker and held it out. "If you would like to take over, Mary Alice, be my guest," she said.

"We're tired and jet-lagged," I said, taking the marker from Helen. "We're going to sit and eat ice cream and drink wine and see if we can find any holes in this," I said, pointing to the notes under Günther Paar's name. It was thick with detail, while the section under the heading THIERRY CARAPAZ was less comprehensive. Under Vance Gilchrist's name there was a wide expanse of white.

"What's that?" Mary Alice asked, peering at the emptiness.

"That blank space represents what we don't know yet. We'll get there."

The ice cream helped settle everybody's mood, but the wine did the heavy lifting. By the time we'd finished off two bottles of extremely bad Rioja, we were feeling much chummier.

"God, this wine is terrible," Helen said, pouring out the last of it. She upended the bottle, looking for any stray drops.

"It's getting the job done," I told her.

Natalie took the bottle and looked at the label. "Monos Muertos. What does that mean?"

"Dead Monkeys," I answered, pushing my glass away. "We've been drinking dead monkey wine."

Natalie shrieked and dropped the bottle.

"It's not *made* from dead monkeys," Mary Alice said. "It's a marketing gimmick."

"It's nasty," Natalie answered.

"Not as nasty as that bathroom upstairs," I said. "We'll need to get that sorted out so we can at least shower without worrying about tetanus or Lyme or rabies."

"None of which they have in the British

Isles," Helen said. She sighed. "I know the house is a shambles and it's freezing and I'm ninety percent sure there's a dead rat under my bed upstairs, but I am still glad we came back. I've missed this place."

We looked around the kitchen. When Natalie had been looking for plates, she'd found a stash of jam jars and stuck candles in a dozen of them. She'd clustered them on the mantelpiece, next to an aggressively ugly cuckoo clock, a china shepherdess with most of her fingers broken off so she was flipping the bird, and a basket of dingy wool balls stuck with a pair of vicious-looking knitting needles. But the candlelight had softened the cracked walls and the dirty windows and the fire Mary Alice had kindled in the fireplace had warmed the room and made it seem almost cozy.

Draining the last of her wine, Helen grabbed a fresh marker from the pack — a juicy green that smelled like watermelon — and went back to the wall. PROBLEMS, she lettered neatly.

We worked through the night, going over the plan and back again. Günther, blessedly, was a creature of habit. He always did a post-holiday detox at his favorite health spa. A few clicks around their website and we had all the information we needed, including a map of the property and a smiling photo of the spa staff in plain black scrubs — austere and businesslike.

By the time dawn worked its grey light through the kitchen windows, we were finished. The details had been plotted out on the murder wall, as Natalie had taken to calling it. We stepped back and surveyed it, plugging various holes and running the plan backwards and forwards until it was smooth as butter in a Texas summer.

"Holy shit," Mary Alice said, eyes skimming the wall. "I think it's going to work."

"Damned straight." I grinned at her.

"We just have to decide who's running point," Natalie said.

Mary Alice raised her hand. "Me."

She had her stubborn face on and I understood why. If she could get out there and *do* something about the situation we were in, it would go a long way towards making her feel like she was getting her life back.

We all nodded agreement and she went on. "Helen, we'll need a second pair of hands —"

"I'll do it." I cut Mary Alice off quickly.

Natalie spoke up. "I think that should be up to Helen."

"I don't. I said I'll do it," I countered.

279

"Jesus, what did you have for breakfast? A bowl of Honey Bunches of Bitch?" Natalie grumped.

Helen put a hand to her arm. "It's fine. If Billie wants it, she should do it."

"I do." Nobody argued. I wasn't about to rat Helen out for losing her nerve in Jackson Square, but I wasn't willing to gamble the success of this mission either. She could take a back seat until she'd proved herself.

Our plan meant another errand run and a fair bit of preparation. I started with the jar I'd unearthed in the garden shed — an old glass carboy that somebody must have kept for brewing cider or storing wine. I scrubbed it out with a long-handled brush and snapped on a pair of vinyl gloves. I filled the carboy with water from the outside tap and opened a fresh pack of cigarettes, breaking off the filters. I used a knife to slit each of the cigarettes, carefully emptying the tobacco into the jar, watching the brown flakes swirl into the water. It was oddly relaxing, disemboweling each cigarette into the carboy. A few of the hardier birds were singing and the winter sunshine was the color of a pale lemon. I might have even whistled a few bars of "American Pie" as I gave the sludge in the jar a good shake and covered it. I set it in a bright patch on the step like I was making sun tea. I would bring it in at sundown and set it on the back of the stove to keep it warm, steeping it as carefully as the best top-leaf Earl Grey.

I went back into the kitchen, stamping my feet and blowing on my fingers, to find Helen making a series of phone calls.

"What are you doing?" I whispered.

"We tried to make a booking online, but the spa is full," she muttered.

I opened my mouth but she made a shushing motion at me as someone apparently picked up the phone on the other end. "Yes, is that the Spa at Courtempierre-les-Bains?" Helen had adopted a cut-glass English accent, deliberately mispronouncing the French in a way that only British aristocrats can get away with. "This is Lady Henrietta Ridley and I am ringing to see why I haven't yet received a confirmation email of my booking. Ridley. Riddddddley," she said, drawing out the syllable in apparent annoyance. "What? Of course I am certain. My assistant, Cassandra, made the booking last week. For all I know, you are the person with whom she spoke. Now, kindly confirm my booking."

There was a faint series of squawks from the phone, and Helen cut in sharply. "My good man, do not make excuses. The booking is for four ladies, myself and three companions. We wish to take the waters and perhaps a little light massage, but that is all. We will be coming to *rest*. I presume you can accommodate that?" More squawks. "I realize it is a busy time of year, but it is hardly my fault that you have lost the booking. By all means, yes. Put me on hold," she finished acidly.

"Are we getting rooms or not?" I hissed. She looked at me, frowning, and shrugged her shoulders. The entire enterprise hinged on being able to get access to the spa. Minka was sitting opposite with the laptop we had picked up for her in Poole. I signaled her to pull up the spa's feed on social media. The latest post was an image of a snowy landscape with a thermal pool gently steaming against a crisp blue sky.

I skimmed the comments — hearts, praise hands, little emoji with towel turbans — until I found what I needed. *Can't wait to see you this weekend for my hen party!* chirped Debbi Williams, followed by a chicken emoji and heart eyes. I went to her profile and found her location listed as Cardiff. A few more clicks and I saw the engagement pic, Debbi glowing in the arms of a pleasant-looking guy as she flashed a small, bright diamond at the camera. A few posts later was a group photo of Debbi with five other girls captioned, *My best mates and bridesmaids!* Six girls altogether, which meant at least two rooms and probably three. It would do just fine.

I scrolled back to the spa page and clicked the link in their bio to their website. Just then Helen started to speak again. "Yes, I am still here, and I intend to be here until you find my booking." I made a frantic gesture at her to keep stalling, and she launched into a genteel tirade while I kept hitting buttons until I found the link to the phone number and dialed.

I motioned to her that it was ringing and she broke into her own rant. "Go and answer that other line immediately. I cannot hear myself think. Yes, I will hold."

The desk clerk answered my call in French and German but switched to English immediately, his voice harried.

"Yes, this is Debbi Williams from Cardiff. I have a booking for this weekend for a small block of rooms for a hen party. I'm afraid I have to cancel. No, I don't have the confirmation number handy, but I suppose I could look. It might take a few minutes . . ." I trailed off, but the desk clerk cut in.

"It is policy to use the confirmation

number to cancel a booking," he began. The Swiss and their rules. I rolled my eyes at Helen.

"It's not my fault he canceled the wedding," I said, letting my voice break on a sob. "I've had to tell all our friends and it's been so humiliating, and now you're going to make me pay for this booking that I can't afford anymore because he left with all of our wedding money —"

The desk clerk might have been Swiss, but he was also a man, and I haven't met a man yet who could handle a crying woman — especially when he already had an irritated woman on the other line and I was handing him available rooms on a silver platter. I threw in a few stuttering, dry-eyed sobs for good measure. "He cheated on me, you know. With my sister," I sniffled. The poor desk clerk didn't stand a chance.

"I suppose I could make an exception just this once, Miss Williams," he said hastily.

I started to babble my thanks, but he cut in. "We have canceled your booking. Thank you and we hope to welcome you to the Spa at Courtempierre-les-Bains on another occasion." He hung up and went straight back to Helen. Even muffled, his tone sounded relieved and Helen practically purred.

"Well, I am very glad we could get that

straightened out. Yes. We will see you this weekend. Two rooms. And a complimentary scalp massage for my trouble? How kind."

She hung up and turned to me. "Who the hell is Debbi Williams?"

CHAPTER TWENTY-THREE

Two days later, my tobacco tea was finished. I strained off the solids, burying them in the garden. The liquid that was left was pure poison. We gathered around the kitchen table, gloves on and Kevin shut in the pantry to keep him from killing himself. The six of us worked slowly, using kitchen funnels to decant the murky liquid into an assortment of opaque toiletry bottles. Face wash, toner, astringent, mouthwash — all got filled and then capped, the lids sealed with melted candle wax to make them spill-proof. A few miniatures with Irish whiskey labels got the same treatment. We were going by train instead of flying, but we weren't taking any chances on raising eyebrows at Customs. Altogether we had more than enough to do the job.

When we finished, we cleared up the kitchen and poured the rest of the poison down the sink. Natalie sluiced it out with boiling water and did the same for the carboy, eliminating any traces of what we'd done. We were packed and ready, with fresh papers, disguises, and everything else we needed, all folded into a single carry-on each. The rest of us looked away as Mary Alice and Akiko said a stilted good-bye. Akiko had hardly said two words to her since we'd been in England, but I hoped a little time apart would help her to wrap her head around the fact that this was her new normal — at least for now.

Minka drove us to the train station, where we traveled in separate carriages to London. We got ourselves to Zurich by slightly different routes and rendezvoused in the train station before piling into a hired car service — Lady Henrietta Ridley would never Uber. Helen took point, striding along purposefully while the rest of us scuttled behind. We'd scoured the local thrift shops to find tweedy English clothes, and a set of wigs from a firm that supplied Beyoncé took care of our hair. Natalie found an oversized bra she padded out with water balloons nestled into a pair of socks while I tucked prosthetic ass pads around my hips to suggest flesh that had settled with age. We looked like a girl gang that would have the Queen as our leader, all low heels and no-

nonsense curls. Mary Alice had even tucked butterscotch candies in her purse, which she handed out to porters in lieu of tips.

We checked into the spa without incident. The desk clerk that Helen had gently terrorized as "Lady Henrietta" was nowhere in sight. We signed in and were given keys by a slim young woman whose name tag said she was Ji-Woo. She gave us complimentary glasses of alkaline water and Natalie deliberately tripped, spilling hers all down Ji-Woo's tidy black suit.

"Oh, I *am* sorry," Natalie drawled.

Ji-Woo gave her a thin smile. "Not at all, madam. If you will excuse me, I will just go and change my blouse."

We waved her off, telling her we would find our own way upstairs. As soon as she disappeared through the door behind the front desk, Natalie nipped around, kneeling in front of the computer while the rest of us studied the brochures of spa treatments, keeping watch on the elevator, front entrance, and office door.

"Hurry up," Mary Alice muttered. Natalie pushed herself to her feet, her knees giving a creak of protest as I grabbed a couple of Ji-Woo's business cards.

"Got it," Nat said. "He's in Room 217."

We took our keys and brochures and

headed up to our rooms on the third floor. Mary Alice and I bunked together, while Helen and Nat took the second room. There was a handy communicating door, which we left open, and in a matter of minutes we were ready. Each room had a writing desk with a thick leather portfolio, and inside was a full complement of spa stationery, stamped with the resort's letterhead. I scrawled a note addressed to Günther explaining that the water would be shut off for a short while the following day and that as compensation for the inconvenience, I was arranging for him to have a complimentary mud wrap in his room at five PM this afternoon. I signed it with Ji-Woo's name and stuffed it into the envelope with one of her business cards. I addressed the envelope, careful to cross the seven in his room number like a proper little European. I handed it off to Natalie, who nipped down and slid it under his door before hurrying back.

We were sitting on the edge of Helen's bed, waiting, when she returned.

"Was he in there?" I asked.

"Oh yeah. I could hear him snoring like a freight train," Nat said.

"What if he doesn't wake up in time to see the note?" Helen asked. She sounded like a fretful toddler, and Nat gave her a comforting pat.

"I thought of that. I knocked on the door to wake him up. I was hiding in the stairwell when I heard his door open." She turned to me. "Billie, you're up."

I picked up the phone and punched in his room number. When he answered, I spoke quickly and brightly, putting an accent on my English that was vague enough to have been anything from South African to Latvian. "Mr. Paar? This is Elsa with Spa Services. I am calling to confirm your appointment at five PM today with Annike for a mud wrap. Yes, it is complimentary, courtesy of Ji-Woo at the front desk. The mud wrap is one of our superior services, a value of two hundred seventy-five euros. No, Annike will bring everything with her. Thank you, sir. Your service is confirmed."

I looked to Mary Alice. "Showtime."

CHAPTER TWENTY-FOUR

The clock showed five minutes to five when Mary Alice and I headed out. We were both dressed in the plain black scrubs of the spa staff. Mary Alice's wig was a severe ice-white geometric bob, and her face had been carefully contoured, the shading making her cheekbones high and angular. Her breasts were strapped down and she was wearing steel-rimmed glasses. The effect was severe in a Scandi-chic way. I had opted for a low dark brown bun threaded with silver and cheek pads to make my face fuller. A dusting of pale powder gave me a washed-out, fatigued look. The fact that I was lugging a collapsible treatment table helped sell the impression I was giving of a tired older woman just waiting for the end of her shift. Mary Alice carried a tote with our supplies. We paused in front of Günther's door and rapped softly.

He opened the door at once, and I ducked

my head to hide my surprise. I wouldn't have known him if he'd walked up and slapped me on the street. It had been more than fifteen years since our paths had crossed, and in spite of his obsession with his health, he looked like shit. He was carrying extra weight, which might have suited someone cheerier, but he looked bloated. His skin was splotchy and there were heavy bags under his eyes. He was wearing one of the spa robes and it gapped a little, showing a chest furry with white hair. His feet were bare, the toenails thick and yellow, and when he smiled, I saw that his teeth were the same.

"Good afternoon, I am Annike," Mary Alice said in a clipped voice. "You are ready for treatment?"

"Yes, yes," he said, stepping back and waving us in. "And this is complimentary, correct?"

"Except for the tip," I said. Mary Alice would have kicked me if she'd been closer, but she merely signaled for me to set up the table. "My assistant will help me to set up. You are being naked?" she asked with a finger pointing at his mid-section.

"Yes," he told her, holding the belt of his robe.

"When the table is ready, you will lie

under the sheet facedown," she told him. "We will prepare the muds in the bathroom."

He nodded and I hurried to lock the legs of the treatment table, spreading it with a folded blanket and a sheet. Then I laid out layers of plastic wrap, the kind caterers use for food. I ducked into the bathroom after Mary Alice and we pulled a bucket out of the tote bag. It was full of dark green spa mud, powdered and ready to mix. I turned on the tap so he would hear water running while we snapped on gloves and the small noseclips swimmers wear. They weren't as good as respirators, but they would keep us from inhaling the worst of the nicotine. I poured the poison in slowly, letting Mary Alice mix it with a wooden spoon until it made a thick, gloppy paste. I dumped in half a bottle of lavender oil to mask any odor, and we were ready.

We pulled off the noseclips and carried the bucket out to the bedroom, where Günther was relaxing under the sheet. We could see the back of his head, and when Mary Alice pulled the cover back, there he was in all his dimply, mottled glory. Some men age well, but Günther wasn't one of them. We started scooping up the mud and slapping it on his back, larding him up like we were glazing a Sunday ham.

"That smells unusual," he said, his voice muffled by the treatment table.

"A new blend," Mary Alice said smoothly.

"Only for VIPs. Perhaps we will put it on the menu for the spa, perhaps not," I added.

We worked fast, layering on more and more mud until the back of his body was coated with it from neck to feet. "Turn over," Mary Alice instructed. He struggled to flip but Mary Alice gave him a hand. She tucked the sheet discreetly around his crotch as we worked, mudding up his legs and torso, finishing with his arms. When the last of the mud had been packed onto him, we folded the plastic wrap around and drew the sheet up over his feet at the bottom, then wrapped each side tightly across, tucking it under him to make a sort of burrito.

He opened his eyes. "How long is the treatment?"

Mary Alice consulted her watch. "Thirty minutes. We will return to check on you then."

But we didn't make any move to leave, and he turned his head, his eyes blinking in confusion. "Wait, I don't feel good. My heart," he said. "It is beating very fast."

"That's the nicotine," Mary Alice said in her own voice.

He blinked several times more. "Wha—what?" His voice was thick and slurred. Recognition flickered in his eyes and he groaned, understanding at last what was happening.

"The nicotine," I told him. "It's in the mud and we've slathered your entire body in it. It's one of the transdermal poisons, you know. I mean, the buccal mucosa or the rectum is the best way to administer it, but why would you even bother when the average adult has twenty-one square feet of skin and every pore is right there, just waiting to be used? You're probably already getting queasy. Don't worry. That just means it's working."

He opened his mouth — to yell at us, I think — but all he managed was a gurgled shriek. I went to the desk, where a bowl of apples was sitting, and stripped off my glove to choose one. I polished it on my uniform and took a bite. Fresh and crisp as new snow. I ate it down to the core as Günther continued to struggle for breath.

"Why?" he managed to pant once.

"You know why," Mary Alice told him. "You ordered our termination."

"Had to," he gasped. "Vance —"

"Don't worry," I said brightly. "We'll deal with him too."

Mary Alice checked her watch again. "He's taking too long. Did you make the poison strong enough?" she asked, frowning.

"Yes, Mary Alice. At least I think so. I didn't exactly have a lab, did I? We're doing this old-school, remember? Down and dirty. I did the best I could with what I had." I didn't mention the fact that she was usually our poison expert but she'd been too preoccupied with her marital trouble to be of much help.

"Well, maybe we need to speed things along," she suggested. "We have a train to catch and we still have to clean him up."

He made a mewling sound then, followed by a rattle, but he kept breathing and I stuffed the apple core in my pocket. "Fine. Shoot you for it. Odds."

She sighed and we each made a fist. "One. Two. Three. Shoot."

We held out our hands and Mary Alice grinned. "Even. You lose. Finish him."

He bucked a little then, although I would have thought he was past hearing. I pulled off a fresh length of plastic wrap and held it tightly over his face. It didn't take long. When it was over, I peeled away the plastic and stuck it in my pocket with the apple core. Together we unwrapped him and hauled him into the shower, using loofahs to scrub the mud off. There were a few red spots on his face — petechiae, the classic symptom of asphyxiation.

"That's not part of the plan," Mary Alice pointed out sourly.

"I'll handle it," I promised. We dried him and tucked him into bed before scrubbing down the bathroom to remove all traces of the mud. Everything — sheets, loofahs, plastic wrap, gloves, mud and poison containers, spoon — went into a garbage bag. I found the note from Ji-Woo and added it to the rest before tying it neatly.

As a final flourish, I grabbed another apple with the hem of my shirt. I put it into his hand, pressing it firmly to get good fingerprints onto it. Then I lifted it to his mouth, manipulating his jaw to take a hefty bite with his toothmarks in it. It took a little maneuvering to get the bite stuffed down in his throat, but it was a pretty touch. At first glance, anybody would think he'd died of a heart attack or stroke, but anyone taking a closer look would assume he'd choked — and that would square with the modest amount of petechiae.

"Handled," I told Mary Alice. She rolled her eyes and made a final sweep of the room.

"That's everything." She ushered me out,

and I looked at the time.

"It's 6:04. Not bad for a couple of old broads," I said with a grin. We left the treatment table in the stairwell — some poor spa employee would probably get an ass chewing for that, but it was better than hauling it around. Back in our rooms we changed and bagged up our black uniforms and wigs. We resumed the clothes we'd traveled in and the four of us headed down with our bags.

A girl with thick bangs was arguing tearfully with Ji-Woo. "But I wouldn't have canceled — it's my hen do! What do you mean you don't have any rooms left?"

Ji-Woo's jaw was tight as she tried to placate the girl, who was surrounded by a clutch of annoyed-looking bridesmaids.

Helen strode through them and dropped our keys on the front desk. "I am afraid the rooms are not to our satisfaction," she said loftily. "Kindly arrange for a taxi. We will be leaving."

Ji-Woo snapped her fingers for a porter to flag a taxi and turned to the weeping bride. "Good news, Miss Williams. Two rooms have just come available."

The bridesmaids cheered and we tottered out into the early evening. Natalie had been carrying the garbage bag in her suitcase, so

298

we dumped it in the first trash bin we saw at the station. We caught the next train to Geneva, where we had booked into a small, discreet hotel and made late reservations at the Taverne du Valais for charbonnade and red wine. We toasted our success with a single glass each and turned in by midnight. By seven the next morning, we were on a train, headed back to England via Amsterdam.

One down. Two to go.

CHAPTER TWENTY-FIVE
JULY 1981

"Zanzibar," Mary Alice says, letting her breath hang on the last syllable. "Can you imagine? I've never heard of anything so romantic in my life."

"Romantic? We're going to kill an old woman," Billie reminds her, but she is smiling. It is the first time they have worked together since killing the bishop in Rome fifteen months before, and it feels good to be reunited even if they have been relegated to supporting roles. They are backing up Vance Gilchrist and Thierry Carapaz, a Frenchman they met up with at the airport in London. Carapaz carried their documents identifying them as a group of graduate archaeological students excavating the ruins of an old clove plantation in Zanzibar. The plantation is adjacent to the house of their target — Baroness Elisabeth von Waldenheim, a prominent Nazi whose whereabouts have been unknown for the better part of forty years.

But the Provenance department has done its job well, positively identifying the reclusive baroness through the hairdresser who comes once a week to wash and set her hair. The baroness lives with her art collection and a pair of servants who have worked for her since she sat at the center of the Führer's inner circle. The art collection — pieces purloined with the help of Hermann Göring — is to be saved but the servants are not. The dossier prepared by Provenance is thorough, and the Volkmars' guilt is never in question. Their crimes, and those of the baroness, are detailed at length. Included in the dossier are maps of the house and its grounds and photographs of the targets and the art collection.

One photograph in particular has captured Billie's attention. It is poor, black-and-white and blurred — no doubt a fourth- or fifth-generation photocopy — and inked around the border are the words *The Queen of Sheba Arising by Sofonisba Anguissola*. The notes say the photograph was taken in 1931, the last known image of the painting. The subject is a common one in Renaissance and Baroque art. Claude Lorrain, Tintoretto, Lavinia Fontana — all have painted the Queen of Sheba garbed in elaborate clothing contemporary to their time, rich brocades and heavy velvets giving witness to her legendary wealth as she makes her first appearance at the court of King Solomon.

But Anguissola has chosen differently. To begin with, she has painted a woman with dark skin, Billie sees. Where other artists have chosen to depict the queen with the fashionable blond tresses of the Renaissance ideal, Anguissola depicts her as she would have been — an African queen. And where others have painted her arriving at the court of Solomon, received with fanfare and lavish ceremony, Anguissola has chosen to portray her rising from her bed after her tempestuous night with the king, grasping a white sheet for contrast against her skin. Her hands and wrists are hung with gorgeous jewels, rubies and emeralds, Billie guesses, although it is impossible to tell from the black-and-white reproduction. One enormous pearl hangs from a tiny chain threaded through her curls, resting voluptuously on her brow. There is a knowingness in the eyes that says she understands and knows you do too. Behind her is a stately bed, gilded and hung with swags of velvet draperies. And just visible in the tangle of tousled bedclothes is the bare thigh of a sleeping man, his luscious robes and hastily discarded bits of armor strewn about the floor. The queen's heavy-lidded eyes say it all. She hasn't slept because she has been too busy conquering a king. It is sensual and yet domestic, an intimate moment of grand people, and Billie is glad that her job will be helping to restore the painting to its rightful owners.

She does not think about the baroness or the Volkmars as they make their preparations. They are camping at the clove plantation in the ruins of the overseer's house, planning to use the punishment cells beneath to access a tunnel that runs from the main house to the area that once housed the enslaved farmworkers. Vance has explained that the original owner, not wanting his gardens spoiled by workers coming and going, ordered the tunnel dug to keep them out of sight. It has been decades since the tunnel was in use, but they will have a week to shore it up and surveil the baroness. Carapaz will take care of dispatching the Volkmars while Vance has reserved the baroness for himself. She is the first Nazi the Museum has targeted in over a decade, and taking her out will ensure a promotion. Money, status — these are important to Vance, but nothing means as much as going down in the history of the Museum as a

Nazi killer. It is the reason the Museum exists, and it is a demonstration of the board's faith in him that they have assigned him leadership of the mission. The women are to give weight to the cover story as a student expedition and to secure the paintings and that is all.

Their duffel bags and backpacks are full of nondescript clothes from charity shops, dull reference texts from university presses — purchased new but carefully aged — and excavation tools. There are no weapons, no liquor, no pills. Even Natalie's copy of *Scruples* has been surrendered. Zanzibar is an Islamic country and they do not want to attract any attention from the authorities.

They are traveling cheaply, as any academic group on limited funds would do. Their tickets have been purchased in bucket shops and they route them through Naples, connecting on to Cairo and then Mombasa before the bus to Dar es Salaam and the ferry to Zanzibar. By the time they arrive, they look like college kids, wrinkled and dusty and smelling rank. But the sea air is fresh and they have a night booked at a hostel in Stone Town before they have to camp out. In his dual role of mission leader and dig supervisor, Vance gives them a few hours to play tourist. They explore the

Zanzibari markets and admire the Gujarati doors throughout the town, carved of teak and heavily embellished with engraved brass ornaments. They take photos of the House of Wonders and bargain badly for souvenirs, coming away with leather slippers and sarongs. Mary Alice buys a handful of colorful beaded bracelets, one for each of them, and helps Vance find a present for his bride — a tiny star sapphire on a thin chain.

The next morning they are up and packed before the first call to prayer. The drive to the former clove plantation where they will be based takes two hours, the last half over bumping, pitted roads that wind north and east, away from the coast and into the interior of the island. They pitch camp with practiced ease, erecting three tents — his, hers, and mess. In case anyone happens by, they set out survey equipment and dig a few test pits, marking them carefully with a string grid.

The days drag by, long and mercilessly hot. They are sick of the waiting, the fitful hours, and the pests. Carapaz has read up on them, taking great pleasure in detailing all the things a yellow sac spider or red-clawed scorpion can do.

"Would you shut up already?" Natalie demands over dinner the third night.

"Come on," he says, poking an elbow into her ribs. "Don't you want to hear about the baboon spider? What about the spider wasp? Do you know it has the most painful sting of any insect except the bullet ant?"

Natalie dumps the rest of her food into the fire and stalks off. They are getting on each other's nerves, tired of the bush bathroom and the nights of broken sleep. And worst of all is the endless waiting, the hours of poking listlessly in the trenches they have dug, pretending to excavate. They casually watch the Volkmars move around the property, the old man clipping listlessly at a clump of ginger lilies, the wife pegging out laundry on a sagging clothesline.

One evening, Billie steps out of the mess tent and inhales deeply. The air in Zanzibar smells different than anywhere else. The sharp green fragrance of unripe spices, the salt of the sea. And above it, something else, the thin odor of cigarettes. She follows the smell to a stand of banana trees and parts them. She is not far from the baroness's veranda, maybe twenty yards. And she can see the old woman sitting in the shadows, hunched in a wheelchair. Someone has rolled her outside to watch the sunset, or maybe it's to keep the stink of her cigarette out of the house.

As she watches, the caretaker's wife comes outside. Frau Volkmar flaps her hand, saying something in German. It is not the northern German that Billie knows. Instead, it's an Austrian dialect, and it sounds irritable. She shoves the old woman forward, moving a thin pillow around before stuffing it back into place and stalking off with another few words flung over her shoulder.

The baroness doesn't respond. She simply sits, smoking, the gray worm of the ash dropping to her nightgown. She was beautiful once. There is a studio portrait of her in the dossier, blond hair swept back and held in place with a diamond clip in the shape of a parteiadler. Her expression is one of perfect contentment. She knows exactly who she is and what she wants. It is taken at the height of her power, although she doesn't know it.

It is hard to reconcile that woman with the shrunken figure huddled in the wheelchair. She doesn't always remember to take the cigarette out of her mouth to tap the ash, but when she does, a thin silver thread of drool stretches from her lip and Billie almost wants to pity her.

Almost. She sees the indignity of old age, how life becomes very small until there is nothing left of independence and power and

307

beauty and freedom except a shell of a body that relies upon others for everything. It is terrible to witness, but it is *hers,* Billie reflects. Whatever it looks like, this life has been lived. And that is something the baroness took from others when she had the chance.

The baroness slowly lifts her old lizard eyes to Billie, and their gazes meet across the soft expanse of grass. She might call out or become agitated, and Billie's breath stops in her chest.

But the baroness does nothing. She simply sits and drops ash on her lap, staring into the grove of banana trees at the figure she assumes is a ghost. There are so many of them now, ghosts who come and go, reminding her of things that ought to be forgotten. She doesn't even recognize this one. Is she a girl from the camps? One of those who rode a boxcar and never came back?

The baroness doesn't know and she hardly cares. The past and present are the same to her. She hates people who have been dead for sixty years and she forgets the girl who cuts her hair. Maybe that is who is standing in the banana trees, the girl who comes once a month with her sharp, shiny scissors and trims the thin wisps on her scalp. She doesn't think it is time for her haircut, but she could be wrong. She turns away and smokes again and when she looks back, the girl is gone.

Billie draws back in the cover of the banana trees and turns away, anticipation rising.

The baroness will die tonight.

Sometime after midnight, Thierry Carapaz, who has been gone since afternoon, returns with a van. It is rusted and patched and bears the faded logo of a Tanzanian coffee brand. He has rented it with a small wad of used notes of three different currencies. His beard has grown in, thick and dark, and he could easily be mistaken for a local. There is a legend in Zanzibar that a Persian prince once married a Swahili princess and their union resulted in the Shirazi people, traders who inhabit the islands of the Indian Ocean. The beaches are creamy white sand, soft as talc under the feet, and the water is a brilliant turquoise. In a few months, when the news of what he is about to do has faded to a memory, he will return to snorkel along the eastern shore and spend his nights with tourist girls. The locals are prettier, but he has run afoul of too many outraged fathers and brothers. He will try his luck instead with the models who come to shoot catalogs on the beaches. They will untie their bikini strings and uncap their cocaine vials for him, and he will be very happy until they summon him to work again. He is not like Vance Gilchrist or the four women. He doesn't kill because he is good at it; he kills because it pays well and he has a plan, one that will enable him to rise within the organization and live in the kind of luxury his parents could only have dreamed of.

He brakes the van near the stand of banana trees, making sure it is screened from the baroness's house should anyone care to look out. But the house is shrouded in darkness, and he imagines he can hear the fitful, restless sleep of the old people inside.

He is standing outside the van, holding an unlit cigarette, when Billie walks up. He mimes a light, but Billie simply shrugs and he pockets the cigarette. She rests against the van, hands thrust into her pockets.

"If you came for a shag, it'll have to wait until the job is done." His voice is a whisper, so low it does not carry beyond the banana trees. Her answering laugh could be mistaken for a bird, startled out of sleep.

"God, you have a high opinion of yourself."

He rests next to her against the van. She is not entirely relaxed; she's learned never to let her guard down completely, but he doesn't make a move to touch her.

"I have a pretty good track record," he tells her.

"I bet you do. Vance sent me to see if there were any problems."

"Tell Vance he is not my babysitter. If there were problems, I dealt with them."

"If you want to have a dick-swinging contest with Vance, you'll have to start it yourself. I'm not telling him anything of the kind."

It's his turn to laugh. "You're a hard woman, Billie."

"Softness is overrated."

"Not where I'm from."

She pauses and they listen for a moment to the night sounds — birds, wind in the banana trees, and far away, the small, slight whine of an engine on the ocean. A fisherman, setting out for his nightly catch.

"Where are you from?"

He shrugs. "Here and there."

She doesn't reply and he feels the weight of her silence until he can't stand it. "France. Burgundy, to be precise. My mother was Algerian and my father was Spanish, from the Balearics. That's why I like islands," he says. "It's in my blood."

"Was? Your parents are dead?"

"Yes. Before I joined the Museum."

"So you grew up in Burgundy?"

He makes an impatient gesture. "You ask a lot of questions."

"I'm curious about people."

"Yes, I grew up in Burgundy. On a wine-making estate. Don't get ideas — it didn't belong to my family. My parents worked for the people who owned it. Maman scrubbed floors and did the laundry. My father worked in the vineyard, spraying the vines with some toxic shit that ended up killing him. It was slow and ugly. Maman's cancer was fast." He paused and gave her a close look. "You don't seem sad for me. Usually when I tell my tragic story, a girl would already be unbuttoning her blouse by this point."

"I have sad stories of my own," she says.

"Tell me and maybe I'll unbutton my blouse," he offers.

She smiles. "I like you a little more than I want to but not nearly as much as you think I do."

"Fair enough." He pauses and cocks his head, studying her face in the dim starlight. "So what do you want out of this job, American girl?"

"Well, I like to travel and the money's good."

He nods and she lobs the question back. "What do you want out of the job, French boy?"

"Money. Girls. A really nice car. And a house — a town house in Paris. I even know the exact one." Billie raises a brow and he goes on. "The family in Burgundy, the one my parents worked for, they owned this town house. Like three hundred years of the same assholes living there, lording it over everybody. It's abandoned now. But someday, I'm going to have enough money to buy it." He pauses and cocks his head. "So, how did they find you?"

She tells him, giving him the bare facts of her arrest for assault, and he grins again. "Same. Only I was eighteen and it was for arson. It is why the Museum decided I should specialize in setting fires."

"What did you burn?"

"The vineyard where my father worked."

"Jesus."

"And the house. With the family in it. That's why the town house in Paris is abandoned."

"They died?"

"All of them. Even the dog."

He consults his watch and pushes away from the van. "Come on. It's time."

CHAPTER TWENTY-SIX

"Alright, we got lucky finding Günther. Any suggestions on how to find Carapaz?" Helen threw the question out to the table. Akiko was wrestling with the stove at Benscombe, cooking dinner while Minka sat on a stool and pretended to help. The rest of us were throwing ideas at the wall, but so far nothing was sticking. Carapaz liked women and wine, but that wasn't much help. Museum board members didn't exactly have their addresses in the phone book.

"Let's start with what we know," Mary Alice said reasonably. "He lives in Paris."

"Three million people in forty square miles. That narrows it down," Natalie said.

Mary Alice smiled thinly. "You can be constructive or I can staple your lips together. I don't much care either way."

Natalie stuck her tongue out, but I spoke up before she could make things worse.

"He always wanted to buy a house in Paris

— a specific house, I mean. It belonged to the people who owned the estate where his parents worked."

Helen perked up. "There might be something in that. What was their name?"

I shrugged and looked around the table. Nobody else knew, so I pointed to the laptop. "His parents both died in Burgundy. I can't imagine the name Carapaz is common there. I think it's originally Spanish."

Mary Alice sighed and reached for the laptop. She clicked around for a while, muttering to herself, until Minka took pity on her. There was a rattle of keys and suddenly the cheap printer in the corner was spitting out pages. They were a little blurry and the French was provincial, but I translated easily enough.

"It's a death notice for his father. It lists his address as the Château d'Archambeau in Burgundy." I pointed to Minka. "Now find us a property in Paris owned by the same family. Start with the 7th arrondissement."

She worked with one hand and ate shepherd's pie with the other. By the time we polished off the last of the apple crumble, she'd found it. She didn't crow; she just printed it off along with a map of Paris showing the neighborhoods and dropped it on my empty plate.

"Is 15th actually," she said with a smile. She pointed to where the 15th arrondissement bulged out into a U shape formed by the 7th on one side, the 6th on another, and the 14th on the last. "Near Montparnasse Cemetery. Owned by d'Archambeau family until 2008. Then it was sold to private holding company chartered in Panama."

"Carapaz," Mary Alice guessed.

"Most likely," Natalie agreed. "He made director that year and that comes with a nice juicy bonus. He would have been able to afford it then."

"And no director would have bought it outright," Helen added. "A holding company is pretty convincing."

I turned to Minka. "See if you can turn up anything else on that address in any database anywhere. We're looking for a link to the name of Carapaz."

She nodded and bent back over her laptop. The rest of us cleaned up and went about our business. I knew better than to pressure her while she worked. It took her another three hours, but just when we were ready to turn in, she had it.

Minka handed me a printout and I skimmed the dense lines with Nat reading over my shoulder. "What is this? It looks like a chat room."

I pointed to the map Minka had provided with the d'Archambeau house circled in red. "It's a message board for people who live in the neighborhood but it seems to be geared to expats. They're all complaining about their French neighbors." I skimmed the text until I came to the relevant line. "Here, one of them is complaining about the man next door, a Monsieur Carapaz, who puts out food for the stray cats. They keep coming into her garden, and she blames Carapaz."

Natalie touched the woman's signature line. "She's at number twenty. What number is the d'Archambeau house?"

I grinned. "Twenty-two. We've got him."

CHAPTER TWENTY-SEVEN

We spent the rest of the night passing around various printouts. We found detailed maps of the area, downloaded a brief history of the house in an out-of-print book on Parisian architecture, and took a Google Earth stroll down the Rue d'Archambeau, a tiny cul-de-sac tucked off the Avenue du Maine. It was Mary Alice who noticed the problem first.

"The entrance to the cul-de-sac is adjacent to the train station," she said.

Helen raised her brows. "So?"

"So that's a TGV station, high-speed, state-of-the-art. It's going to be crawling with CCTV cameras."

Helen was skeptical. "You really think Carapaz has had somebody hack into public security cameras for him?"

"He doesn't have to," Mary Alice said. She was reviewing the Google Earth tour and stopped, pointing to a tiny black spot above his front door. "He's got cameras of his own." She whizzed us around his house, looking from every angle, then popped across the street to look at the neighbor's house. "Seventeen cameras. At least seventeen I can see. Now, some may be dummies and put there just for show, but at least a handful of them are going to be live and monitored, especially now that Günther is dead."

Natalie had been quiet, surveying an old map of Paris she had unearthed from Constance Halliday's study. "What are you doing with that?" I asked. "It's not up-to-date. It doesn't have any Starbucks on it."

She grinned. "Nope, but it has exactly what I needed. I know how to get in."

Mary Alice gave her a look. "Sprout wings and fly?"

"No, smartass," Natalie said smugly. "Exactly the opposite. We're going underground."

The reactions were not positive.

"What do you mean we're going underground?" Helen asked.

Natalie pushed her map over and traced a route with her finger. "The house is here, on Rue d'Archambeau just off of Avenue du Maine. The Avenue du Maine intersects with the Rue Froidevaux. And look where

319

the Rue Froidevaux ends up."

She tapped the map triumphantly. Mary Alice twisted her neck, reading upside down. "Les Catacombes de Paris. Oh, *hell* no."

She folded her arms over her chest, but Natalie was undeterred. "It's a brilliant idea."

"It's a grotesque idea. Have you ever been in that place?" Mary Alice demanded. "It's just miles of tunnels full of bones. Bones, stacked upon bones, piled on top of — guess what? More bones."

"The operative phrase being 'miles of tunnels,' " Natalie replied. "Besides, how can you be squeamish about bones?"

"I just don't like them," Mary Alice said stubbornly. "The skulls freak me out. They seem like they're looking at you but they don't have eyes. It's not natural."

"It's completely natural," Natalie argued. "It's actually the definition of natural. It's what happens when we die."

"Not me," Mary Alice said. "I'm being cremated and letting Akiko put my ashes in a nice urn. Maybe something from Pottery Barn. I can sit on the mantel and she can decorate me for holidays."

I studied the map. "It's not a terrible idea," I said slowly.

Natalie preened. "Thank you."

"What made you think of it?" I asked.

"The last time I was in Paris I went on a date with a cataphile."

"A what now?" Mary Alice asked. "I thought that was a mountain lion."

Natalie rolled her eyes. "A cataphile is a Parisian urban explorer."

Mary Alice blinked. "Then what am I thinking of?"

"You're thinking of a catamount," Helen said helpfully.

"Not to be confused with a catamite," Natalie added. She turned back to the map. "There are more than a hundred kilometers of tunnels under the city. Some folks go on tours, but the guy I went out with was one of the outlaw types, dropping down into the tunnels to explore on his own. He found us a very nice manhole cover in the Marais."

"Sounds romantic," I said.

She nodded, her expression suddenly dreamy. "It really was. We climbed around for a few hours, then had a lovely picnic supper and had some naked time together. I didn't go out with him again. Uncut," she said, making a sad face and pulling her sleeve over her fist to demonstrate.

"Too much information," Mary Alice told her sternly.

"Back to the plan," I ordered. "Now, Nat, what do you know about the tunnels in this area? Where do they lead? Do they go into houses?"

"Oh yeah. Loads of them go right into the cellars. A lot of folks used them for bringing in wine barrels, firewood, coal — anything that would be too messy to haul through the house. Some people used them as escape routes or hideouts during revolutions or World War II. And lots of people used them to store valuables. That's half the attraction for the explorers — the idea that there could be treasure stashed down there."

"And lots of people know about this?" Helen asked.

"Loads," Natalie assured her. "There are even parties. Not legal ones, but the fines are pretty small, so people are happy to risk it."

Helen shook her head. "It seems dangerous."

"Well, of course it's dangerous," Natalie said. "There are utilities down there. Some routes are flooded or caved in. And don't get me started on the rats."

Helen went pale. "I really hate rats."

Natalie patted her hand. "It's fine, honey. You can't go down there anyway."

"Why not?"

322

"You had a bad case of pneumonia last year," Nat reminded her. "There are at least five varieties of mold down there that aren't found anywhere else in the world. The air is too bad unless you've got strong lungs."

"Oh, that's disappointing," Helen said. But she looked relieved.

"Fine," I said, folding my arms and looking at Natalie. "That leaves you and me. First, we'd have to do a recon to figure out if we can even get as far as his house through the tunnels. Then we'd have to see if there's a means of getting in."

Natalie shrugged. "I'm ready when you are. Let's get this party started."

CHAPTER TWENTY-EIGHT

The party actually got started two days later. It took some time to make preparations and pack our bags. Akiko was not at all thrilled that we were leaving again, and Minka threw a full-on pout.

"Why do you not let me come with you? I am very strong."

"You are strong," I agreed as I finished throwing things in a bag. "So strong that it's best if you stay here and protect Akiko. She's not as tough as you are," I said, lying only a little. "And we've taken every precaution to make sure it's safe here, but just in case, she might need some looking after. You can do that, right?"

Minka sulked but she looked secretly thrilled that I had put her in charge.

"I will teach her duets," Minka said, pulling up *Frozen* on her laptop. "She will be Anna. I am Elsa."

Akiko still seemed a little dazed, so maybe

the idea of sitting around having a Disney sing-along wasn't the worst idea. Besides, somebody had to look out for Kevin.

We used a fresh set of papers to hop the ferry from Dover to Calais and took the bus into Paris, arriving on a chilly evening that was spitting sleet. Paris is a beautiful city when she feels like it, and that evening she was spiteful. We were all wearing jogging suits with clunky white tennis shoes and fanny packs, a group of German lady tourists intent upon the winter sales. We had found a moderately priced hotel on the edge of the 14th arrondissement, a few blocks from the entrance to the catacombs. The morning after we arrived, Natalie and I put on our curly grey wigs and took our fanny packs to the main entrance in the Place Denfert-Rochereau. There was a wait while everyone passed their belongings through security, and a single guard in a black coat surveyed the snaking queue.

"That man looks like Tom Hardy and I am dressed like Jessica Tandy," Natalie hissed.

"You are also working," I reminded her. I gave her a little shove to push her up in the line.

"There's a rumor Tom is going to be the next James Bond. He could shake my martini anytime," she said, waggling her eyebrows. She had powdered them white, but they were still effective.

"Give your libido a rest," I said. "And you're supposed to be speaking German." The Paris guide I was carrying had a German flag emblazoned on the front and I tapped her with it.

"Ja, meine herrische Dame," she said, saluting.

I pushed her again and in a few minutes we were through the security queue. A bored employee sat on a stool, recording the number of entries on a silver clicker as we rebuckled our fanny packs. There was nothing more interesting in them than wallets stuffed with coupons and credit cards, and a few toiletries and small craft projects each. I was also carrying a pair of plastic ponchos printed with Eiffel Towers bought cheaply from a sidewalk vendor just off the Pont des Arts. We'd made a stop at a sporting goods store for a few extras including kneepads, neatly hidden under our jogging pants. The catacombs tours were self-guided, and we started down the tall circular staircase, descending 131 steps until we hit stone. The air was dank and chilly, and there was an odor unlike anything I'd ever smelled before.

"What the hell is that?" I muttered in Natalie's ear.

"Death, darling," she said.

But this wasn't the kind of death I was used to. We dealt it out, quick and clean. Depending on whether the mark had been shot or stabbed or poisoned, the smell would be different. Blood was sharp and metallic; poison could be pleasant — I had a soft spot for botanicals. Hang around too long and you'd smell other, worse things as the body settled into the relaxation of death. But the first few minutes could be perfectly tolerable if you weren't too squeamish about the odor of blood.

Blood, I could handle. But Mary Alice had a point about the bones. There was a short exhibition on the history of the catacombs, explaining that the crowded cemeteries had become vectors for disease by the time of the French Revolution and a plan had been formed to exhume the dead and relocate them to an ossuary. Approximately six million of them had found their way to this city of the dead. Then we turned a corner and *WHAM.* Bones from the word go. The catacombs were a series of low, wide chambers with bones piled in patterns against the walls, maybe six feet deep. Each room opened onto at least one other, with heaps of bones locked behind fences. Some of the rooms were themed — nothing but piles of skulls, grinning at the visitors. Beside them was a plaque reading, STOP — THIS IS THE EMPIRE OF DEATH. I hoped there were replicas in the gift shop because I wanted to buy one for Mary Alice to hang in her kitchen.

"This must be the femur room," I said as we turned a corner and came upon a heap of heavy, long bones with knobby ends.

We paused, making a show of peering interestedly at a set of bones as a group of Canadian tourists moved past, snapping pictures as they went. One girl fell a little behind, posting her selfie ("#romancingthe bone"), and I fought the urge to trip her.

When they had moved on to the next room, Natalie peered back the way we had come and gave me a quick signal. She led the way around a lacy pillar of vertebrae to a small gate set in the stone wall. I pulled a set of circular knitting needles out of my fanny pack. The work in progress was a Möbius scarf in a dull, stony shade of wool. Mary Alice had prepped it, and she had explained how to unravel the scarf, popping the stitches free until the needles were bare. A quick twist and the ends of the needles were unscrewed. Inside each was concealed a thin piece of sturdy wire, and I handed them over as Natalie whipped a credit card out of her wallet. I pressed the corner and it lit up, a miniature flashlight we'd found at the hardware store where we'd bought the wire. She bent to work, wriggling the wires into the keyhole of the gate. She closed her eyes and did it by touch while I held the light steady.

From the room beyond, I could hear the faint sounds of a tour guide reciting facts in Japanese. I didn't hurry Nat along; I just kept the light pointed where she was working and listened as the noises of the tour group got louder. I could make out the shutter clicks of their camera phones, the rustle of their raincoats.

Natalie swore softly.

"You've got about four seconds," I said finally.

She closed her eyes again and took a deep breath, flicking her wrist. The lock turned and she yanked the gate open. The metal made a hideous scraping noise, but we'd come too far. We dove inside, pulling the gate closed behind us and flinging ourselves flat on the ground. There was a tiny depression there and the gate was deep in shadow. As long as nobody came close to investigate, we could wait until the tour group passed through and then go on our way.

We lay next to each other, eyes squeezed closed, hardly daring to breathe. Suddenly, I knew we weren't alone. Squeaky footsteps were coming closer, and when I peeped through my eyelashes, I saw two small sneakers, lights blinking around the soles.

A small face bent to peer through the bars of the gate. It was a boy, maybe seven or eight. "Who are you?" he demanded in Japanese.

"A lady demon. And I'm going to eat your soul," I said, smiling. I made a claw with my hands and he ran away, shrieking for his mother.

He tugged at her coat, pointing towards us as we hunkered in the shadows, but his mother gave him a scolding for telling lies and shoved him into the next room.

Natalie forced herself to her feet, brushing at her clothes. "Was that really necessary?"

"It got rid of him," I said, tying the end of the yarn to the gate. I tossed her one of the plastic ponchos. "Now let's go exploring."

CHAPTER TWENTY-NINE

Four hours and about fifty wrong turns later, we stopped. Natalie rummaged in her pack for a water bottle and a few of the energy gels we had bought at the sporting goods store. They were nasty but they did the trick, topping us up as we took stock of our surroundings.

Natalie was comparing a dozen printouts of various maps and overlays with the step counter we'd brought and a tiny compass she wore on a chain around her neck.

"This is it," she said, pointing towards a small flight of steps cut into the stone. We climbed, dodging a few broken steps, until we got to an ancient door cut into the rock. A doorjamb had been fitted and the door itself was stout, old oak. The lock was rusted and the hinges were crumbling into piles of red dust. Natalie wanted to pick the lock, but I was tired at that point and picked up a handy piece of broken stone. Two good hits and the lock dropped off.

"Subtle," she said.

"Natalie, I am tired, I am covered in mud that is at least seventy percent dead people, and I am hungry. Do not test me."

The hinges were so wonky it took two of us to open the door enough to slip through. We didn't leave it entirely open — no point in advertising our presence in case anybody else happened along. We hadn't seen anyone during our recon and I was happy to keep it that way. We emerged into a wine cave, long abandoned, the barrels empty and cobwebbed. I flashed the light onto the name stenciled on the barrels and nearly whooped out loud. D'Archambeau. Natalie pointed and gave me a smug look.

"Natalie, you are flaky as a Pillsbury crescent roll, but you have a damned fine sense of direction," I told her. Tactfully, I ignored the hours we'd spent making wrong turns and hitting dead ends. We'd found it and that was all that mattered.

We moved through the wine cave and up a flight of stairs into the cellar proper. It was stacked with broken cribs and empty demijohns and piles of rotting copies of *Paris Match* and newspapers curling with age. There was a fair bit of scuttling around — mice, no doubt — but no other signs of life. We picked our way carefully around the piles towards the door in the opposite wall. It was all beginning to feel a bit too easy, and I was a little relieved when we hit a snag. I'm not a pessimist, but all jobs have complications and it's better to get them out of the way early. Our complication was a bright, shiny new biometric lock set in a heavy door of reinforced steel.

Natalie turned to me and swore. "I can't pick that, and even if I could, I don't have the tools."

I looked around for another way in. Sometimes when a lock is impossible, the gods will smile and the hinge will be on your side of the door. Hammering out a hinge pin is heavy work, and we didn't have mallets, but it didn't matter. Scars on the doorframe showed where the door had been reset, the hinges safely inside the house proper.

I shook my head. "It's locked up tighter than a Baptist virgin. Come on."

We took our time moving around the cellar, searching for any sign of another way in. We had given up and were about to leave when Nat saw it. She lowered to her knees, groaning only a little, and pushed aside a stack of magazines. A few rodent bones went flying and I slapped them away.

"If I never see another bone, it will be too

soon," I said, kneeling beside her. "What have you found?"

She was working her fingertips around a panel set into the rock wall. It was no more than three feet square, flimsy wood that gave way as soon as she pushed. Air, stale and clammy, rushed out from the dark cavity behind.

"Natalie, if you have just opened the seventh seal and kicked off the End Times, give me a heads-up," I told her.

She flashed a light inside the opening, her head and shoulders disappearing. When she popped back, she was grinning.

"It's a utility chase. Plumbing," she informed me, pointing to where the tangle of pipes snaked through the darkness. "I'm going to follow it. Stay here, and if I don't come back in fifteen minutes, go for help."

"Go for help? Shouldn't I come and get you?"

"Nope," she said, wriggling through the opening. "If I'm not back it means I got stuck, and if I got stuck, you're *definitely* not fitting through there."

"Did you just call me fat?" I asked her ass as she disappeared. The small glow of her light disappeared and I sat back, checking the luminous dial on my watch. I clicked off my light and sat in the darkness. There was no point in wasting the batteries. The only threat down there might be an overzealous mouse or a spider that mistook my wig for a handy place to hang out.

I checked my watch every five minutes, testing myself to see how accurate my sense of time was. It's easy to lose track when you're not relying on visual cues. There was no sign of Natalie as the minutes ticked past. I had already decided to ignore her instructions to go for help — how exactly was I supposed to explain this to the authorities? And neither Mary Alice nor Helen were good with tight spaces. I didn't much care for them either, but I never stepped away from a job that required pushing myself, testing the edge of that tiny tendency towards discomfort when I couldn't move freely. It was a way of toughening myself up, and I had just about made up my mind to go after her when I saw the glow coming back. She was a mess, poncho shredded and sneakers covered in cobwebs, but she was smiling.

"Got it?" I asked, putting out a hand to haul her back through the opening in the wall.

"Got it," she said, smiling even bigger. "And he'll never see it coming."

We scrambled out of the cellar, through

335

the wine cave, and back to the catacombs, following the grubby yarn trail I'd left until we reached the gate. The trip back was much faster, maybe twenty minutes now that we knew the way. We took off our torn ponchos, rolling them up neatly and stashing them in our pockets. Fresh ones went over our clothes, hiding the worst of the stains, and we dusted off our wigs, cleaning the streaks of dirt from our faces with baby wipes. We were pink-cheeked and only a little the worse for wear when we emerged from the catacombs into the gift shop, chattering in German about the atmosphere. A sleepy staff member made two clicks on their counter and we gave a little smile and wave.

As we took the long way back to the hotel, strolling casually down the Boulevard Raspail, Natalie outlined the plan. I poked holes in it wherever I could, but she had an answer for everything.

"It's a damned good idea," I admitted finally. "But it's going to be hard."

Natalie grinned. "Just like old times."

CHAPTER THIRTY

We slept most of the next day before the four of us set out in the late afternoon for the catacombs. We were dressed in fresh jogging suits with plenty of supplies stashed in various pockets. Food, water, and new Eiffel Tower ponchos from our favorite vendor. Mary Alice and Helen came with us to make a group of four. We had already explained to them the necessity for a couple of extra bodies the night before when we gathered for dinner and a council of war in Helen and Natalie's hotel room. Nat and I had each showered twice and our hair was still wet as we dug in.

"The catacombs staff tracks entries and exits with those little silver clickers," Natalie said over cartons of carryout Vietnamese food.

Mary Alice frowned into her bún bò huê. "Like they do for the carnival Tilt-A-Whirl?"

"Exactly," Natalie told her. "It's low-tech. They have cameras, but there's no reason for them to check the feed so long as the numbers match up."

Helen was picking listlessly at an order of gòi cuôn. "Mary Alice and I should take care of that. It's the least we can do since we can't do the actual hit."

"I did the last one," Mary Alice pointed out as she grabbed one of Helen's spring rolls to dunk in her beef broth. She eyed my food and I put a protective hand over the container.

"Touch my bún cha and you'll draw back a bloody stump," I warned her as I scooped up another pork patty.

She grumped but settled back into her chair. "Why can't you" — she pointed at me with a spring roll — "and you" — the spring roll swiveled to Natalie — "just do what you did tonight and come out through the catacombs? Then the clicker will be accurate."

"Because the catacombs close at eight thirty PM and we won't be able to get to work until well after midnight," I told her. "If this is going to work, Carapaz needs to be asleep."

Natalie ran through the rest of the plan and we worked out the details over tiny coconut jellies in the shape of smiley faces. Mary Alice made a long list of supplies we'd have to restock and which stores would have what we needed. But Helen didn't say much. Most of her coconut jelly was left on the plate, and Mary Alice gave me a look when we got back to our room.

"What?" I was dog-tired and I realized there was a faint, nasty smell in the hotel room.

"I'm worried about Helen. She's still hardly eating. It's like the light has gone out."

"She's in mourning," I said. I breathed in again. There was definitely something hanging in the air. I moved to the curtains and sniffed. Nothing.

"It's more than that," Mary Alice said, dragging a sleep shirt over her head. She'd lost her Snoopy shirt on the *Amphitrite,* but she'd replaced it with a soccer jersey that stretched to her knees. "But I don't know what the problem is."

"She's got the yips," I said absently.

"The yips?"

"It's a baseball term. Sometimes pitchers will lose a pitch. Maybe they've always been able to hum a fastball right over the center of home plate. But one day they wake up and it's just . . . gone. No matter what they do, they can't find that pitch. They've got the yips. Helen has the yips."

"You think this is about work?"

I went to the bed and started sniffing sheets. "I know it is."

I looked up and Mary Alice was giving me a quizzical look over her half-glasses. I sat down on the bed. "Fine. I didn't say anything at the time, but in Jackson Square, I gave Helen the signal to hit Sweeney."

Mary Alice blinked. "You did?"

"Yes. And she balked. She froze up. That's why I took him out."

She gave a low whistle. "Damn. But we accused you of poaching him. Why didn't you say anything?"

I shrugged. "Calling Helen out isn't exactly going to do her any favors. You have to be careful with the yips. The yips are *delicate.*"

I picked up the pillow and sniffed it. Nothing but detergent.

"So how do pitchers fix the yips?"

"They don't. You wait them out and hopefully one day you wake up and they're gone."

"And if they never leave?"

"Then you get busted down to the minors where you sit on the bench until the end of your contract and you wind up coaching

Little League to six-year-old assholes."

"Six-year-olds can't be assholes," Mary Alice says. "The fact that you think they can says a lot."

"Yeah, it says that you've clearly never met a six-year-old." I reached for the corner of the bedspread to give it a good sniff.

"Billie, I care about you, but this is an intervention. That smell is you. Go take another shower."

CHAPTER THIRTY-ONE

The next day we followed the routine Mary
Alice had laid out. We ate well and worked
our way methodically through the shopping
list and preparations. Natalie and I stuffed
our pockets as full as we could of all the
supplies we needed, and wore double fanny
packs, hiding the extra bulk under our
windbreakers. The weather had turned cold
and damp and we huddled together in line,
each of us wearing one of the brightly pat-
terned ponchos. We put our steel-grey wigs
back on and a few minutes with a contour
kit aged us up about a decade. A group of
Italian teenagers cut in line in front of us
and I stared down the leader of the little
wolfpack as he stepped on my sneaker to
get to his friends. I was just reaching for my
knitting needles when Mary Alice gripped
my arm.

"Play nice," she murmured.

"I wasn't going to kill him," I muttered

342

back. "But a little light stabbing might teach him some manners."

"Focus on the job. I'll trip him when we get inside," she promised.

"That's real friendship," I told her.

We passed through the security screening and made our way through the exhibition and into the rooms of bones. Helen was pale, her breath shallow, and I gave Mary Alice a nudge. "Hurry her to the end. The air is shit down here and she doesn't look good."

Helen overheard and managed a tight smile. "I'm fine, Billie. It's just a little smelly."

"Moldy bones," Nat said cheerfully. She looked around. "Ready?"

"Ready," the rest of us said. Mary Alice and Helen gave us one last look and moved away, slowly circling the stacks of bones. It took a while for them to find the right marks, but about half an hour later, a pair of younger women wearing Disneyland Paris sweatshirts wandered in. They were fussing about the dirtiness of the place and I could practically feel Mary Alice beaming from across the room. They were *perfect*. She approached with the extra ponchos and spent a few minutes chatting brightly. The women looked wary at first, probably expecting she'd want money, but after a bit they accepted the ponchos and put them on. The plan called for Mary Alice and Helen to jostle the counter out of the staff member's hand at the exit. It would be child's play to pick it up and add two quick clicks as they were handing it back, but if that failed, and they realized two guests were still in the catacombs, they'd pull the video. And video would show four women going in wearing Eiffel Tower ponchos and four Eiffel Tower ponchos coming out. They'd do a sweep at that point and when the catacombs staff didn't find anyone, they would probably shrug and lock up for the night.

We waited for a bit, letting the last rush of guests move through before the quiet of the dinner hour. There would be another rush of evening tours, but we were long gone before that, using the break between groups to slip through the gate again. It was much more difficult to relock than it had been to pick it in the first place, but it was essential to leave no indication anyone had come that way.

We wound our way through the tunnels, up and down and around, always bearing northwest. We stopped in a cozy little nook to hunker down under space blankets — it was *cold* down there — and pack in some nutrition. We played word games and took turns dozing off until it was time to head off again. When we got to the d'Archambeau wine cave, we stopped and checked our gear one last time, then entered the cellar. A quick look around showed that nothing had been moved since the day before. The spiderwebs were intact, the stacks of *Paris Match* still teetering. Natalie whipped off the wooden panel and we paused long enough to strap headlamps on. Then we eased into the utility chase, Natalie in front leading the way.

There wasn't much room and we had to move sideways, backs against the stone walls as our fronts brushed the pipes. After we'd gone twenty feet or so, they took a vertical turn and so did the chase. This part had clearly been a chimney at one time, lined with old bricks, the mortar in between crumbling. I pulled out a chalk bag and dipped my fingers in before passing it to Nat. We both wore climbing shoes, thin-soled and grippy, and as we made our way up, finding hand- and footholds in the gaps between the bricks, I could almost imagine I was on the gym's climbing wall. We didn't have far to go — only fifteen feet or so — before Nat stopped, wedging her feet on a ledge. The pipes bent at a ninety-degree angle; we were just outside a bathroom. In front of Natalie was a cutout, about the same size as the opening from the cellar, blocked with a piece of metal that was held in place with a series of clips.

Nat took out a Swiss Army knife, flicking it open to the flathead screwdriver attachment. She had just raised her hand to wedge it under the first clip when we heard the whistle. Nat froze, tool in hand, and gave me a wide-eyed stare. It was just one low note at first, then it slid into a loose melody. It took me a minute to place it, but when I did, I almost laughed out loud.

" 'Uptown Funk,' " I mouthed to Natalie. We waited until the notes trailed off. There was a pause, a rattle of something metal, and then a *whoosh* as the toilet flushed. The wastewater rattled down the pipe next to us and Natalie made a gagging motion. "God, I hope that was just pee," I muttered. She flapped her hand at me and I made the universal gesture for zipping lips. She tapped her watch and I nodded. It was just past one AM and hopefully that late-night bathroom trip meant Carapaz would be out again soon.

To be safe, we gave it half an hour before Natalie started to work again. She took ages, prying open each little metal clasp. She alternated sides, then did the top. When that was finished, she motioned to me, and I squeezed in next to her. The metal panel wasn't just a sheet, it was a box — the medicine cabinet of Carapaz's bathroom. Together we eased it forward slowly, working it free. The hardest part of the entire job was maneuvering the medicine cabinet into the bathroom and setting it on the vanity in perfect silence. The opening where the medicine cabinet had been was a vacant rectangle and Nat popped her head through, surveying the bathroom. She gave me a thumbs-up and we moved on to phase two. I laced my hands into a cat's cradle for Nat, giving her a boost over the edge of the opening. She shimmied through, and after a minute, a hand came back through, giving me another thumbs-up.

A little taller than Nat, I had an easier time getting myself up and over. The vanity was a modern slab of concrete, studded with tiny fossils and empty of any toiletries. A sleek, smoked-glass sink sat on top, and I straddled it as I eased my way onto the vanity. Nat held up a hand to help me down, and I dropped to my feet on the flokati rug. We stood in the silence, listening for any sound of movement. There was a faint rustle as Carapaz turned over in bed and a long, rippling fart followed by a snore.

God, I love men, but they are disgusting. We waited another few minutes to make certain he was settled again before we crept out of the bathroom. The bedside light was still on, glowing softly. We paused at the doorway, taking in the scene. He must have fallen asleep reading. A file folder was open on the bed, reading glasses still perched on the end of his nose. Natalie went first, moving noiselessly across the parquet floor. After the modern atrocity of the bathroom, I'd been afraid he had remodeled the heart out of the old house, but I was glad to see he'd kept the original floors. There was a long expanse to cover before reaching the end of the room where the bed stood — a wide, low California king, which seemed excessive in Paris. The room was warm; he'd obviously sprung for central heat at some point, and he'd gotten the duvet twisted around his legs, probably when he was trying to kick it off. It made me wonder if he was sleeping poorly.

Something on your conscience, bitch? I moved in Natalie's wake until we reached the end of the bed, where we divided. She went right, I went left. He was flat on his back, snores bubbling gently from his open mouth. One hand was tucked under his pillow and I gave Nat a quick nod. It didn't take a genius to realize a gun was stashed under there, and he was clutching it, even in sleep. A well-trained, fully alert person could react in maybe a second and a half to a situation. Add another few seconds for Carapaz to wake, maybe one or two more to account for age. I still didn't like it. Five seconds wasn't much time to disarm him, especially at our age. I had done fine during the climb, but my legs and arms were shaking with the effort, and I didn't figure Nat was in much better shape.

Nat looked at his arm and nodded. His gun hand was on my side, which meant it was up to me to keep him neutralized while Nat finished him. She reached for her trusty Swiss Army knife again, this time choosing the longest blade. It was only two inches long, but she'd sharpened it to a razor's edge. While we'd been passing time in the tunnels, we'd debated at length where she should hit him. I was partial to the subclavian artery, but Natalie preferred the carotids.

We looked at each other across the bed and mouthed a count.

One. Two. Three.

We probably should have discussed

whether we were going to *on* three or *after* three. I assumed it would be *one-two-three-go!*, but Natalie jumped right on three and I was half a beat behind. She leapt on the bed, thrusting the blade up under his jaw and slicing down hard at a slant. His eyes flew open and he let out a roar just as I rushed him. His hand was still under the pillow but he must have squeezed the trigger reflexively because a bullet whizzed out, puncturing the pillow and sending feathers flying into the air. His neck was putting out blood like a gas pump as his free hand went for Nat's neck and she sliced at his arm, laying open the sleeve of his pajama top. She got lucky; she hit his ulnar artery and blood spewed in an arc.

All of that happened in a few seconds, but it was enough for pandemonium to erupt. He was bleeding out, sitting in a fountain of blood, yet he managed to hit a button on the nightstand. An alarm sounded, piercing and shrill, and from downstairs I could hear a guard dog howling like the Hound of the Baskervilles. Footsteps pounded up the stairs and we scuttled off the bed. For reasons I couldn't explain, I snatched up the folder as we ran. He was dying, but Carapaz didn't give up easy. He still had his gun and he got off two shots, one of them just grazing the top of my shoulder as we hit the bathroom at a dead run. Natalie slammed the door closed and locked it as I dove for the window, wrenching it open.

Nat had flung herself through the opening into the utility chase and was hissing at me. "What the actual shit are you doing? *Hurry!*"

I shoved the folder inside my shirt, using my bra to hold it in place. Then I hauled myself into the utility chase just as the first crashes came against the bathroom door. We hoisted the medicine cabinet back into place. There was no time to secure it, and there was nothing to do but cross our fingers and hope it would stay.

We scuttled down the chase, half falling in our hurry to get to the bottom. Natalie had edged out of it, backing into the cellar just as the medicine cabinet flew back in a fusillade of gunshots. The mirror on the front shattered against the bricks, showering me in glass as I ducked my head. I was almost to the bottom but Carapaz's bodyguards were already leaning through. They were big boys, thick as linebackers, and there was no way they could get into the chase. But they had guns, and they started shooting immediately. They were shooting into the dark and the bullets ricocheted off the brick, chipping off bits that flew into my hair. It was only a matter of time before one of them thought to get a flashlight, but before they did, hands grabbed my ankles and yanked hard. Natalie hauled me into the cellar and we scrambled to our feet, wheezing. We didn't dare stop in case one of those hired guns realized how the chase fit into the fabric of the house.

So we raced through the cellar, tipping over stacks of *Paris Match* as we went. As they fell, I got a brainstorm and flicked open my lighter. The paper was damp and moldy, but it caught. The wine cave was filling with smoke by the time we made our way out, wedging the door closed behind us. We hurried on, twisting and turning for hours through passages too narrow for them to follow even if they tried. The air got colder and wetter, heavy with odors I didn't even want to try to identify.

We came to a stop when Natalie had to catch her breath. Her color was bad and she was holding her side like she had a stitch. My sweatshirt was soaked in blood from the wound in my shoulder and Nat pointed, gasping out the words. "You . . . okay?"

"Graze," I said shortly. I looked around, but nothing about this spot was familiar. "Do you know where we are?"

She shook her head and I would have cursed but I didn't have the energy. Instead I shoved a power gel into her mouth and we started again. We came into a tunnel which was wide enough for a small road with lots of doors leading off of it. I pushed through the first one and found a flight of stairs. I dragged Natalie up until we came to a locked door. She was nearly spent, but she rallied, rubbing her hands together to get some warmth back into them until she was able to maneuver the wires in her fanny pack to pick the lock.

The door led into a stone hut, small and windowless, a few rusted hand tools sitting with a stack of flowerpots in the corner. "It looks like a groundskeeper's shed," I said. There was a door on the opposite wall, but this one wasn't locked. I wasn't surprised; there was nothing inside worth stealing. We opened it and icy cold air rushed in, but it was fresh. We emerged into an otherworldly landscape, a sea of pale stone crosses as far as we could see. In the center, on a low rise, was a circular tower.

I grinned.

"Welcome to Montparnasse Cemetery," I said, looping an arm around her shoulders. "We made it."

CHAPTER THIRTY-TWO

JULY 1981

Wearing their darkest clothes and rubber-soled shoes, they slip out of their tents and into the excavation pit. The entrance to the tunnel has been shored up with lumber, and they ease inside. Thierry Carapaz is carrying a small backpack; the rest have flashlights and a few tools small enough to fit into a pocket. The air in the tunnel is stuffy and damp, and they are all rolling in sweat by the time they reach the cellar. They are moving in silent single file by the light of the miner's torch Vance Gilchrist has strapped to his head. He turns it off when they emerge into the cellar of the main house and they wait for several minutes, crouching in the cool darkness and letting their eyes adjust. This is the third time they have been in the cellar on reconnaissance. Apart from a stack of empty olive oil cans and a flurry of dead flies, there is nothing in the stone-walled room. The telephone line

354

snakes down one wall, and Mary Alice snips it. The baroness's villa is cut off now from the outside world.

A short flight of steps ends at the door into the house, and Natalie is dispatched with a set of tools to gently oil the hinges and pick the lock. She works by touch, and when she finishes, she gives a soft whistle. They join her on the steps and wait for Vance to give the signal, another whistle that mimics the birds in the garden. At his mark, they slip, one by one, into the kitchen, where a low night-light is burning. The kitchen is small and grimy, carved out of the dining room by a flimsy partition wall. The stove is tiny, tethered to a tank of gas by a cord, and Carapaz kneels next to it. He silently begins to unpack his tools while Vance and the women separate. Mary Alice is to provide any backup that Carapaz requires, and Helen and Natalie wait for the signal to begin removing the art.

Three months earlier, a Provenance agent posing as a plumber gained access to the house and drew a map from memory — a map they have all memorized. Billie has walked these shadowy rooms a thousand times in her mind, and she counts off the steps as she follows Vance through the dining room and down a low, wide hall to the baroness's bedroom. Vance pauses, his hand on the knob, waiting until they hear the squeak of bedsprings and a low, rattling breath.

He eases open the door and steps over the threshold. Instantly, the bedside light snaps on. The baroness is awake, holding a revolver in one hand and the telephone in the other.

Vance holds up his hands, smiling. "Good evening."

He doesn't reassure her with lies or pretend everything is going to be okay, and Billie respects him for it. The baroness unleashes a litany of German, spitting the consonants as she shouts at the phone, at her caretakers. But no one is coming, and at the last moment, she seems to understand that.

She drops the phone, cupping her free hand under the revolver to steady it. She points it squarely at Vance, and Billie moves into the room. It is standard procedure in such situations, and it is how they have been trained to respond. Two possible places to shoot confuses a target, buying them extra time.

"It's alright," Vance says confidently. "If she hasn't shot yet, she won't."

He almost finishes the last word before

the baroness fires, clipping his collar. "I'll be damned," he mutters, clapping his hand to where the bullet has skimmed his skin, burning it before burying itself in a painting on the wall behind.

Before she can pull the trigger again, Billie puts her hand over the baroness's. It feels like a collection of bird bones in Billie's palm, the skin cold and lifeless, the spare flesh winnowed away until only the brittle framework remains.

She looks up at Billie with eyes that are black and bright with hatred. She says something that Billie barely hears, her ears still ringing from the sound of the shot in the small room. In the time it has taken Billie to reach the baroness's side, she has swept the night table and seen the basket of knitting, balls of wool impaled by a pair of long steel needles.

Billie raises her hand and the baroness feels nothing, only a small punch angling down behind her collarbone. Then Billie removes her fist and the warmth comes, gushing wetly. The subclavian artery, nicknamed "the well" for how much liquid it pumps, is severed cleanly. A young and healthy person will bleed out in as little as two minutes from such an injury, but the baroness is already sinking. Her mouth opens several times but she says nothing else. She does not close her eyes but watches Billie as the life drains out of her, and the last thing she sees is a blond girl smiling in satisfaction at a job well done.

Vance's hand is clapped to his neck, red seeping between his fingers; his face is a mask of fury and Billie realizes too late what she's done. It has been more than a decade since the Museum has found a Nazi to execute and it should have been Vance's kill.

"She was mine," he says hoarsely.

"She shot you —"

Vance looms over her, putting his face so close to hers she can see her reflection in his pupils, upside down and very, very small.

"She. Was. Mine."

For an instant Billie thinks he means to hit her, and her fingers tighten on the knitting needle still in her hand. She won't strike first, but if he touches her, she won't go down without a fight.

He glances down at the knitting needle and his grin is humorless and cold. "Little girl, if I wanted to punish you for this, you'd be dead before you ever saw me coming. You are not my equal, and don't you ever make the mistake of thinking you are. I've forgotten more about how to kill people than you will ever learn, so finish the job and stay out of my way," he orders. He points to the painting on the wall. "Get it down. It's on the manifest."

She grabs the painting off the wall and hurries out to the dining room, where Natalie is wrapping the last of the paintings. They form a chain, hauling the artworks into the cellar under cover of darkness until the house is stripped. They shift the paintings down the tunnel, barricading the cellar behind them as they go with piles of debris. They stack the art carefully and build another pile of debris to shield it from the excavation side.

Filthy and tired, they move to the stand of banana trees and wait. Carapaz has timed it perfectly, and just as they settle in beneath the wide green leaves, the gas tank explodes. He has left a trail of fuel through the house and it catches quickly, climbing the walls and lighting the roof. There is a muffled whoosh when the fire reaches the baroness's room. The windows blow out from the heat and the warmth of it touches their faces as they watch.

"Holy shit," Natalie breathes.

The walls of the house seem to inhale, puffing outwards as smoke billows into the night sky. Billie edges forward, but the roof suddenly collapses in a shower of sparks.

The beams crash down with a roar and the night itself erupts.

But the plantation is isolated, the nearest neighbor several miles away, and no one comes. When the fire settles to smoldering ash, they turn to the paintings. Vance Gilchrist has the manifest, and as they identify each of the recovered pieces of art, he marks them off.

"Van Gogh. *The Woman in the Wood.* Caravaggio. *The Gorgon Tisiphone.* Bruegel. *The Plague Doctor.*"

To ship the paintings, they have purchased a set of Gujarati doors, heavily carved but not particularly valuable. Each door comprises a front and back panel, held together with strips nailed around the circumference. Their evenings have been spent carefully removing the nails securing the bottom strips, the section the Customs inspectors are least likely to scrutinize. The same small prybars are used to remove each heavy frame from the paintings and unpick the tacks securing the canvases to their stretchers. Freed, the canvases are slipped inside the opening in the doors. The doors will be crated up and shipped to an import furniture company in Milan that is owned by the Museum. From there, the paintings will be cleaned and remounted and quietly restored to the families from whom they were looted. The Provenance department prides itself on finding the lost owners, searching immigration records and gallery catalogs until they can piece together the rightful claims. Any art they cannot restore to its owners is held in a climate-controlled Swiss warehouse in the hopes they will someday be able to place it.

The last to go in is the painting that has been nicked by the baroness's bullet.

"Sofonisba Anguissola. *The Queen of Sheba Arising,*" Vance says. He does not mention the bullet hole in the corner, and neither does Billie, but she watches as the painted face disappears into its hiding place.

It will be almost forty years before she will see it again.

CHAPTER THIRTY-THREE

Two down, one to go, I repeated to myself as I made tea. It drummed in my head, relentless as the rain that pounded down day after day. We'd only been back for three days, but England was getting on my nerves. To begin with, I was feeling every last second of my sixty years after the hit on Carapaz. Muscles I had forgotten about were stiff and sore, and my knuckles and knees were bruised to hell and back. Mary Alice had stitched up my shoulder — neatly, with tiny, precise stitches. But it itched like fire, and the more it itched, the crankier I got.

The fact that days were passing with no plan on how to find Vance Gilchrist was also a solid nuisance. We started to snipe at each other, but that didn't help. Soon the house was filled with the sound of slamming doors and everybody's spite music turned up to drown out the others. Natalie was blasting

Lizzo from her phone over the Babymetal Minka played through her laptop. Helen unearthed a portable record player from the attic which still worked, and she even found a half-warped Carole King album to play on it. It couldn't compete with Mary Alice's Baroque opera on BBC Radio in the kitchen. Dido was just screeching her last when I tapped out, taking a pack of cigarettes and a notebook to the garden shed along with the folder we had lifted from Carapaz's house. I stacked a few moldy bags of mulch to make a sort of sofa and sat, listening to CCR and smoking with my fingers going numb. If it had been summer, a curious rabbit or a friendly mouse might have kept me company, but there was nothing Beatrix Potter about that shed. It was drafty and damp, and the tip of my nose burned with the cold.

Whenever a hit was ordered, a packet would come with the preliminary information put together by Provenance. The packet always looked like something your great-aunt would send, a chatty letter on personalized stationery and a selection of newspaper and magazine clippings, recipe cards, knitting patterns. Every squad of Museum recruits had their own theme devised during training. All communication with us came on notepaper headed with an illustration of a young girl looking over a flock of sheep. It was a play on Constance's code name of Shepherdess, and the letters were always signed "Aunt Constance" although the actual writing was done by some grunt in Provenance. We ignored the text of the letter and paid attention to the picture at the top. It varied subtly depending on the information it was supposed to convey. The number of sheep told us how many weeks until the hit needed to happen; the direction the shepherdess was facing, the color of the ribbon on her crook — all of them gave us another piece of the puzzle. And every page in the packet added more detail until we knew exactly who we were supposed to kill, complete with suggestions on locations, the subject's patterns of behavior, personal interests, and obvious vulnerabilities.

Once the packet was decoded, it was up to us to devise the actual plan. We coordinated with Acquisitions for supplies and logistics of carrying it out, and a team from that department was always tasked with getting whatever we needed as well as monitoring for further developments. Initially, our plans had to be approved by the head of the Exhibitions department, but once we'd proven ourselves, we were left on our own to develop our plans, and I had a routine for mine.

The day a packet came, I cleared my schedule. I canceled appointments, rescheduled deadlines for my freelance translating work. Then I settled in with a pack of Eves and the silver lighter my mother had accidentally left behind the day she walked out. Next to the lighter and cigarettes, I would arrange a fresh notebook and a new Ticonderoga, sharpened to a needle point. Then I would pour a glass bottle of Big Red over ice and settle in. The ideas didn't come until I had sat for a while, smoking and listening to the ice crack, the air smelling of burnt tobacco and the cotton candy tang of the soda. I turned the lighter over in my hand as I thought, wearing down the chunks of turquoise like worry beads.

After the first glass was half-drunk and a couple of butts had been ground into the Bakelite saucer I used for an ashtray, I'd start jotting ideas. Random words at first, questions, possibilities. I didn't censor this part, just wrote whatever came to me. I would keep at it, smoking and writing and drinking until I had a headache from the Eves and a stomachache from the soda. And the plan would be there, rough, but with all the major parts working. It usually took several more days to finish it off, smoothing out the ragged ends and tucking them in until I had a neat little scheme. It had been my method for forty years and it had never failed me.

But now I didn't have a Ticonderoga or a pack of Eves, and I sure as hell didn't have any Big Red. I had a notebook from the pound store with a picture of a basket of puppies on it and a marker that smelled like bubble gum. And I had my lighter. I pulled it out of my pocket and lit one of the god-awful cigarettes left from the brew we'd made for Günther. It was cheap and rough and I coughed until my eyes streamed before stubbing it out on the sole of my boot. I rubbed my thumb over the lighter, noting every lump of turquoise, rubbed smooth from years of handling. It was heavy and not particularly pretty, and I was sure my mother had stolen it from one of the men she referred to as her "boyfriends." There had been so many of them, all vaguely the same, with flashy cars and unsuspecting wives. She would take up with them for a weekend or a year, however long they managed to convince her that this time she'd met a good man who would really take care of her. She never saw the clues, or maybe she just didn't want to. She would shake out her blond hair and put on another coat of frosted lipstick and get into yet another Camaro, thinking this time it would be different.

But it never was. She got older but never any smarter, and with age came desperation. She just wanted so badly to be loved, but the love of a child wasn't enough, wasn't the right kind of love. So I learned to keep it back, not to burden her with it. She loved me best when I didn't ask anything of her, so I carried that love alone until the day she up and walked away for good. She left with a man, of course, this one heading for California. He had a paunch and a shirt open to his navel, but he drove a Cadillac and had a plan to make money. The fact that a kid was a dealbreaker didn't stop her; it probably didn't even slow her down. She took whatever she could carry that would pawn easily, which is how I know she forgot the lighter. It would have gotten her a few bucks for gas money or a Stuckey's pecan log.

At first, I hoped she might send for me. I used that lighter on a birthday candle. I didn't have a cake — Meemaw's budget didn't stretch that far and she hadn't even remembered my birthday. But I found a broken candle from a faded box in the pantry and I lit it with my mother's lighter, making the same wish I'd made when I'd stolen a rabbit's foot keychain from the five-and-dime just so I could rub it.

The wish never came true. I used the lighter to burn the postcard she sent from Venice Beach telling me how wonderful it was but how she just couldn't afford the bus ticket for me to visit. After that I stopped checking the mail and I stopped looking backwards. But I kept the lighter. I used it when I wanted to burn my bridges, torching report cards and disciplinary notes, rejection letters and pink slips. I glued back the turquoises when they fell out and refilled the fluid and kept it polished. I moved a lot during my first years with the Museum. I preferred furnished rentals and kept my possessions light — just a single box of things I could ship easily from place to place. Over the years, the things in the box changed, but the lighter was the constant, the one item I always carried in my pocket. I used it to burn intel and light signal fires and flaming shots when the occasion called for it. It lay on the nightstand the first time I spent the night with Taverner, and I used it to light a cigarette the last time I said good-bye to him, my hand shaking so badly I could hardly get it to catch. It was a talisman of sorts, and it never failed me.

Until now. I turned it over and over in my hand, but it just felt cold and heavy. There was no inspiration for how to find Vance, only the biting cold of the shed and the weight of the lump of silver in my hand. I flicked it, kindling the little flame. I passed my hand over it, warming it a bit but mostly killing time, bringing my palm closer and closer with each pass.

I flipped open the folder from Carapaz's house and paged through it. Whatever instinct had prompted me to snatch it on the way out had paid off. It was our dossier, the one prepared for the board, alleging we were on the take. Like all material prepped for the board, it was almost clinical in its tone, laying out the evidence like a trail of bread crumbs for the directors to follow. There was a section on each of us, complete with murders we were supposed to have committed for pay. I skimmed my pages again, going over the lurid details. They were laughable — targets I had never even heard of, methods I rarely used. The whole thing smelled sloppy to me, like it had been assembled too fast or by somebody with no time to spare.

I lit another cigarette — it might have

been nasty but I needed the nicotine — and blew out a mouthful of smoke slowly, making rings. Smoke and mirrors, that's all the dossier was, a prop to keep on hand in case anybody asked questions about us. The file was the old-fashioned kind, pasteboard covers with a long metal bracket down one side. The arms of the bracket were threaded through holes punched in the pages inside, keeping everything neat and tidy, with little clasps to hold the bracket arms down and form a temporary binding. It meant the pages could be flipped through like a book, complete with a snug little gutter on the inside. I flicked the clasps off and straightened the bracket arms before I slid the front cover off. I pulled each page free until I saw it, a tiny set of coded characters running vertically along one of the inside margins. Every dossier came with a code like that, a series of letters and numbers that could be interpreted if you knew what you were looking at. Every person who had a hand in compiling it added their initials and the date to the code. By the time it got to a field agent, the code could take up the entire length of the page. This one was short — one set of initials and one date. One person had compiled the dossier.

I ran my finger over the initials, remembering my conversation with Naomi Ndiaye, searching for anything I might have missed. After a while, I put the dossier back together and clipped the cover into place. I had some answers, but there was only so much I could do without more information.

I pulled out the phone Minka had set up for me and dialed in Naomi's number. There was a long moment of silence, then an automated voice.

"This number is no longer in service. If you believe you have reached this message in error, please hang up and dial again."

I jabbed the "off" button and swore. The bitch had changed her number, no doubt to keep me from calling her again.

I figured it was a long shot, but I was running low of options. I punched in the number of the answering service I'd given Martin. When it picked up, I keyed in the pin, expecting to hear the usual snippy recording. "You have *no* new messages." Instead, she perkily told me that I had a new message and asked if I'd like to hear it.

"Yes, you stupid bitch," I muttered.

The recording didn't like that. "I did not recognize that response," she said, sounding offended as a recording can sound.

"Yes, please and thank you, with sugar on top and cream on Sundays," I said.

"One moment, please."

There was a long few seconds of staticky silence before Martin's voice came through, sounding younger than I remembered and hushed, as if he were afraid of being overheard.

"Billie, it's Martin. I think I heard something, or maybe I didn't. I don't know. But I had to bring some files to Vance and I went to the bathroom and when I came back, he was on the phone. He didn't hear me, so I . . . shit, I eavesdropped, okay. I don't know what it means, but he said the same phrase twice. Toll mash. I know it sounds stupid and I'm probably going to hate myself for even thinking it might help, but I feel bad. I mean, you were always nice to me, Billie. I — I have to go. Toll mash. I hope it helps."

I pressed "end call" and stared at the phone, rolling the phrase over in my mind. Toll mash. I couldn't even begin to imagine what it might mean. It sounded like a wrestling move or something to do with a chocolate chip cookie.

"Toll mash." I tried saying it out loud and that didn't help. I closed my eyes and pictured the letters, but they didn't look right. Instead of TOLL MASH, I kept picturing something different.

TOLLEMACHE.

The name was vaguely familiar, but I couldn't remember why. I clapped my hands together to get some warmth back into them, then plugged the word into the search bar of my phone. There were 775,000 results, but the first was what I wanted. Tollemache's Auctions and Private Sales. Along with Christie's and Sotheby's, it was one of the big three auction houses in London, specializing in paintings and jewelry. I pulled up their website and the landing page featured an exquisite Boldini woman in pink satin and tulle. Tollemache's was traditional, stuffy even. They'd sooner burn the house down than sell contemporary art. No stuffed taxidermy sharks or canvases streaked with menstrual blood for them. They were strictly old-school.

And they meant nothing to us. I'd never even set foot in the place, and to my knowledge neither had any of the others. Tollemache's was old money, housed in a sagging Tudor building that made Liberty look postmodern. I clicked through the site for maybe a quarter of an hour before I found it.

It was on the Events page, an announcement of their annual January sale. This year's theme was female painters and it was titled *A Celebration of Five Centuries of Women in Art, 1500–1950.* I clicked through the online catalog, translating the estimates in pounds sterling to dollars as I read. There was a luscious O'Keeffe predicted to hit mid–eight figures, with works by Gentileschi, Cassatt, and Vigée Le Brun expected to fetch a little over five million dollars each. A Vallayer-Coster was projected to roll in the range of $900,000, with a Fontana bringing up the rear at a cool half a million.

At the bottom of the listing was a line in bold. *Recent addition to the sale.* I clicked it and stared. I took off my reading glasses, polished them carefully on my shirttail, then stared some more. And suddenly I knew exactly how we were going to find Vance Gilchrist.

CHAPTER THIRTY-FOUR

The others were in the kitchen when I came in, waving my phone and doing a little victory dance.

"What the hell are you so excited about?" Mary Alice asked. Her temper was getting sourer by the day as Akiko kept her distance.

"I know how we're going to find Vance," I told her, turning my phone. The others gathered around and I heard three women suck in their breath at one time.

Only Akiko and Minka didn't understand. "So?" Minka said, handing back the phone.

Akiko peered at the tiny screen. "Nice painting, but what does it have to do with Gilchrist?"

I smiled. "This is not a nice painting. This is *The Queen of Sheba Arising* by Sofonisba Anguissola." I cleared my throat and started to read from the catalog entry. " 'Commissioned by Elisabeth of Valois, Queen of Spain, *The Queen of Sheba Arising* was painted by Anguissola during her tenure in Madrid as court painter. Upon the death of the queen, Anguissola returned to her home in Cremona with the painting, where it remained until her death in 1625. It was inherited by her stepson, Guido Lomellino, and was passed down through the Lomellino family, remaining in private hands.' "

Helen peered at the small screen. "Are you sure that's our *Sheba*?"

"It's her alright," I said. I flicked to the tab where the condition of the painting was described. I skimmed the mention of crackling and the lack of original frame — all to be expected with a piece dating to the Renaissance. I highlighted the relevant section and passed it to Natalie to read aloud.

" 'The painting is in overall good condition with only minor damage due to age. One small repair appears to have been made to the canvas in the lower left corner, a circle approximately .75 centimeters in diameter where the canvas was at some point completely punctured. Damage was only done to the draperies of the composition and none of the figures nor the artist's signature was involved. The repair is only detectable under laboratory conditions and is not expected to affect the value.' "

"The gunshot," Mary Alice said. "Holy

shit. It *is* our *Sheba*."

I nodded while Akiko looked perplexed. "Why do you keep calling this painting your *Sheba*?"

We filled her in briefly on the Zanzibar mission and the damage inflicted on the painting when the baroness's shot had gone wide.

"Most of the other works recovered have been repatriated, returned to the rightful owners, the heirs of the families whose collections were looted during World War II," Helen explained. "But not the *Sheba*. The family who owned her were all killed during the war. Provenance investigated for years, but they never found anyone who might have a claim on her."

"So where has she been?" Akiko asked. "I'm guessing she hasn't just been hanging on a wall in someone's den."

"There's a facility in Switzerland," Natalie said. "A free port."

"What is that?" Minka asked.

Nat explained. "A free port is a place where deals are made and money changes hands but there are no taxes to be paid."

"Wait, there's actually a place where that happens?" Akiko asked.

"Hundreds of such places," Helen told her. "They're nothing new. They've been around since antiquity."

"But all governments love taxes," Minka put in.

"Yes," Helen said, "but they love commerce more. So they permit free zones to be established in order to boost trade."

"One of the largest in the world is in Geneva," Natalie explained. "It started off as a big ugly grain warehouse where people could stockpile common goods like food and coal, but when World War II came, folks started stashing more interesting things — gold bullion, jewels, vintage wines."

"Art," Mary Alice put in.

"Art," Natalie agreed. "And it's a great place to store your goods. They have storage that is strictly controlled for temperature and humidity, so it's safe to keep your paintings or manuscripts, paper currency. And it's convenient because everybody likes their secret Swiss bank accounts. If you're already in the area, doing a little modest banking, moving a few hundred million around, it's easy to pop in and visit your Van Goghs or your South Sea pearls."

"It's also very secure," Helen added. "Barbed wire, armored doors, heavy security. Impossible to steal from."

"And your painting is there?" Akiko asked. "The *Sheba*?"

"It was," I told her. "The Museum rents space there because maintaining a storage facility of that caliber is expensive and could draw attention. By storing things at the free port facility, the Museum is just another client. And the Museum doesn't have many pieces to store. Over the decades, hundreds of paintings have been recovered, but only a dozen or so haven't been restored to their rightful owners. *Sheba* is one of them. After we recovered her in 1981, she was sent directly to Geneva and she's been there ever since."

"Until now," Mary Alice corrected.

"Until now," I agreed.

Akiko's brow furrowed. "But how do you know Vance Gilchrist took her out? Maybe her owners were found and this is all just a coincidence."

I ticked off the replies on my fingers. "First, Vance had to remove her personally because the security is biometric and only the Museum directors have access to the collection in storage. Two directors are dead, and that painting was added to Tollemache's listing at the last minute. Second, when art is restored to the owners, we get an update if it's a piece we recovered. Nobody here has heard a thing about the *Sheba* for almost forty years." I held up a third finger.

"Third?" Akiko asked.

"Third, I don't believe in coincidences. Not where Vance is concerned. He's done this on purpose to draw us out. Auction houses don't like to talk too much about damage to the artworks. But the description of the *Sheba* is very specific. It was a bullet hole in that corner, and Vance made sure that fact was put into the catalog. He wanted us to find it."

"Why? I thought he would be hiding from you. Isn't he in fear of his life?" Akiko protested.

Mary Alice moved her hand to touch Akiko, then seemed to think better of it. "He knows we're after him. We've already taken out Paar and Carapaz. He doesn't want to keep looking over his shoulder. He's initiating a fight on his own terms."

Minka scowled. "This is not safe."

"No." I smiled. "No, it isn't safe at all." I paused. "There's one other thing you should know." And then I told them what I'd found in the folder, the coded identity of the person who had prepared the dossier.

Mary Alice was the first to speak. "What are we going to do about it?"

"Add another name to the hit list," I said,

picking up a marker that smelled like cotton candy.

I wrote the name in pink block capitals. Then I turned back. "Anybody got a problem with that?"

CHAPTER THIRTY-FIVE

The auction wasn't for another week, and I was glad of the chance to work out the details. We started with what we knew for sure — the setting.

"This will be a big sale," Mary Alice mused as we gathered in Constance's study one evening after dinner. Akiko and Minka were in the kitchen clearing up and working on a duet from *Tangled.* Helen was skimming Tollemache's website, looking for anything we might have missed, while Mary Alice flicked through the printouts we'd compiled. I was sitting behind Constance's desk, idly turning pages in an art book I'd found on the shelf. *The Art of the Female Painter.* The title was sexist as hell, but I was hoping for some inspiration.

"Lots of people will be crowding in the sale, collectors, journalists," Mary Alice went on.

"And a shit-ton of security," Natalie said.

"Clearances, CCTV, the works, and all of it state-of-the-art."

"And livestreamed," Helen said, pointing to a hyperlink on the website. "For people who want to watch or bid at home."

I thought for a minute. "That's a lot of witnesses — too many for an organization that prides itself on discretion. They'll have to take us out and kill us somewhere else."

"You think he'll come in person? That's a big risk," Helen said.

"Vance is an arrogant SOB. And he's been pissed at me since I poached his Nazi in Zanzibar. Of course he'll come in person. He'll underestimate us, and that's our biggest advantage," I said.

"So," Mary Alice said, "we need a plan to get into Tollemache's without alerting Vance's people. Then we need a way to kill Vance without anybody noticing."

"Surely it's better to abduct him and kill him elsewhere," Helen said. "Much more discreet."

"Much more dangerous," Nat corrected. "If we hustle him out, there's always the chance we'll be followed or he'll escape. I say we hit him at the auction house."

"With the whole world watching?" I raised a brow at her. "Not exactly subtle. And we can't take the chance of bystanders getting hurt."

Natalie's face was wearing its stubborn expression, but she didn't argue. The first rule of Museum work was that we never touched innocent people. It was a pain in the ass — there's nothing easier than hurling a bomb into a crowd — but it forced us to be careful and creative in our missions.

I turned the page and stopped cold. It was a color plate of a painting I had only seen once before. I'd been in Venice, taking a few days' leave after quietly killing the head of an Armenian crime syndicate who was there on his honeymoon. I had planned on seeing the sights, but the rains came and I spent most of my time wandering around museums to stay out of the wet. I had found myself in the Guggenheim late one afternoon, meandering from gallery to gallery, when I spotted it.

The caption identified it as *Shepherdess of the Sphinxes* by Leonor Fini.

She'd been painted in 1941 but she had lavish '80s hair, rising up tawny and tousled. She was wearing a sort of armored piece over her genitals, a metallic bathing suit if you squinted while you studied it. Between her legs, she held a shepherd's crook like a witch preparing to mount her broomstick, and she was looking over her little flock with a calm, watchful gaze. Nothing would happen to her girls while she was around, although from the looks of things, the herd of sphinxes could take care of themselves. They had the bodies of lionesses but the pouty faces and poutier breasts of supermodels. Their expressions were serene as they surveyed their gentle pasture dotted with flowers and the bones of the dead men they'd eaten. It was ghoulish and beautiful, a perfect representation of the terrible feminine power of life and death. The sphinxes had crushed men to bone and sucked out the marrow, all without messing up their hair. I smiled as I looked from one to the other, noting the line of a lazy tail, the assessing gaze directed to a possible meal waiting just out of frame. And yet, they weren't the predators. They were gathered in a herd, lovingly watched over and guarded. They weren't evil, after all. They were simply true to their nature. Something in the protective stance of the shepherdess had spoken to me, I guess. I'd bought a postcard of the painting in the gift shop, carrying it with me for years until it had gone soft with age and eventually I'd lost it.

I hadn't thought of her in years, but here she was in all her ferocious glory. I remembered then something that Constance Halliday had told me the last time I had stood in that room. We had just gotten our orders for our first job, the mission out of Nice, targeting the Bulgarian. My nerves had been jangling, and Constance found me working out in the garden, throwing punches at the sparring dummy until my knuckles were bruised. She'd forced me to come in, ordering me to soak my hands until the swelling went down. I'd expected a lecture, but for the first time, she didn't say anything. She had sat with me and given me a quiet, confident silence instead.

It unnerved me. I jerked my hands out of the basin of cold water and stared her down.

"Aren't you going to give me some advice? Tell me how to handle this?" I demanded.

She got up and went to the door, giving me one last look.

"True leadership, Miss Webster, is not about trusting yourself. It is about trusting your team."

Trusting your team. I looked at the painting in the book, running a fingertip over that beautiful, murderous herd of sphinxes.

I slammed the book shut. "I've got it." The other three looked up expectantly. "You won't like it. But it's the only way. Here's what we're going to do . . ."

After I laid out the plan, we argued for a few hours before they gave in. I should have slept like a baby, considering the fact that I had just gotten my way, but instead I tossed and turned awhile before heading down to heat some milk. I don't drink it — warm milk is disgusting. But you have to stir milk constantly to keep it from scorching and I do find that relaxing. I found Helen sitting at the table, address book in front of her, expression thoughtful.

"You got an idea?" I asked as I poured the milk down the sink and got out the bottle of brandy.

"Maybe," she said. She tapped her thumbnail against her teeth and fell to thinking again.

I didn't ask her for more. I knew she'd talk when she was ready. My only mistake was thinking she'd talk to me.

CHAPTER THIRTY-SIX

I came down to breakfast the next morning, following the smell of toast and Earl Grey. I pushed open the kitchen door and stopped, staring at the two people seated at the table. Helen lifted her chin and her companion turned slowly to face me, hands wrapped around a mug of tea.

"Hello, Billie," Taverner said. His voice was flat and his eyes were anything but friendly.

"Am I hallucinating?" I asked. "What are you doing here?"

"I called him," Helen said, lifting her address book with a nervous smile. "Now, you are free to yell at me later, but I'd appreciate it if you'd hear me out first."

I sat down across from them, folding my arms over my chest. "Alright." Helen poured another mug of tea and pushed it towards me.

"Drink this. Or save it and throw it at me

when I'm finished, if you must."

She attempted another smile and I waited until she let it fall before I reached for the cup. I didn't look at him.

Helen cleared her throat. "We need reinforcements. Vance is expecting trouble — specifically, he's expecting *us.* He isn't expecting Minka or Akiko, and that makes them valuable to what we're about to do. It also makes them vulnerable. They're not pros, Billie. They need protection. Besides," she went on in a reasonable tone, "he isn't expecting Taverner."

He was staring down into his tea, his knuckles white where he was gripping the mug. I didn't say that he looked good, but he did. He'd kept his rangy build. The shoulders were still broad, the hips still narrow. He looked a little softer through the middle, but hell, who didn't at our age. And he'd kept all his hair although it had gone pure silver, the ends of it curling like they had when he was thirty. I kept up the inventory until I got to his face to find he was watching me watching him and I jerked my attention to Helen.

"What sort of fee did you promise him?" I asked.

"Are you *kidding* me?" Taverner said suddenly. He looked up and I realized he was angry. Livid, actually.

Helen rose. "I think I'll give you two a minute," she said. She slipped out of the room.

"She was always the tactful one," I said.

"Really? That's how you're going to do this?" He shoved his mug away, sloshing a little of the tea over the side.

"I'm not mad at you," I said calmly. "I'm annoyed with *them.* I wasn't even consulted about including you."

"And including me isn't exactly your strong suit, is it?" He placed his palms flat on the table and pushed his chair back. He stood and I did the same.

"What's that supposed to mean?"

"Did it ever, for one moment, enter your mind to let me know you weren't dead?" he demanded.

I opened my mouth and closed it again. It was a full minute before I spoke. "That's why you're angry."

"Angry? I'm not angry, Billie. Angry is when you find out the dry cleaner lost your favorite shirt. What I'm feeling is the sort of emotion you don't even admit to your confessor. Five days after Christmas I get a call from Sweeney telling me you four are dead. That's all, just the bare fact of you no longer being in this world. It is now the middle of January," he said, pointing to the calendar tacked on the wall to make his point. "That's weeks later. *Weeks* of thinking you were gone."

I might have pointed out that all of this could have been avoided if Sweeney had bothered to call him back after I'd made contact and he knew we were alive, but Sweeney had been after the bonus. No way he would have taken the risk of Taverner either taking the job himself or tipping us off. But I figured none of that would make him feel better, so I said something else instead.

"I'm sorry."

He folded his arms over his chest and gave me a long look. "Do better."

"I am sorry, Taverner. I didn't think —"

"No. But then, you never do."

It was a good line and he was smart enough to use it for his exit. When he'd gone, Helen crept back in. I flapped a hand at her.

"It's fine, Helen."

"Is it?"

"No. If this place had a woodchipper I'd feed you to it."

She sat down and took my hand. "I wish I could have told you, but I knew that wouldn't be possible. You'd have said no, and it's a good idea."

"It is a good idea," I agreed. "A very good idea. I wish you could have told me too. You can't just go off on your own —"

"I didn't," she said gently.

"Mary Alice?"

"Dialed his number."

"Natalie?"

"Picked him up from the station this morning."

"Wow." I slipped my hand from under hers.

"I know you're angry. We expected this. We knew we were taking a risk by bringing him in. But we also knew that there is nobody in the world who would be better suited. He's cool in a crisis, smart, capable. The fact that the two of you have unfinished business —"

I cut her off. "I wouldn't call it that. We made our choices and we made our peace with it. Decades ago."

"Yes, I can tell how relaxed you are," she said mildly.

I made a face at her. "Okay, I'm pissed, but not at you and not because you brought him in. I'm pissed because we're supposed to be a team and nobody mentioned the idea of bringing him in."

"And?" She raised a brow.

392

"And I'm pissed at myself because he thought we were dead. I never thought to tell him otherwise."

"I know," she told me. "He was a little surprised to get my call." A tiny smile touched her lips and I relaxed.

"I feel like a bitch, Helen. It just didn't occur to me to call him."

"Lonesome is habit," she said with a shrug. "One that can be broken."

She left then and it was probably for the best. I stubbed out my cigarette before I went to find Taverner. He was in the garden, chucking knives at a tree stump. His form was still good, but the fact that he was doing something as visceral as knife throwing meant he was still feeling testy.

"So, I hear you're into philanthropy now," I said, coming to sit on the edge of the grass. "Giving away murders, no charge."

"Well, every fifth murder is free, and I've already killed four people this year," he said.

"Good to keep your hand in," I agreed. I blew out a breath that sounded ragged and felt worse. "I really am sorry, you know. I should have thought and I didn't. I guess I'm so used to pushing you out of my mind that I've gotten really good at it."

"Well, that stings," he said, coming to sit next to me. I handed him a bottle of water.

He smelled like clean sweat and something else. Lemons?

"How are the twins?" I managed.

"Grown. Planning their thirtieth-birthday bash. Kate is a television producer living in London and is engaged to a nice young man I don't much like. Sarah is a garden designer. She married an American and lives in upstate New York. She has twins of her own who just turned three."

I couldn't help it; I laughed. "You're a grandfather?"

"Yes. They call me PeePaw. I hate it."

"You should. It's awful. Do you see your grandchildren much if they're in America?"

He shrugged. "Not as often as I'd like. But they're busy."

"What about you?"

"I live in a cottage in Yorkshire, where I bake bread and refinish antiques and shock the neighbors with naked tai chi in the garden."

"Retirement sounds like it agrees with you."

He was quiet a long minute. "It's an adjustment. I have considered freelancing. You know, picking up the odd murder here and there just to keep busy."

"Oh, so we're the first. Hey, if you do a good job, you can use us for a reference."

"I'll be sure to put that on my CV," he said. He paused. "For what it's worth, I'm sorry about Vance. I never much liked him, but I didn't think he was bent."

"Me either. He was never my biggest fan, but I understood why. I just feel so . . . stupid. My entire career, all those years, and for what? No pension. Reputation shredded."

"Hey, you killed some really deserving people. That's got to be worth something."

I laughed until I felt the tears gathering in the corner of my eyes.

"God, I needed that. Thank you."

"It's what I'm here for," he said, almost touching my shoulder with his.

"I'm sorry about Beth," I told him finally.

He nodded. "I got your card. I should have answered it, but with the funeral and all, I never got around to it."

We were quiet for several minutes and it felt good, being with him. Too good. It was time to get back to business. "We've dotted all the *i*'s, crossed the *t*'s, Taverner. The plan is solid. We did the work."

"Yes, you did."

"So, you're in." I didn't want it to be a question, but I had to know. I kept my voice just neutral enough.

"I'm in," he said. Something knotted up

in my chest started to unravel.

"I know you told Helen you wouldn't take any money," I began.

"I've never yet killed a woman who didn't have it coming," he said lightly. "Don't make me rethink that."

"We're in charge," I told him. "No going rogue."

"I get it," he said, pushing himself to his feet and going to retrieve his knives from the stump. "I'm just the pretty face."

"And don't you forget it." I rose and brushed off the seat of my pants. "So what kind of firepower did you bring?"

He stared me down. "Are you asking if I brought guns?"

"Well, yes. It wouldn't have been smart for us to travel with them internationally. Too many questions. I assumed you had a nice little arsenal you were going to share."

"Of course I don't have an arsenal. I'm a responsible grandfather and this is England. There are no guns in my house."

"Jesus, Taverner. Then why are you here?"

He rolled his eyes. "In case you've forgot, I'm skilled at more than pulling a trigger." He wasn't talking about sex — at least I don't think he was. He went on. "But I may have something that will work in the boot of my car."

He took me to where he'd parked his car — a vintage Jaguar that looked like it had almost as many miles as we did. He popped the trunk. I looked in and laughed. "Seriously?" I picked up the packet of firecrackers. Small poppers that would deliver a bit of a bang and not much else.

"I told you. I'm a grandfather. Actually, I'm the *cool* grandfather," he informed me.

"You let three-year-olds play with firecrackers?"

"Of course not. I let them watch from a safe distance." He propped one hip against the car. "No special resources for this job. You'll have to work with what you've got."

I hefted the pack of firecrackers in my hand, thinking of the last time I'd seen a fireworks stand on the side of the road. A tired-looking woman at the wheel of a station wagon full of snot-nosed little boys had looked the other way as they loaded up on the crackers, stuffing them into apples and tossing them out the back window at passing cars.

I looked at Taverner and shrugged. "Story of my life. Why should it be any different now?"

CHAPTER THIRTY-SEVEN

Helen and Taverner made a run to the grocery store for supplies — potatoes, a huge beef roast, individual Yorkshire puddings, apple tart, nondairy creamer — because for the last night at Benscombe we decided on a special dinner. Taverner did the cooking, a bath towel wrapped around his waist in place of an apron. Nobody had much of an appetite, but we always remembered Constance Halliday's golden rule: eat, sleep, and use the facilities at every opportunity. The Duke of Wellington, she'd explained, had told his troops to make water whenever they could, and it was pretty good advice. You couldn't always count on a toilet or a cruller when you needed one.

So we forced ourselves to eat, and when the dishes were done, the others wandered off, leaving Nat, Helen, Mary Alice, and me. Natalie emerged from the cellar with a cobwebby bottle. "Guess what I found?"

She wiped the bottle clean and Helen rousted out the good glasses, giving them a quick wash. I proposed the toast.

"Tomorrow has been a long time in the making," I began. "Forty years." I paused, thinking of the Shepherdess and everything she had taught us. I cleared my throat and started again. "Forty years ago, Constance Halliday set us on this road and created her squad of Sphinxes. It hasn't been exactly what any of us expected. But we have done our best, and we will make her proud. She challenged us to make justice our priority, and tomorrow, justice will be done."

"Justice," said the others. We clinked glasses and drank. Then we took out our phones and opened our Menopaws! app. It was time to sync our cycles.

The next day I woke and stretched, a good two hours of yoga to get me limbered up. Then I took a long shower and dressed in jeans, a white silk shirt, and a suede jacket the color of burnt caramel. I put on a pair of flat boots and brushed out my hair. There were a few extra grey ones in the mix, but I figured I'd earned them. I clipped half of it back with a simple silver barrette Natalie brought me; the rest hung down, brushing my shoulders. I didn't bother with jewelry or perfume.

The others were scattered around the property. Taverner was busy in the kitchen, sharpening a boning knife, while Mary Alice and Helen were tinkering with a decrepit old tractor, unscrewing a heavy panel of steel from the side that was painted with the word "Bettinson." Natalie was keeping busy with some knitting needles and a skein of yarn she'd found in the attic.

I looked at the knotty shape she was making.

"Scabbard?" I guessed.

"Penis warmer," she told me.

I laughed and went to the garden shed for a long time, having one last cigarette and clicking through my phone as I ran through the plan. I was gambling, not just with my life, but with everyone's. I couldn't afford to get this wrong.

I pulled my jacket around me and stubbed out my cigarette before saying my goodbyes. I thumbed through the apps, opening the one for text messages. I keyed in a few sentences and hit "send." When I was finished, I left my phone with Mary Alice.

"You ready for this?" she asked.

"Nope."

She grinned. "Neither are we. Now, get going."

I went to the driveway to find Taverner

waiting, swinging his keys in his hand.

"I thought Minka was taking me to the station."

"She's busy working on her fastball with Akiko," he said. "I'm driving you."

I got into the passenger side without waiting for him to open the door.

"So we're spending some quality time together?" I asked.

"It looks like it." His voice was casual, but he was tapping his finger on the steering wheel and I knew exactly why.

Those last few hours before a job goes down, the adrenaline is pumping and there are limited ways of releasing it. Sex and exercise are effective, but they're a bad idea before a job. They can leave you tired and rubber-legged. Alcohol can also take the edge off, but it can also dull the sharpness you need for the work. There's only one solution and that's to sit with it, that simmering feeling of wanting to jump out of your skin. It's the reason I took up meditation, and most of the time it worked, but not with Taverner sitting next to me, eighteen inches and thirty years of history between us. We'd been good together in a way that I could never have explained to anybody. The sense of recognition, of the world slotting into place when I met him, was something I'd never felt before or since.

We'd lasted three years, stealing time between jobs to meet up in out-of-the-way places since romantic entanglements between field agents were strictly prohibited. Our last rendezvous — in a dive lodge in Mozambique — ended with him proposing for the fourth time and me packing my bag two days early. He'd driven me to the station then too, kissing me on the cheek and telling me he understood. It wasn't complicated. We wanted different things. He was six years older and ready to settle down, build a life, and make some babies. And no matter how hard I tried, I couldn't figure out how to make myself small enough to fit into that picture.

Two years later, he'd left a message for me when I was on a job in Venice. When I called him back, he'd told me it was his wedding day, and I wished him luck. I very nearly meant it. He didn't say the words, but I was fluent in Taverner and I could hear the subtext. *I loved you first and I will love you last.*

I'd hung up the phone and gone on to kill my mark in Venice with my bare hands, probably around the time he was cutting his wedding cake.

I turned to face him, studying the profile

that had somehow gotten better with age. "Do you ever regret it?" I asked him. "Breaking up, I mean."

He paid me the compliment of at least thinking about it before he said no. "If we hadn't broken up, I wouldn't have my girls. I would have missed thirty good years with Beth — and they were good, most of them."

"Was it everything you wanted? The picket fence? The PTA?"

"What's the PTA? Some sort of cult?"

"Pretty much." I waited as he navigated a roundabout.

"Yes," he said finally. "I got my rose-covered cottage and my happily-almost-after." He flicked me a sideways look. "You?"

My mind skimmed like a bird over the past thirty — almost forty — years. Jesus, where had the time gone? The scenes passed in front of my eyes like a movie reel, some in faded black-and-white, some in a riot of Technicolor, the places I'd seen, the people I'd known.

"I have had exactly the life I wanted for myself," I told him.

He was quiet a long moment. "I'm glad."

"You know," I said lightly, "I always wondered if you were really that upset when I turned you down. I half expected you to chase after me and drag me to the altar against my will, but you never did."

"Oh, I thought about it," he admitted with a smile. "But I knew if I pushed, you would wind up hating me for it, and I wasn't about to take that chance. Besides, I always figured we'd find our way back to each other in the end."

I couldn't form an answer to that so it was just as well that we'd arrived. He eased to a stop in the drop-off lane at the station and I opened my door. I cleared my throat and managed to sound passably normal. "It was good of you to come."

"There was never a chance I wouldn't," he said. He grinned, and I smiled back, meaning it.

"Thanks for the ride, English."

"See you on the other side."

CHAPTER THIRTY-EIGHT

It had rained in the late afternoon and the pavement smelled like wet cement. I made my way on foot from the station, turning the corner to see Tollemache's lit up like a birthday cake. The windows facing the street were permanently shuttered, but lanterns, glowing softly, hung on either side of the door. Someone had set out a line of boxwood topiaries hung with fairy lights — an intern, probably. The door was propped open and a decorative young man dressed in a tight plaid suit was standing just inside, repeating, "Welcome to Tollemache's," every five or six seconds like he was stuck on a loop.

I passed inside and grabbed a glass of champagne from a girl circulating with a tray. It was early yet, but the room was buzzing with anticipation and prospective buyers crowded around the paintings. I stood against a wall, letting the crowds pass in front of me as I sipped my champagne and took stock.

Tollemache's had taken the mock Tudor theme to the extreme. The interior was designed to resemble the Globe Theatre, with an open stage in the center surrounded by galleried walkways. The upper gallery was reserved for sellers and Tollemache's executives, with the lower gallery providing a sort of corral for onlookers and the press. There was even a wide stretch of wine-colored velvet curtains along the back of the stage with a podium set just in front for the auctioneer.

Next to the podium stood an empty easel. It was flanked by a long table outfitted with a phone bank. Most auction houses had a large computerized sign to display the reserve and current bids in various currencies, but Tollemache's was too old-school for that. The reserve and current were shown in pounds sterling only, and if you didn't know your euros from your yen, well, sucks to be you, I guess. More than one bidder had gotten burned by failing to calculate the exchange correctly, but Tollemache's got away with it because it was supposed to be part of their eccentric charm.

After I'd downed half my drink, I joined the queue to see the paintings. It moved quicker than I expected and not many people were focused on the *Sheba*. They wanted the big-money pictures — the pushing to see the O'Keeffe had resulted in a shoving match. But the *Sheba* hung in a smaller alcove, grouped quietly with Vallayer-Coster's pineapple still life. The pineapple was . . . well, it was a pineapple — yellow and green and surrounded by an assortment of other fruits and a sullen-looking lobster.

The *Sheba* was different. She had the quality of all of Anguissola's women. They stare out with their painted eyes — not at you, through you. They stare so long and so hard you almost believe they're real and you're the creation from some artist's imagination. They're entirely alive in the way only great art can be. Most of Anguissola's portraits have black backgrounds, but to set off the queen's dark skin, she had painted a domestic scene behind, the soft white of the bed-sheets a reminder of just what the queen had been doing — and who. Solomon's naked thigh was a tanned olive against the tumbled linens, his muscles relaxed with fatigue and satisfaction. Sheba's eyes were calm and watchful, a tiny smile playing over her lips. A spilled pitcher of water alluded to the story that Solomon

407

had tricked her into bed, making her promise to sleep with him if she took anything belonging to him. Then he fed her spicy food, ensuring she would need to help herself to a cup of water in the night — a tiny theft with enormous consequences.

This Sheba didn't look like a woman who'd been tricked into sex. She looked like a woman who had gotten exactly what she wanted. The king's weapons were lying on the floor, useless and abandoned, a signal that war had been vanquished by love. Everything about the painting was sexy, from the glow on Sheba's skin to the bowl of ripe peaches next to the bed.

I bent near to the bottom left corner, but I couldn't find the repair. If you didn't know it had been shot, you'd never suspect a bullet had once pierced the canvas. I was sad that the Provenance department had never unearthed any survivors from the family who had last owned it, but I was glad the *Sheba* was getting out in the world again. She deserved to be seen.

As I straightened, I realized someone was standing at my elbow. She was tall and wearing five-inch stilettos that put her easily over six feet. Her pantsuit was white, the trousers tight through the thighs but flaring from the knees. She wasn't wearing a shirt under the low-cut white blazer, just a thin gold chain that clasped under her breasts and behind her neck. Her hoop earrings were diamond, as were the rings on her fingers. Her Afro formed a perfect circle around her head and she had frosted the ends in gold, giving her a glimmering halo. Her lips were the same shimmering gold. A flunky stood behind her holding a custom oversized white ostrich Birkin bag that Helen would have given her right arm for. It took me a minute to place her, and then it came to me — Mona Rae. The last time I'd seen her, she had been on the cover of *Entertainment Weekly* for winning the Golden Globe for Best Director.

A bell rang and the music system was flooded with the sound of Elgar's "Trumpet Voluntary," Tollemache's signature piece. Like cattle, the bidders made their way towards the seating area. Heavy wine-red ropes kept the journalists and tourists at a distance, and girls wearing plain black dresses and holding clipboards were stationed at each gap in the ropes. They directed every bidder to a specific numbered seat, ticking people off as they passed. Mona Rae, I noticed, was sitting right up front, perfectly positioned for journalists to get a spectacular photo of her when the *Sheba* made an appearance.

But the Anguissola wasn't coming up until the second lot. The crowd settled into their seats, the air vibrating with energy. Suddenly, the music crashed to a crescendo and the red velvet curtains parted. Behind was a line of porters dressed in racing green coveralls, Tollemache's logo stitched in gold on each breast pocket. Making her way through the gauntlet of porters was the auctioneer, Lilja Koskela.

She was fortyish and thin like a whippet with a nose like one too. I didn't know Finns came with black hair, but this one did, and she was sporting a pair of Verdura necklaces — heavy gold chains dotted with a variety of gemstones. Later I looked them up and found out they were worth about eighty grand. If I'd known that at the time, I might have at least considered branching into jewel theft. Lilja Koskela strode to the podium like an Oscar favorite accepting her statue. She looked coolly at the crowd and made a few announcements, her English only barely tinged with a Finnish vowel here and there.

I was half listening to her as my gaze wandered over the crowd. I would have missed him if it hadn't been for the quick flash of white cuff. He was dressed with nondescript good taste, plain Burberry trench, dull plaid scarf, navy trilby pulled down over his brow. I sipped at my champagne and waited. He was discreet; only another pro would have noticed the small, sweeping scans he made of the crowd. But I kept behind a pillar, one of the floodlights positioned just above me, throwing me into shadow.

At the podium, Lilja Koskela finished her announcements and there was a sudden rousing blare of Handel's *Water Music* as a pair of porters carried in Vallayer-Coster's *Pineapple.* They set it on the easel and the crowd leaned forward. It was the only still life in the group and about as exciting as you'd expect a pineapple to be. But Koskela was a born storyteller, and by the time she finished describing the composition and the provenance, bidders were reaching for their paddles.

She started them at £400,000 and suddenly we were off to the races, bids flying all over the room. At first, it seemed like there were eight different bidders, but some of them may have been chandelier bids — a technique Mary Alice had explained. It's when the auctioneer pretends to accept a bid from a phantom bidder in order to drive the price up. It was a risky proposition if you weren't sure someone in the room would top it, but Koskela worked the crowd, milking them like dairy cows until she got them up to £750,000. At an exchange rate of one pound sterling to $1.308, plus fees, the *Pineapple* might look like SpongeBob's house, but it was working its way towards a cool million.

She brought the hammer down at £775,000 and the crowd went nuts, at least nuts for an auction crowd. There was a brief interlude before the music blared — Handel again. *The Arrival of the Queen of Sheba*. Koskela read through the provenance. She opened the bidding at £300,000. There were a number of bidders to start — a few museums, a couple of private dealers. Representations of Black women in Renaissance art weren't all that common, after all. And Anguissola was a good bet to appreciate in value. She wasn't well-known outside the art world, but female artists were increasingly in vogue and Anguissola was one of the best.

I could have made a move then, but I was feeling sentimental. I wanted to see the *Sheba* get her due. Mona Rae had her paddle in the air when the hammer came down: £1.2 million. A new record for Anguissola, Koskela announced in a throaty purr. Mona Rae threw up her hands in victory and was immediately escorted out by a senior staff member to arrange payment and gloat over her win.

Everyone's attention was focused on the auctioneer as the marquee painting — a sentimental Cassatt — was brought out. It was time. The chair next to Vance was open and I slipped into it.

"I'm glad the *Sheba* went for so much," I said conversationally. "A nice little bonus for the Museum. And it's getting such a good home. I really think Mona Rae feels what Anguissola was going for."

I gave him a sideways look, happy to see that he looked older than I'd expected. He hadn't run to fat. There was no paunch underneath that Burberry. But the eyes had seen a lot. They were hard and flat as he flicked a glance in my direction.

"Hello, Vance."

"Billie."

I lifted the edge of the file out of my bag so he could see it. "I have a copy of the dossier you have on us. It's bullshit, by the way. It accuses us of things we never did."

"Oh, and where did you get this copy?" he asked. His mouth was twitching like he wanted to smile. It's the sort of look a man gets when he's got a winning hand at poker

413

and can't hide it for shit.

"I took it from Carapaz's house," I admitted.

"Presumably the night you killed him," he replied.

"Well, okay. That looks bad, I'll give you that much."

He didn't say anything, but he hadn't shot me yet, so I figured that was a good sign.

"Vance, all we want is a chance to prove we're innocent."

He turned to me with a tight smile. "Innocent of what? Paar's death? Carapaz's?"

"There is an order out for us," I said evenly. "We are just trying to stay alive."

Suddenly, the smartwatch on his wrist chimed and he looked down. A text message scrolled by and he read it, smiled, then pulled his cuff down over his wrist.

"I appreciate your courage in coming in here like this. Truly. I expected some ridiculous, theatrical caper, and instead you're taking what's coming to you like a man." He leaned closer and I could smell the strong menthol of Fisherman's Friend on his breath.

"You starting a cold?" I asked. "If so, I'm going to need you to sit way back. And keep your germs to yourself. I really don't want to catch anything."

The smile tightened. "You don't get it, do you? That message was from Benscombe. I have a team there and they've just taken the others. Whatever you thought you were doing here" — he paused and made a circle with his forefinger — "is over."

I let my face fall as I turned away from him, staring straight ahead. He slid his hand under my elbow.

"Now, I'm going to get up and you're coming with me. I have four associates in this room, so please know that if you decide to try anything stupid, you won't make it out alive."

I swallowed hard and forced myself to sound casual. "Where are we going?"

"Where else? Benscombe. I thought it would be nice for all of you to die together."

"Shouldn't you be twirling a mustache when you say shit like that? Maybe petting a fluffy white cat?"

His nostrils flared a tiny bit, the only show of annoyance he allowed himself.

"Relax," I told him. "I see your goons." I moved my gaze around the room, nodding to three people arranged at different vantage points. "Upstairs is Wendy Jeong. I haven't seen her since Marrakesh. Nielssen is mingling in the crowd, dressed as a cater waiter. He just missed me in New Orleans, you know. And Carter Briggs is sitting two rows back, across the aisle. By the way, I think he just bid on some silhouettes and they're way overvalued."

"You missed one."

"No, I didn't. Eva Nowak, by the phone bank. Wearing knockoff Chanel and not even bothering to try to blend in. The bitch never did know how to dress, but then I'm not exactly winning any awards for my fashion sense. A little piece of advice for you, Vance — I can see every one of them is packing. You really should tell them to be more discreet."

His hand tightened on my upper arm. "I know you don't want to see any of these innocent art people get hurt. So let's get up now, nice and easy."

I did as I was told. He guided me through the crowd and out the front door. A luxury SUV with smoked glass was waiting at the curb a little way down the street, the motor idling. We stood outside as he searched me, running his hands through my pockets and a lot of other places, checking for weapons. As soon as we appeared, the foursome I had spotted were on our heels, opening doors and piling in. I got shoved to the back, where someone was already sitting, folded into the corner and taking up as little space as possible. A hand in my back shoved hard and I caught myself by grabbing on to the person in the shadows.

"Sorry," I said reflexively.

"So am I," the figure said.

Just then the interior light clicked on and I got a look at him.

"Hello, Martin."

CHAPTER THIRTY-NINE

Vance sat on my other side, so the trip to Benscombe was pretty cozy. We didn't talk beyond a polite offer of water on their side and an equally polite refusal on mine. I was thirsty, but the last thing I wanted was to have to pee. I knew Vance would never authorize a bathroom stop and you shouldn't hold it too long at my age. That's how you get UTIs.

So, I checked out. When I was a kid, I never counted sheep. Instead I silently recited the presidents in order. Then I moved on to English monarchs, elements of the periodic table by atomic weight, counting to a thousand in various languages. It doesn't really matter what the mental task is — the point is to occupy your mind just enough to keep it from wandering off. This time I worked my way through a list of my kills, starting with the Bulgarian job out of Nice.

We turned off the main highway towards Benscombe. I looked around and stretched a little before turning to Martin.

"So, I'm guessing you were working with him the whole time?" I asked, jerking my head to Vance.

I could only see him in silhouette, but I could tell he was biting his lip.

"Not at first," he said quietly.

"You prepared the dossier against us?" I made it a question, but I already knew the answer. I had seen everything I needed in Carapaz's file, starting with Martin's initials right at the start of the coded string of characters in the margin. MF — so appropriate, as it turned out.

"Yes. Naomi didn't brief the board for the last meeting. I did. She had morning sickness and couldn't travel," he said, lowering his head.

I poked him in the sweater vest. "It was a shitty thing to do to us. Was it your idea or Vance's?"

I turned and saw that Vance was watching us.

"Martin came to us," he said. "With evidence that the four of you were taking payments to conduct hits on the side."

"And you believed that bullshit?"

Vance shrugged and I turned to Martin.

419

"So you faked information that we were working freelance. Why?"

"Because the little shit thought he could outflank me," Vance said, a smile in his voice. "He thought he could turn the board against the four of you and get us to issue a termination order. Then he would give you just enough information to come after us, using the four of you to take us out so he could take over the organization. I mean, exterminating the entire board would leave a hell of a power vacuum, wouldn't it? You see, Billie, this was never about you. It was about Martin, thinking he could use you like his very own little puppet, jerking your strings to make you dance. You and the other three would remove the board and leave him in charge of everything." Vance leaned over to speak to Martin directly. "But you underestimated me, didn't you?"

Martin said nothing and Vance reached across me to give him a quick slap. A passing streetlamp threw a patch of light onto Martin's face and I could see a line of dried blood beneath one ear. He had the look of a man who'd been roughed up a little and hadn't enjoyed it one bit.

"And now you've gotten caught with your hand in the cookie jar," I said to Martin. "What did you think, that you could move everybody around on the chessboard and when the smoke cleared, you'd be the last one standing?"

"Something like that," he said, his jaw tight.

I looked at Vance. "So if we agree that Martin was playing us against each other, maybe we could come to terms."

Vance shook his head. "No chance. This was too good of an opportunity to pass up."

I nodded. "Of course it was. You're happy we took out Carapaz and Paar. What's the matter? Board getting too crowded and you'd like to run things alone?"

"Billie, the Museum started as a noble endeavor, but in the last few years, it's gotten tired. And do you know why? Too many cooks. There has always been a Provenance department to identify targets, a board to vote on issuing termination orders — and that only once every quarter. It's just so goddamned *slow*. That might have worked back when the Museum was founded, but it's a whole new world now, and we're still stuck in the dark ages. It's time to modernize, to streamline, to overhaul and build it back up with the right leadership. The Museum has the potential to be a private army of the greatest assassins in the world."

"Under your command," I finished.

I saw the gleam of his teeth as he smiled in the darkness. "Somebody has to be in charge."

I turned back to Martin. "Wow. You really got played."

He choked back a laugh that might have been a sob. "You're one to talk. The only reason we even found you is because you were stupid enough to send that text message." His voice rose as he mimicked the words. *"Thanks for all your help. Next time I see you, drinks are on me."*

I gave him my best outraged-old-lady look. "I didn't tell you where we were."

"You left your location services on," Vance said, his voice scathing. "As soon as Martin traced your phone to Benscombe, I had a team en route to secure the others."

The car braked to a stop. The driver stayed inside, but Vance, Martin, and I piled out with the other four. A guard was standing at the front door of the house and he stepped up to brief Vance.

"The property is secure. Three subjects in the kitchen."

Three. I let out a breath in relief. Mary Alice, Natalie, and Helen. That meant Akiko and Minka were safe with Taverner. Whatever Vance had managed to do, he hadn't gotten his hands on them.

I was herded into the house ahead of the others, and Martin was somewhere in the middle. I didn't know what they planned to do with him, but I was sure it wouldn't be pretty.

We moved down the hall and into the kitchen. Mary Alice, Helen, and Natalie were seated at the table, the surface covered with a piece of flowered oilcloth. Two guards stood against the wall, weapons unholstered. Clean dishes were stacked in the drainer, but baking goods were arranged on the worktops, and somebody had left a candle burning on a saucer in the middle of the table. And coffee had been made at some point and not cleared away. A pot stood next to a sugar bowl and a few bottles of powdered creamer, but the mugs were empty.

I sniffed the air. "Bath and Body Works?"

"Marks and Spencer," Mary Alice said. "They were having a sale."

"It's nice," I told her. Somebody nudged my back with a gun and I joined them at the table. Vance took a chair also and we looked around at each other.

"So, shall I fill them in?" I turned to the others. "Correct me if I leave something out. Martin," I said, pointing to where he stood, sniveling a little in his sweater vest, "started it all. He decided to take over the Museum. So he faked evidence that we'd been working against the board, which he presented to them, causing them to issue a termination order against us." I looked up at him. "I guess you were thinking that once Vance was dead, you could just slip into his office and nobody would care?"

"There is an interim director clause," Martin said quietly. "When I first came to work at the Museum, my job was digitizing the founding documents. I came across the section dealing with what would happen in the event of a succession crisis and I thought that was kind of useful information to keep handy."

"A succession crisis?" Mary Alice raised her brows. "That sounds so official."

Martin went on. "When a board member's seat is unexpectedly vacated, their immediate subordinate is automatically advanced to interim board member in their place."

Helen pursed her lips. "So if the whole board were terminated, then you and Naomi would take over? Only Naomi is out on sick leave, so that means you would have the entire control."

"And it wouldn't be too difficult to push out a pregnant woman working remotely," Natalie finished. "Pretty misogynistic, if you ask me."

"But instead," I went on, "Vance clocked what he was up to and let him use us to take out Carapaz and Paar, leaving Vance free to revamp the Museum however he wanted."

I leaned forward. "What was it, Vance? The money? Director's salary not stretch as far these days?"

He shook his head. "I don't usually hold grudges, Billie. I make an exception for you."

I rolled my eyes. "Are you still pissed about Zanzibar?"

He leaned close and I realized the Fisherman's Friend smell was long gone. He smelled like old man. "You took my Nazi, Billie. That was *my* assignment, my mission. You were there as backup only. You were supposed to handle the art and fill in our cover story. That's all. But you couldn't help yourself. You rushed in and took her."

"I saved your life," I said quietly.

He slammed a hand to the table, causing the mugs to jump and the candle flame to flicker. "You really think I couldn't handle one old woman? She got off one lucky shot and she wouldn't have gotten another. I had everything under control. And you ruined it. The very last Nazi ever taken by the

Museum. And you got the credit."

"Vance, she's dead. That was the mission. What does it matter who made the kill?"

"It mattered."

"Enough for you to decide to plot my death four decades later?"

He grinned. "No. But enough to make your death completely acceptable as part of what happens now."

"And what does happen now?" Helen asked quietly. "You kill us and take over the Museum?"

"Something like that," he said. He rose, thrusting his hands into his pockets. "With Martin gone," he said, flicking a glance to Martin, who flinched, "and Naomi on leave, it will be easy to institute a few changes."

"Such as abolishing the other two board positions," Natalie suggested.

"And rolling their functions into one job — yours," Mary Alice finished.

He shrugged. "Downsizing. It happens to every organization sooner or later."

He motioned for us to stand. "Up on your feet. It's time."

"It's not the worst plan in the world," I told him. "And you'd have gotten away with it too, if it wasn't for us meddling kids."

"What's that supposed to mean?" He gestured around the room. "Four assassins and two guards, five more guards outside. And that's not even counting me. Look, you played and you lost. There's no shame in that. But it's over now."

He turned to go, leaving the wet work to the others. My gaze dropped to the phone on the table. Mary Alice's. The Menopaws! app was open, the little cat circling as numbers counted down.

"Vance," I called.

He paused in the doorway. "What? You got any last words?"

"Yeah." I looked at the other three. Mary Alice. Helen. Natalie. Then I turned to Vance. I took a deep breath and smiled. "Assuming that because a person is sixty she doesn't understand location services is ageist bullshit."

Just then, the numbers on the app hit zero and the little cat on the app meowed. Helen's phone meowed too, and at the same second, Natalie's joined in. Outside, Minka had my phone, set to sync with the others, and as the four mechanical cats yowled in unison, we dove under the table just as the window shattered and the room erupted into flame.

The fight was over faster than you might expect. To begin with, we had the element of surprise. Mary Alice and Helen had screwed the tractor panel to the underside of the table, reinforcing it and buying us some time as we flipped it on its side and sheltered behind. The window blowing out was a nice little diversionary tactic thanks to Taverner's prep with the potatoes and Akiko's throwing arm. Each potato had been fitted with a firework, giving a nice little pop and a nasty amount of smoke as they came flying through the window. Taverner had built Akiko a snug bunker in the garden, and the plan was for her to keep lighting and hurling while he lay in wait for whatever guards Vance had sent ahead. I suspected Taverner had brought a few toys he hadn't shared with me, but he would be lethal enough with just the boning knife from the kitchen. Minka stayed with Akiko, lighting and pitching. One of them hit Nielssen squarely in the face, and he charged outside, one hand clapped to the bloody crater where his eye used to be. A quick gasp told me Taverner had finished him.

That left Wendy Jeong, Carter Briggs, and Eva Nowak. Martin had ducked out through the smoke and confusion, and I wasn't sure where Vance was. Nat grabbed the oilcloth and dragged it off the table, catching one container of coffee creamer in midair. She pitched it directly at Eva, the powder exploding as it hit her faux Chanel. Mary Alice followed with the lit candle and the whole thing went up like the Fourth of July. (Most people don't realize exactly how flammable nondairy creamer is. Consider this a PSA.)

Nielssen had left the back door open as he ran, and we had a clear line to it as long as we stayed behind the table. With a heave, we lifted it in front of us like a Spartan shield, running as fast as we could as Wendy and Carter emptied their guns at us. Bullets ricocheted around the room, and one of them winged Carter. Just then, Wendy's gun jammed, and as she worked the clip, Mary Alice noticed the small bit of powdered creamer burning near her shoe. Her aim wasn't perfect, but it didn't have to be. The bottle of cooking oil she threw smashed at Wendy's feet, splashing her up to her knees. Carter had transferred his gun to his non-dominant hand, and he emptied another clip. The table was giving way, the wood splintering to hell, and I knew it wouldn't stand another round.

I looked around for something to throw, but before I could lay hands on anything, Mary Alice snatched up a heavy iron skillet and swung it like she was batting cleanup.

There wasn't much left of his head after the second swing, and she turned to Eva, finishing her off where she'd fallen while Nat took care of Wendy. Helen looked shell-shocked, but I grabbed her hand and hauled her outside, my other arm around her waist.

"It's almost over," I promised her.

Just then a bullet winged through my hair, clipping the very bottom of my earlobe. It was Vance, coming through the garden at us. I shoved Helen aside, and she stumbled back into the house. Mary Alice and Nat were putting the fire out, and Akiko must have run out of potatoes. God only knew where Taverner was, and I realized it was probably always going to end like this.

I stood up, shaking with adrenaline and fatigue because, let's face it, I'm not as young as I used to be.

I squared up to Vance, blood dripping down my shirt. "Goddammit, Vance. That was silk."

"Smartass, right to the end," he said, raising his gun. He squeezed and nothing happened. He didn't try again. He tossed the gun aside and reached inside his pocket, coming up empty. He must have miscalculated or misplaced his backup because he had nothing, and as he straightened, he stripped off his jacket and cracked his neck.

And then the bastard smiled at me. He smiled the same smile I'd seen a thousand times, a hundred thousand. The smile that said, *I know best.* The smile that said, *I'm better than you.* The smile that said, *I'm safe here and you're not.* The smile that said *I have a dick, so I win.*

Rage rolled up in me like the sea and I felt it sweep over my head, threatening to drown me. And then I heard a voice, small and still, a voice I hadn't heard in forty years. I closed my eyes and listened.

It isn't your anger that will make you good at this job. It is your joy.

The rage ebbed and, in its place, only happiness. Fierce, rampant happiness.

It wasn't the prettiest fight I've ever been in, but it was the most ferocious. I hit him with everything I had and he damned near won. We were on the grass, wet with dew and slippery, his legs locked around mine, his hands squeezing my throat until my vision was going dark. He'd managed a few good hits to my ears and they were ringing so loud I couldn't hear anything except my own heartbeat.

I could tell he was surprised I'd held my own for so long. But then, Vance always did underestimate women.

I waited, holding my breath and lolling

my head to the side, sticking my tongue out just a little for effect. He eased the pressure in his hands. They were shaking and I reminded myself that he was five years older than I was and carrying a little martini weight.

The instant his hands relaxed, I jerked my head back and slammed it into his nose, breaking it in a gush of blood and cartilage. He staggered back as I got to my feet, grinning. "That can't really be the first time a woman has faked it with you."

He came at me with a roar, and I let him. Twenty years ago, I could have countered with a hurricane maneuver, running my feet up his torso and wrapping my legs around his neck to fling him to the ground. But that shit takes stamina, and I was tiring fast. I had one good move left and then it would be game over, one way or another.

He put his hands out to take me by the throat again, shaking me like a doll, the blood spraying from his broken nose. I let him bear me down to the ground, landing on me, hands squeezing, tighter and tighter, narrowing my vision to a pinpoint of blackness. I grabbed at his hands with my left, scrabbling at his fingers, but they were like iron. With my right, I reached up into my hair and took out the barrette, flicking it open. Natalie had sharpened it for me, honing it finer than a razor, and when I snaked it into Vance's armpit to slice the axillary artery, it slipped in like butter.

He didn't know what had happened at first, but I brought the blade out, holding it in front of my face, the metal wet with his blood. The sight of it threw him off and he loosened his grip. Before he could regroup, I twisted my hips and flipped him onto his back. Our legs were still locked and I used mine to hold him in place, my hip flexors screaming as I rose, looping one arm under his chin, just like Mad Dog had taught me. I put my other hand on top of his head, and as I looked down into his eyes, I realized he knew exactly what was coming.

He opened his mouth, but he didn't say anything. And then I jerked hard, snapping his neck with a quick flick of the wrist. His body settled against mine, before he slid slowly down, like a rock coming to rest on the bottom of the sea. I laid him on the grass, rolling onto my knees. I was bleeding and out of breath, the stitches on my shoulder popped open and part of my earlobe entirely gone. Mary Alice and Natalie, bruised and bloody, were standing on the edge of the garden. Mary Alice was holding an axe and what was left of two guards was stacked up like cordwood between them.

I lifted a hand to wave, too tired to call out. Just then I felt a cold muzzle against my neck.

"Get up, slowly," Martin said. The gun shook in his hand and I didn't like it.

A nervous hand is a hand that will accidentally pull the trigger. Mary Alice hefted the axe, but Martin jerked his gun around to her. "Don't move. And don't come any closer. I just want to get out of here."

"You tried to get us killed," Natalie pointed out. "I don't think we're going to let that happen."

"Jesus, Nat, you could *lie*," I muttered. He jammed the gun into my neck and Nat and Mary Alice stayed where they were.

"In case you haven't noticed," Mary Alice said patiently, "we have friends here. You won't get out alive."

"I will if I have her," he said, pushing the gun further. I wondered if he'd managed to pick up Vance's spare. I doubted Vance would have let him keep his own piece.

"Martin," I said, "let's just be reasonable. I'm happy to come along for a little ride, okay?"

His laugh was shaky, edged with hysteria. "And have you kill me when we're alone?

You might be old, but I don't like those odds."

"Then I think we're at an impasse," I pointed out.

He held me tightly, so tightly I could feel the hammer of his heartbeat. "Stop talking. I just have to think."

"Well, do you think maybe you could ease up on your grip?" I asked. "That gun in my neck is uncomfortable."

"Shut up, shut *up,*" he said. He dragged me to the edge of the garden where the rosebushes had grown up in a thicket like Sleeping Beauty's. There was a little gap and I realized what he meant to do when we got there. Both of us would never fit. He was going to shoot me and drop my body, using it as a shield as he made his escape alone.

He paused, raising the barrel of the gun to the back of my head. I felt the exhalation of his breath against my hair as he prepared to fire. A flash, a bang, and blood, hot and metallic, on my neck. It was over. I turned to see him slide to the ground, a hole in his forehead the size of my fist. I put a hand to my neck and brought it back wet. His blood, not mine.

And behind him stood Helen, holding Constance Halliday's beloved Colt revolver and smiling.

It really was just like old times.

CHAPTER FORTY

A figure moved out of the shadows and Helen swung her gun to cover it.

"Hey, now, you wouldn't really shoot a pregnant woman, would you?"

Naomi Ndiaye moved to stand over Martin's body. She was wearing a Burberry trench coat slung over her shoulders. Her fitted T-shirt hugged a generous bump.

"Should you really have flown in your condition?" Natalie asked.

Naomi shrugged. "It's not usually a problem until you're past the second trimester. I know I look huge, but that's a third baby for you." She lifted her hands where we could see them. "I'm going to reach into the pocket of my coat, and you aren't going to shoot me, Helen," she said, giving Helen a long stare.

Helen nodded and Naomi's hand slipped into her pocket. She came out with a bottle of something green. She twisted off the cap and for an instant I thought of gasoline or napalm or any one of a hundred nasty things she could have brought with her. But then she drank from it, a deep gulp, and gave a huge belch.

"Damn, that feels better. Ginger ale," she explained, showing the label. "For the nausea."

"Still?" Mary Alice asked.

Naomi made a face. "Hyperemesis gravidarum."

Natalie nodded. "Princess Kate gets that, poor thing."

"I get sick as a dog with each one of these babies. I'm usually done with it after the first trimester, but traveling can bring it back on," Naomi added with a significant look at each of us.

"Well, we didn't invite you," I pointed out.

"No," she said, nudging Martin's foot with her sneaker. "I was following him." She glanced at Helen. "I know you're good with that, but it makes me a little nervous to have it pointed my way. Maybe you could just lower your hand and I promise not to make any sudden movements."

Helen considered a moment. "Let Natalie pat you down."

Naomi shook her head. "I think not. I have flown across the Atlantic, but that's as much as I'm going to jeopardize this baby. I'm not carrying a weapon because I have no intention of getting into a fight. I've only had dry toast for the last twelve hours and I'm barely keeping that down. I haven't slept since yesterday, and I think my pregnancy hemorrhoids are flaring, so the last thing I'm in the mood for is being groped by anybody. No offense, Natalie," she added.

"None taken," Natalie assured her.

"You poor thing," Mary Alice said. "Would you like something to eat? Maybe you could manage an egg?"

Naomi shuddered. "Thank you, no. I intend to get this sorted and get the hell out of Dodge." She looked at the gun in Helen's hand. "I'm Provenance, not Exhibitions," she reminded her. "You might be sixty, but you're properly field trained and you have been killing people since before I was born. If I had to put odds on a fight right now, I'd say you beat me, ten to four."

"Why only ten to four?" Helen asked.

"Because the only way we're fighting is if you start something, and then I'm going to defend this baby until I've got nothing left, and I'm a biter," Naomi told her coolly.

Helen thought a minute, then lowered her arm.

"Thank you," Naomi said dryly. She looked around the circle. "I'm inferring this is your handiwork," she said, pointing to the hole in Martin's forehead.

Helen nodded. Naomi bent, one hand under her belly, and took a good look at the wound. Blood still oozed, moving slowly over his open eye, puddling in the crease of his nose. "A little to the left, but not bad at all. He looks surprised."

"He was," I assured her.

She reached out a hand and closed his eyes. Then she straightened, taking another deep swig of ginger ale. "Dumbass," she said, shaking her head. She took a phone from her pocket and punched in a number. "I need a cleaning crew." She gave the address of Benscombe Hall. "Make it fast and quiet. In the garden." She paused and looked around. "Anybody else we need to take care of tidying up?"

"Bodyguards scattered around the property," I told her. "Pieces of a few folks in the kitchen, but they're probably burned up by now. And Vance Gilchrist is by the greenhouse."

She raised her brows but didn't reply to me. She related the information to the voice on the other end, then hung up without saying good-bye. "Twenty to thirty minutes."

440

She looked around. "I may have gone to Cambridge, but I am from Atlanta and this cold is about in my bones. Let's go inside."

She headed towards the garden shed and the rest of us looked around. Naomi had seamlessly taken charge, and we might have overpowered her — she wasn't exactly fighting fit, and as a member of the Provenance department, her training was much less comprehensive than ours. The bottom line was, we could take her if we chose.

But we didn't choose. Instead, we followed her into the garden shed, where we were joined by Minka and Akiko, who helped us pile up some mulch bags for Naomi to sit on. I didn't bother to look around for Taverner. He'd have done what we asked and slipped away when the getting was good. I just hoped he'd stuck around long enough to see the end.

When we'd gotten comfortable, Naomi started to talk.

"First, I presume that you are responsible for terminating Vance Gilchrist, Thierry Carapaz, and their bodyguards," she began.

"And Günther Paar," I added.

She narrowed her eyes. "That was determined to be natural causes. He choked on an apple during a heart attack."

"I shoved a piece of apple down his

windpipe after Mary Alice and I slathered him in a mud wrap made with nicotine."

Naomi's mouth opened, then closed. And then she burst out laughing. "That is impressive, ladies. Some real old-school shit." She sipped again from her ginger ale. "Alright, that's another notch in the body count. Did you have help?"

"No," I said smoothly.

She looked around the table, but nobody else was willing to give Taverner up either. She nodded. "Okay, y'all are lying to my face, but I get it. You're protecting somebody. That's fine, but I can't protect *you* if you don't tell me the truth."

"Protect us?" Mary Alice asked.

Naomi's expression was cool. "There is an entire organization sniffing after a nice fat bonus for each of your heads. And since I'm in charge now, I'm the one who can call it off. So yes — I am here to protect you."

"Why?" Helen demanded.

Naomi pointed outside to where Martin's body was cooling in the garden. "Because you got rid of that little shit-heel and saved me the trouble."

Natalie's eyes went wide. "You were after Martin?"

"For two, almost three years now, I've

been watching him. He ingratiated himself with the board, taking on extra work, making sure he always saved the day. It was a little too perfect. It got on my tits," she said. "So I started paying attention."

Mary Alice spoke up. "How did you manage to keep tabs on him?"

Naomi smiled. "Every quarter when the board met for me to brief them, Martin was there too. I installed a keystroke logger on his computer and spyware on his phone. Ten minutes' work and I was able to see everything he did, every search, every email, every nasty little move he was planning. I know his level on *Angry Birds,* I know his bank account is way higher than his pay grade, and I know he had a case of athlete's foot that his doctor was concerned about because it took so long to clear up."

"Nasty," Natalie muttered.

Naomi grinned. "I won't tell you about his fanfic. It's pretty out there."

"So you were able to see everything he did," I said slowly. "Including setting us up." I held her stare, but she didn't back down.

"Yes, I was. And I knew I had no way to prove it. Anything I showed the board, he could turn around and say I had installed on his devices in order to frame him for whatever *I* was doing. Besides, you think they were going to listen to me? They were in this up to their hairy eyebrows." She took one last gulp of ginger ale and slowly exhaled a low burp. "This baby is killing me by inches."

Minka spoke up. "You need more ginger." She pulled a tin of ginger chews from her pocket and passed it over. Naomi took one and started to suck.

"I am nice to you as long as you are nice to my friends," Minka said sternly.

"Minka, sit down. Your Ukrainian is showing," I told her.

Naomi looked up. "Ukrainian?" She rattled off a few phrases and Minka brightened, answering her in a chirpy voice I'd never heard her use before.

"You speak Ukrainian?" Helen asked.

Naomi shrugged. "I speak seventeen languages. Most for work. Ukrainian was just for fun."

"Your Duolingo score must be the absolute shit," Natalie said.

Naomi smiled. "So yes, to answer your thinly veiled accusation, Billie, I watched while Martin set you up and the board issued the termination order. I considered sending a warning, but in the end, I chose not to. The board thought four old broads — their words, not mine — wouldn't be a match for Brad Fogerty, so they only sent one assassin on the cruise. They assumed you'd never see him coming. But I thought they were wrong. You have experience and instinct. You knew to keep your eyes open and you saved yourselves. I was betting you would."

"You wagered with their lives," Akiko put in suddenly.

Naomi didn't bat an eye. "I took a calculated risk. We do that in this line of work." She went on. "When they realized you made it off the boat, the board was divided. Paar was inclined to let it go. He had been the most reluctant to issue the termination order in the first place. But Gilchrist and Carapaz pressured him and he agreed to let the order ride. They thought you might turn to a friend for answers, so they were already onto Sweeney."

"They tapped his phone and sent Niels-sen to finish the job in case he buggered it to hell," I guessed.

"Exactly. And when that failed, they assumed you left New Orleans, but they couldn't get a line on where you were. It drove Gilchrist *nuts.* Carapaz decided he would just hole up in Paris and double his bodyguards. Paar never thought you'd be ballsy enough to come out to find them, so he went on with his spa trip. I guess he thought wrong," she said, saluting us. "Paar was a creature of habit. I'm not surprised you found him, but Carapaz must have been trickier. How did you manage that?"

We took her through the process and she looked impressed. "And you grabbed the dossier off the bed without knowing what it was?"

I shrugged. "Maybe subconsciously I recognized it as Museum business. I don't know. It was instinct to take it. And when I read it, I saw the code in the margin and realized it had been compiled by Martin."

"Of course, Martin didn't realize Billie was onto him when he left her the message about Tollemache's," Mary Alice put in.

"He thought he was being subtle," I said with a smile.

"And he needed some way to get you to figure out the painting was at Tollemache's to draw you into Vance's trap," Naomi said, putting the pieces together.

I filled in the rest. "We didn't know where the plot started, but we knew at that point that Vance and Martin were sharing information. And that any plan to take them out would only work if we could turn the tables and get them here."

"So you strolled into Tollemache's bold as

balls and offered yourself up," Naomi said, giving me an approving look. "You've got brass ones."

I shrugged. "The goal for them was the four of us. I figured I was safe until we were all together. Vance has been holding a grudge against me for forty years. Making me watch him kill my friends would be a nifty little bonus for him."

Naomi sucked harder at the ginger chew and rolled her eyes. "I don't know if this is the best thing I've ever had or the worst."

"I say the same about tequila," Minka said.

"You did a good job of making Paar's death seem natural," Naomi went on. "Carapaz and Gilchrist had a debate over how to handle it. Carapaz figured he would just wait you out. He argued that you didn't have the resources to conduct a series of hits, especially against them. Gilchrist was more cautious. When you took out Carapaz, he decided the best defense would be a good offense."

"And the Anguissola went up for auction to draw us out," Helen put in.

"It did the trick," Naomi said, smiling again. "And someday I'd like the whole story of exactly how it went down. But I hear noises in the garden. The cleanup crew is here."

CHAPTER FORTY-ONE

We watched from the shed as the crew, dressed in discreet grey coveralls, rolled the bodies up into tarps and stacked them neatly in the back of a paneled van. They slammed the back door and drove off without speaking to anyone.

"Where will they take them?" Natalie asked.

"There is a waste facility with an industrial incinerator just outside of Bristol. It handles all of our needs in southern England and Wales. Northern England and Scotland are a different division," Naomi explained. "The ashes are dumped in the landfill. Within the hour, every trace of them will be obliterated." She glanced around. "Just out of curiosity, how were you planning on disposing of them?"

"There was some discussion of pigs," I told her.

She nodded. "Pigs are always a good option in the country." She looked around the group. "So, let's discuss the future, ladies. I am here to make you an offer."

Naomi outlined the terms, and after a little haggling, we struck a bargain. Nobody put anything in writing. It was a handshake deal, decided over ginger chews and a vodka miniature Natalie had in her pocket.

"We get the termination order lifted and our pensions reinstated, and you get to take over as acting director until another board can be selected," I summed up.

"We can go back to our lives," Mary Alice said, reaching for Akiko's hand. Akiko let her, and I realized then they were going to be just fine.

"Yes, but not immediately," Naomi cautioned. "I have to make sure everybody gets the word that you're in the Museum's good graces again. So, lay low for a while, will you?"

"I'm going to Japan," Natalie said suddenly. "I've always wanted to study ike-bana."

Akiko looked at Mary Alice and smiled. "Norway for us, I think. We could take Kevin to the land of his ancestors." She raised Kevin's paw and he gave a sleepy growl.

"What about you?" I asked Helen. She

took a deep breath as she looked at the house. The fire hadn't spread beyond the kitchen wing, and the cleanup team had finished putting out the flames. The pall of smoke still hung over the garden, and I figured our hair would smell like it for days.

"I have a house to fix up. I'm ready to tackle it now," Helen said firmly. "You?"

I thought of a tiny Greek island where Taverner and I had spent a month a lifetime ago. We had rented a farmhouse perched on top of a cliff, overlooking a sea so blue you couldn't imagine any other color had ever existed in the world. The wind carried the smell of herbs and salt, and every day the sun had blazed like the chariot wheel of a god.

"Greece," I said suddenly. "I'll be in Greece."

"We will be in Greece," Minka corrected.

I smiled. I'd let her come and stay a little while. Then I would kick her out, gently, and make her see the world. She needed a gap-year adventure, and when she was gone, there would be time, all the time in the world, I decided, thinking of Taverner. A little sun would do him some good, especially if he were doing naked tai chi in my garden.

Naomi excused herself and went to use

the bathroom. When she came back, the others said their good-byes and I walked her out. I took the long way, stopping in the study in front of the painting that still hung on the faded wallpaper. She surveyed it for a long minute. "Astraea," she said, pointing to the scales and sword.

"You know her?"

Her smile was knowing. "My master's thesis was the role of allegory and metaphor in the Italian Baroque."

"Then you understand why this painting was important to Constance Halliday," I said. "And what she stood for. What the Museum stood for. Once."

"I do. And believe me, it will again. I promise."

We shook hands and she left on foot. I don't know where she left her car and I didn't ask. She simply faded out into the shadows as silently as she'd come, and I realized her training might have been better than we'd thought.

I walked outside to catch my breath. It was cold, bitterly so, but I couldn't bring myself to leave just yet.

It was dark in the garden, just before dawn, when the air is grey and the night-birds are singing. They were tired, those nightbirds, and their song was quieter now.

But they were still singing, and they went on singing until dawn broke over the trees.

AUTHOR'S SECOND NOTE

This is where an ordinary author would write THE END in big letters and the story would be finished. But I'm not an ordinary author and this story will never be finished. I've changed just enough so that you can't find us, even if you wanted to. And you really shouldn't try. People have died for less. I know; I was there.

ACKNOWLEDGMENTS

This book was a trust fall, and there were more people than I can possibly count ready to catch me. But special thanks and a round of cocktails to:

Pamela Hopkins, agent, friend, and the first person in this business to wager on me. I hope I have done you proud.

Danielle Perez, gifted editor, who picked up the phone one day and said, "We think you should write a book about older women." You never let me settle and this book shows it.

Jenn Snyder for generosity and editorial perspectives. Our KILLERS are the richer for it.

Claire Zion for encouragement, enthusiasm, and a pep talk over drinks that set this book on its way.

Craig Burke for giving this book the best possible title it could ever have. You are officially godfather to the KILLERS.

The Berkley art department for creating a graphic cover that is absolutely ICONIC.

Ivan Held and Jeanne-Marie Hudson for giving me the opportunity to live large and kill some folks.

Loren Jaggers and Tara O'Connor for cheerleading. Nobody's pom-poms are as fluffy as yours.

Jess Mangicaro for endless patience and unflagging good cheer in the face of my tech-challenged ways. You are a rock star.

Candice Coote for keeping things rolling on.

Michelle Vega for taking the baton handoff to bring this home.

Jomie Wilding and the Writerspace team for attention to detail and keeping the digital house clean.

Angèle Masters for her exquisite work as the voice of the Veronica Speedwell books.

Every person at Berkley and Penguin Random House. Literally, all of you. I am so glad to be taking this journey with you.

Every bookseller, librarian, bookstagrammer, reviewer, and reader who has ever picked up one of my books and had a kind thought. Thank you for spreading the book love.

My go-to resource for all things physical and the pal who never flinches when my text messages start, "So I need to kill a guy . . . ," Travis Staton-Marrero.

Ariel Lawhon and Lauren Willig, who both fielded terrified phone calls that included the question, "BUT HOW?"

Tasha Turner, Felicia Grossman, Jenny Rae Rappaport, Lauren Conrad, Stacey Agdern, and Brina Starler, for kindly sharing insights about their Jewish faith with me.

Blake Leyers, my beloved friend, you are as supportive as good pantyhose. Thank you for the phone calls, the texts, the brainstorming, and above all for the note "If you are writing authentically, you cannot fail." It's still taped to my computer.

The rest of the Blanket Fort. For gifs and in-jokes and utter ridiculousness. You are my people.

Ali Trotta, for shrieking with excitement so loudly when I shared the news about this book, I had to put the phone down, and for regular texts of encouragement.

Twitter peeps, who daily bring me joy and respite. Thank you for being my virtual watercooler.

My daughter and every single "YOU GOT THIS" text.

My parents and all the errands run, the moods endured, the tears dried.

My husband and all the everythings. Every person who identifies female and has rage. I feel you, sister. This one's for you.

ABOUT THE AUTHOR

Deanna Raybourn is the *New York Times* bestselling author of the Edgar Award–nominated Veronica Speedwell Mysteries, as well as the Lady Julia Grey series and several stand-alone works.